THESE GOLDEN DAYS

THE INNOCENT YEARS
★ ★ ★

THESE GOLDEN DAYS

ROBERT FUNDERBURK

BETHANY HOUSE PUBLISHERS
MINNEAPOLIS, MINNESOTA 55438

Cover illustration by Joe Nordstrom

Published by Bethany House Publishers
A Ministry of Bethany Fellowship, Inc.
11300 Hampshire Avenue South
Minneapolis, Minnesota 55438

Printed in the United States of America

Library of Congress Cataloging-in-Publication Data

CIP applied for

ISBN 1–55661–461–6   CIP

To my aunts:
Jewel Rowe, Nita Hall, and Cleta Brewer,
who have the faces and voices of angels.

ROBERT FUNDERBURK is the coauthor of six books with his friend Gilbert Morris. Much of the research for this series was gained through growing up in Baton Rouge and then working as a Louisiana state probation and parole officer for twenty years. He and his wife have one daughter and live in Louisiana.

CONTENTS

★ ★ ★

PART FOUR
A SUDDEN SWEET JOY

PART ONE

★ ★ ★

ONE MISTY CHRISTMAS EVE

ONE

RIDING THE RAILS

★ ★ ★

"Oh—this scares me to death! I just love it!" Jessie Temple leaned out the window, her shoulder-length blond hair blowing in the night wind as she stared down the tracks glinting in the dim light. With her blue eyes, fair skin, and trim figure, she mirrored her mother physically, but her spirit of adventure was totally opposite from Catherine's calm, predictable nature.

Austin Youngblood, wearing faded jeans and a white T-shirt, sat next to Jessie. One arm draped over the steering wheel of his '49 Chevy coupe; the other rested across the back of the seat. The light dancing in his gray eyes reflected the thrill he always felt living on the edge. "This is a walk in the park, Jess. One night we'll do something *really* exciting."

"How'd you ever think of doing this anyway?" Ellis Perry's light brown eyes twitched nervously as he clutched the backseat with both hands. With his sandy hair precisely parted and his gold-rimmed glasses affixed snugly to his protruding ears, he looked the picture of a bookworm, which he was, and the last person in Istrouma High School's junior class to be a close friend of Austin Youngblood's.

"It came to me in a vision, Ellis," Austin smiled, glancing over at Jessie. "I was watching *Your Hit Parade* on television a couple of weeks ago—Snooky Lanson was singing, as I recall, and it just suddenly hit me."

"Aw, go on," Ellis snorted. "It is interesting though, how you got the idea to let just the right amount of air out of the tires so that the car follows along on the tracks. I'll bet you wouldn't even have to steer it."

As though to prove Ellis' point, Austin took his left hand off the steering wheel. The partially deflated tires hummed along the polished steel, following the tracks with the slightest wavering of the automobile.

"Maybe he's smarter than you think he is, Ellis." Janie Simmons' round, freckled face glowed with mischief as she punched Ellis in the side.

"I—I never said Austin wasn't smart," Ellis stammered. "Never said anything like that. Just because he's on the boxing team doesn't mean he's dumb."

"I'm smart enough to have a friend like you. Right, Ellis?" Austin smiled back over the seat. "With all my, ah—commitments it'd be tough to pass this year without your help."

"Sure, Austin," Ellis agreed quickly. "Watch it! We're coming to a street. The other cars won't be expecting us to come flying along on the railroad tracks."

"Oh, don't be such a worrywart, Ellis!" Jessie turned around, leaning over the back of the seat. "Austin knows perfectly well what he's doing."

"Yeah," Janie teased, punching Ellis playfully

again. "We're here to have some fun."

Jessie winked at Janie. "Why don't you do something useful, like kiss Janie?"

Ellis cleared his throat. "I—I couldn't do that. This is only our first date."

"Maybe she wouldn't mind." Jessie flounced the skirt of her blue print dress around her legs as she curled them up on the seat. Then she nodded at Janie. "Would you?"

Janie smiled and fluttered her eyelashes. "Oh, my goodness! Don't even think such a thing, Jess." With that she turned and kissed Ellis on the mouth.

His eyes going wide behind his glasses, Ellis spluttered, "Janie, what's gotten into you?"

"Keeping bad company, I suppose," she replied coyly, glancing at Jessie.

"Pilot to navigator! Pilot to navigator!" Austin called out, cupping his hand over his mouth. "I need a quick fix on our position. We can't have any enemy locomotives sabotaging this mission."

Ellis snatched up the Blue Horse notebook on the seat beside him, turning quickly to the chart and time-tables he had constructed. "Let's see now—we got on the Kansas City Southern tracks at Chippewa Street and we just crossed Choctaw—"

"Gotcha, Navigator," Austin broke in. "And coming up on your left is the new Memorial Stadium where on the twenty-fourth of November last year the Baton Rouge High Bulldogs trounced the Indians forty-seven to twenty-five."

Jessie glanced to her left at the concrete structure where she had spent some of the best times of her junior year on the sidelines, cheering her team on to victory. She could almost hear the roar of the crowd and the thunder of the marching band, could almost feel

the electric thrill of being out in front of all those people, even if it was only leading cheers at a high-school
football game.

Ellis looked up from his notebook, holding his
place with his finger. "You know, Austin . . ."

"Yeah, I know Austin," Austin broke in. "A real
prince of a fellow."

"No," Ellis grinned, "I mean you know there's
something puzzling me about you."

"I'm a real enigma, all right."

"Why would somebody with your athletic ability
choose boxing over football?" Ellis pursed his lips. "I
mean this whole town is football crazy. You could
have gotten a scholarship to Louisiana State University; all the girls love a football hero; the whole thing
is a mystery to me. Why choose boxing?"

"'Cause I can't punch anybody's lights out in football," Austin shot back. "Not legally anyway."

"Oh."

"Besides," Austin continued, leaning over to give
Jessie a quick kiss on the cheek, "I've got the prettiest
girl in town—without football—and, to make matters
even better, my ol' man's made enough money running his bank to send me to any college in the country.
Ain't life grand?"

"I guess so, Austin." Ellis opened his notebook and
went back to his charts.

Jessie rested her elbow on the window, gazing out
across the lake at the State Capitol, rising next to the
mile-wide Mississippi River. The Capitol's limestone
walls glowed faintly and warmly against the night sky.

Turning back, she stared at Austin, his black hair
and deeply tanned face almost a negative image of her
own blond fairness. He looked supremely confident
and in control, and his lean six-foot frame seemed al-

ways poised on the brink of action, even when he relaxed. She had found herself attracted to him, though
he was considered a renegade by the teachers and
most of the students. Perhaps, she found herself
thinking later, it was *because* of this fact and not in
spite of it.

"We're coming to the Boyd Street trestle," Ellis remarked, his finger poised over the notebook. "Let me
double-check the schedules. We wouldn't want to
meet a train there. No way to get down."

Austin placed both hands behind his neck as he
stared straight down the tracks. "Too late, my man.
You had your chance earlier to do that."

Jessie trusted Ellis' meticulous attention to detail
and knew there was little chance for an accident, but
still the remote possibility of disaster made a slight
chill tickle her spine. "That's right, Ellis. It'll be your
fault if we end up as ornaments on the front of a locomotive."

"You'll be famous for a day," Austin added. "Your
name on the front page."

Ellis checked the train schedule for the fourth
time, mopping his forehead with a white handkerchief. "I'd just as soon forego the fame and enjoy my
obscurity right on into old age, if it's all right with you,
Austin."

As they crossed over the trestle, Jessie peered
down to the street level, noticing a city police car
passing beneath them. A head appeared out of the
passenger side window as an officer, his eyes wide in
surprise, stared up at the car passing overhead.

"I think we're going to have company somewhere
up ahead," Jessie warned, pointing down.

Austin glanced down just as the police unit's flashing red light winked on. Two seconds later, the wail of

a siren sounded in the stillness of the late night.

"What's that?" Ellis jerked his head up from his notebook, glancing right and left.

"It's the *po*—leese, Ellis," Austin replied, easing down on the accelerator. "They always manage to show up when somebody's having a good time." The Chevrolet glided smoothly down the tracks, the humming sound intensifying as it picked up speed.

"Don't go so fast!" Janie shrieked. "You'll kill us!"

"Go fast or go to jail," Austin quipped, hitting the brakes. The car slid and swayed toward Boyd Avenue at the top of a hill just ahead of them, lurching sideways with a crying of tires on pavement as it hit the street.

The sound of the siren wailed behind them as the police unit turned, paralleling the tracks in pursuit.

"Turn on your headlights!" Ellis yelled. "You'll wreck this thing and kill us!"

Austin didn't bother to reply. His eyes burned with an intense light as he fought to control the car, still lurching and swaying from the softness of its low tires.

"Do something, Jessie! Make him slow down!" Janie clutched onto the back of the seat, her eyes wild with fear. "We're going to die!"

Jessie stared at Austin, reveling in his coolness and deliberate actions in the face of danger. She found herself so caught up in the pursuit and the thrill of the chase that she had no thought whatsoever of the danger involved. It suddenly occurred to her. *This is why I like being with him so much!*

Numb with fright, Ellis stared straight ahead through the windshield, his eyes as glazed and dull as a man walking out of a beer joint.

Wrestling with the wheel, Austin went barreling

down Boyd Avenue, heading for the Mississippi River. In the rearview mirror he saw the flashing red light of the police unit as it shot up the hill, turning right onto Boyd several blocks behind him. The car slowed as though seeking direction.

With the headlights still off, Austin made a sharp right turn, heading north on Third Street toward the Capitol. Shooting through the traffic lights in the deserted downtown business district, he zipped past the towering capitol building, careening right onto Capitol Lake Drive.

Thirty seconds later, Austin pulled the car beneath an ancient live oak bordering the lake. A line of azalea bushes shielded them from the street.

"Well, we made it!" Austin took a deep breath, expelling it through his lips. "Wasn't that fun, boys and girls?"

Janie wept quietly, leaning forward on the seat, her hands covering her face.

Austin glanced at Jessie and shrugged.

Jessie smiled at him, taking his hand.

In a few moments Ellis broke the silence. "You oughta be committed to the insane asylum, Austin! How could you risk our lives like that?"

"No risk to it if you know what you're doing," Austin replied matter-of-factly.

At that moment the police unit roared by on the other side of the azaleas, its siren lowering in pitch as it followed the road curving around the edge of the lake.

"See what I mean?" Austin announced smugly. "No risk at all for us."

Ellis' face went slack with defeat. "Someday you're not gonna come out on top, Austin."

"Someday we'll *all* be dead, Ellis," Austin replied

abruptly, glancing around toward the backseat.

Ellis and Janie fell into a sullen quiet, glaring at the back of Austin's head.

"Oh, come on now," Jessie remarked cheerfully. "Nothing happened and it's a beautiful night. Let's forget about the whole thing and enjoy ourselves."

"Yeah, let's see who can spot the 'Turtle Man' first," Austin said in an ominous tone.

"The *what*?" Ellis was wary of Austin's deceptions, but he never could figure out when he was being put on.

Austin turned around and rested his forearm on the back of the seat. "You *have* led a sheltered life, haven't you? He's half man and half turtle—lives here in the lake."

Ellis frowned at Austin, then at Janie. "Come on. You think I'm some kind of moron?"

"I'd rather not answer that question, Ellis." Austin stared out across the lake, a smile of disbelief on his face.

"What does he look like?"

"He's kind of hard to describe," Jessie answered in a hushed tone. "He only comes out at night, so nobody's ever had a good look at him."

Ellis was almost beginning to believe in the creature's existence. "Probably just some tramp rambling around looking for a place to sleep."

"Tell you what, Ellis," Austin offered. "If you see him first, give a holler—but not too loud." He motioned to Jessie and she slid over on the seat next to him, settling herself in his arms.

"I don't understand," Ellis whispered to Janie.

She moved next to him, leaning her ear next to his.

Ellis' eyes widened with surprise. Then Janie put her arms around his neck and he fell silent.

★ ★ ★

The morning sky had a bright sheen to it, like a silk covering stretched above the cottony clouds. Songbirds flitted in the dappled light of the ancient live oak that spread its heavy limbs out almost to the scrolled iron railing of the second-story gallery. From below, rising on the barely cool, humid air like sweet incense, the heady, heavy scent of gardenias blended with the smell of damp earth from the flower beds.

"What a gorgeous morning!" Wearing a lavender dressing gown, Catherine Temple sat in a white wrought-iron chair. Spread before her were the remains of breakfast. She pushed her plate back and sipped her tea, breathing in the fragrant air with an occasional glance at her husband.

Lane stared again at the dark headlines of *The Morning Advocate*, "North Korea Invades South Korea," then folded the newspaper and laid it aside. "It pales in comparison to you, my sweet."

"I didn't even think you were listening, the way you had your head buried in that newspaper."

Lane tried to put the war news out of his mind, with little success. "Not much happening."

"What about the situation in Korea?"

"Ah, I don't think much will come of that," Lane replied, trying to convince himself. He unconsciously rubbed the bayonet scar that ran along the right side of his face.

"Well, you're thirty-seven years old and you've already fought your war. Thank goodness for that at least." Catherine stared out across the street. A slim, gray-haired man in khakis and a neatly pressed white shirt pulled a red Radio Flyer wagon laden with grocery bags.

Memories of his days in the South Pacific flashed through Lane's mind. He buried them along with his concern about what was happening in Korea. It was a trick he had learned in combat when he could not afford to lose sleep worrying in the precious little time he had. "Let's just hope that there won't be a war for *anyone* to have to fight this time."

"I'm worried about Jess, Lane." Catherine blurted it out as though she felt she had to share doubts that had been plaguing her for a long while. "She's reached the point where I can't talk to her anymore."

"How does anyone talk to a sixteen-year-old?" Lane smiled. "They all know so much more than we do."

"I'm afraid it's not a joke, Lane," Catherine replied in a somber tone. "Her grades are terrible and she's gone more than she's home."

Lane felt a twinge of guilt at spending so much time with his law practice that there was little left for his family. He knew that Catherine had been left to do the majority of the disciplining of the children when it was primarily his responsibility. "I know it's normal for a girl her age to want to go a lot, but I guess we'll have to keep her home until she brings her grades up."

Catherine sipped her tea from a white porcelain cup with a grapevine pattern circling it just below the rim. She treasured the cup, as it was one of only three she had left from a set given to her as a wedding gift. "This boy, Austin Youngblood, she's seeing now. Something about him worries me."

"I thought he came from a good family," Lane remarked. He turned the newspaper over so the headlines were no longer visible. "His daddy's president of the bank. Seems like you'd approve of him."

"It's something I just can't seem to put my finger

20

on, Lane," Catherine continued, holding her cup with the fingertips of both hands.

"I've only seen the boy a couple of times—and that was when Jess had him moving in a big hurry toward the front door." Lane folded his hands on his bare stomach. He wore only his pajama bottoms, and even though it was not yet eight o'clock, a light film of perspiration coated his chest and arms. He still kept in shape by running and doing calisthenics three times a week, but his South Pacific tan had long since faded, replaced by a mild case of courtroom pallor. "Maybe I should have a little man-to-man talk with the young Mr. Youngblood. See if I can find out what his intentions are toward our daughter."

"Don't be too hard on him," Catherine warned. "It's still just a feeling I have."

"Okay."

Catherine hesitated to continue. "He seems so— well, kind of adventurous, like he's always looking for something dangerous to do, something that normal boys his age would never think about getting into."

"Maybe we should just end the whole thing between them, then," Lane suggested.

"No, that would only make Jessie all the more determined to go with him," Catherine objected, "and, besides, I think he could turn into a fine young man if he could just get over whatever it is that seems to be troubling him."

"Now you've got me really confused," Lane admitted. "I don't know whether to have the boy flogged or recommend him for sainthood."

"I guess it's just a mother's concern for her daughter. I can see why she's attracted to him too." Catherine gazed directly into Lane's eyes. "He's unpredictable and a little wild—kind of like you were at his age."

"I was never wild," Lane objected. "Was I?"

Catherine stood up and walked over to one of the white columns that extended from ground level to the roof. Leaning against its smooth, cool surface, she turned to face her husband. "I was just remembering when I was Jess's age. *My*, how I was in love with you!"

Lane gazed at Catherine's eyes, blue as cornflowers. An errant breeze swirled her light blond hair about her face, suffused with an immeasurable sweetness and serenity. She looked ten years younger than her thirty-five years, and he felt grateful that she had stuck by him through the times when he didn't deserve it. He pushed a faint memory of Bonnie Catelon's dark beauty back into the deepest recesses of his soul. Bonnie was a mistake—a horrible one, for which Catherine had forgiven him. Forgiving himself was another matter. "I hope you still are."

Catherine gave her husband a look of pensive dreaminess, as though the years they had spent together should have been answer enough. "One more problem, before we venture into a more pleasant area."

"Cass."

"Yes—Cass."

"The boy's only eight years old," Lane said wearily. "How can he get into so much trouble?"

"It's not so bad this time."

"You mean they couldn't find the body?" Lane wiped his brow in mock relief. "Good—that means they haven't got any substantial evidence. No body— no crime."

Catherine stared at her husband, shaking her head

in exasperation. "Lane, he's your son. How can you talk about him that way?"

"Sorry," Lane replied sheepishly. "I foolishly cling to the hope that we'll get through a whole week without any problems from that boy."

"Now." Catherine walked over and sat down in Lane's lap. "Can you be serious for a moment?"

"You bet," he grinned back at her, his arms circling her small waist as he pulled her close and nibbled on her earlobe.

"That's not serious." Catherine put her hands against his chest and pushed back. "That's fun."

"Okay, what did he do?"

"Well." Catherine nodded toward the next-door neighbor's house. "He was playing service station and the car—"

"He wrecked the man's car—somehow!" Lane sat upright, almost spilling Catherine onto the floor. "How in the world could an eight-year-old boy wreck a car?"

"Settle down," Catherine pleaded. "He didn't wreck anything. It's not that bad!"

"It's not that bad?" Lane repeated, his jaw set in anger. "That's the same thing you said when he broke a window out of a passing police car!"

Catherine put her hands against Lane's chest, pushing him gently back against the chair. "Just listen, will you?"

Lane took a deep breath, expelling it loudly. "All right. I'll listen."

"Cassidy was playing service station and he put some gas—I mean water—in Mr. Mobley's car."

"With the garden hose—right?"

"Right."

"Of all people, it had to be ol' man Mobley," Lane

moaned. "He'll sue me for a million dollars. They'll haul me off to the debtor's prison!"

Catherine finally realized that Lane had been putting her on, that his near-hysteria about Cassidy's misbehavior was all an act. "You fooled me again, Lane Temple!"

"Who, me?"

"I'll never believe another word you *say* as long as I live!" Catherine pouted.

Lane broke into laughter, throwing his head back, his chest shaking.

"Think you're smart, don't you?"

Lane tried to stop laughing, catching his breath as he wiped tears out of the corners of his eyes. "I wish you could have seen your face—absolutely priceless!"

"Well—what are you going to do about it, Milton Berle, Jr.?" Catherine asked huffily.

"It's already done."

"What?"

"I saw Mobley when I got home last night," Lane explained smugly. "Took care of the whole thing right out there in the driveway."

"He wasn't mad?"

"Not after I told him I'd take care of the garage bill," Lane explained. "Matter of fact, he thought the whole thing was kind of funny."

"He did?"

"Sure," Lane continued, "but there's one little boy who's not going to think it's funny as soon as he wakes up."

"Don't be too hard on him, Lane," Catherine frowned. "After all, he's only a baby."

"He's not quite a baby anymore, Cath," Lane reminded her, "but just to accommodate your fears, I'll use the smallest belt I have on his little behind."

Catherine stood up and began clearing off the table. "At least Dalton and Sharon are toeing the mark."

"We're batting five hundred, then. Ted Williams' average wasn't *that* good."

"Sharon is so quiet I hardly even know when she's around," Catherine remarked, pouring the last of the coffee into Lane's cup and handing it to him.

"Thank the Lord for that! Cass makes enough noise for three kids." Lane sipped the coffee. "I'll bet that girl reads more books than an English professor."

"And Dalton's always too tired from playing to get into any mischief. All that child thinks about is football," Catherine continued, "that or some other sport."

Lane stared down at a yellow cat creeping across the side yard in the deep shadows of the live oak. "He'll get a football scholarship to LSU or I miss my guess."

"That sounds almost traitorous coming from a former Ole Miss quarterback."

"I want him playing *here*, Cath," Lane explained. "If he goes to Oxford I might miss some of the games."

Catherine had finished stacking all the dishes onto a tray. She ran her fingers through Lane's brown hair, still tousled from sleep, and sat back down on his lap. "There's something I've been meaning to talk to you about since last Sunday. You feel like listening to it now?"

"Not about Cass, is it?"

"No, I'm afraid that's all for this week's episode," Catherine replied. "It's about a speaker we had at church last Sunday night. He's a doctor at the leprosarium."

"You mean that leper colony down at Carville?"

25

Lane couldn't imagine why Catherine would be interested in such a place.

"You make it sound so—*biblical*—almost like the patients run around with bells on their necks crying, 'Unclean! Unclean!' It's nothing like that at all. The doctor told us all about it," Catherine explained. "The patients live in dorms and there are even cottages for the married patients."

After seventeen years of marriage, Lane had learned that Catherine didn't approach subjects of this nature lightly. She had already made up her mind that she wanted to *do* something. "Leprosy's communicable, isn't it?"

"Yes," Catherine replied, some doubt creeping into her voice. "But the doctor told us it's transmitted from one person to another only after 'prolonged and intimate contact.'"

"What's your interest in all this?"

Catherine traced the scar on Lane's face. It felt like smooth, pale rubber. "Some of those people never get any visitors—no relatives, no one."

"And you're going to take the place of somebody's dead daughter or no 'count son."

"You think that would be all right?" Catherine leaned on Lane's chest, resting her head against his shoulder.

"I love that perfume."

"You didn't answer my question." Catherine refused to let him distract her.

"No danger of contagion, huh?"

"No. None at all," Catherine assured him. "I won't be treating anyone, just visiting."

"Fine with me, then."

"With all the children in school, I've got extra time to do things like this now." Catherine made tiny circles on Lane's shoulder with her fingernail.

"I *said* it's all right."

"Good." Catherine slid off his lap. "Guess I'd better get this mess cleaned up, then."

Lane glanced through the open French doors into the cool, shadowy bedroom. His voice sounded raspy when he spoke. "Maybe we ought to take a nap first. Dalton and Cass will be up soon and that'll be the end of that."

Catherine blinked slowly, giving Lane a smile that carried a festive tenderness. "Maybe you're right."

TWO

LEPER

★ ★ ★

Catherine drove her black Chrysler south of LSU along the two-lane blacktop that followed the serpentine course of the Mississippi River. To her right, just beyond a barbed-wire fence, the levee rose upward and away from her. Black-and-white Holstein cows grazed in the lush grass on its slope. Farther up, outlined against the blue sky, two boys wearing only faded overalls and straw hats walked along the crest of the levee carrying cane fishing poles over their shoulders.

Turning left off the river road, Catherine drove down a gravel drive toward an antebellum house in the distance. Dr. Curtis Farr had told her about the mansion, built in 1858 and housing the administrative offices of the hospital. She parked beneath a huge magnolia tree in front of a peeling white "Visitor" sign lettered in black.

Walking along the brick path that led up to the house, Catherine saw Dr. Farr step out onto the wide front porch. He looked almost childlike in his starched white smock, except for the fact that his blond hair was thinning on top. His steel-rimmed glasses glinted in the light.

"Hello, Mrs. Temple," Farr greeted her. "So glad you could make it."

"I am too, Doctor." Intrigued by the sparse account he had given her about the man, Catherine eagerly anticipated meeting the patient Farr had assigned as her very own.

"Would you like some coffee?"

"No thanks," Catherine said, glancing about the grounds. "I only have an hour or so."

"Sure, sure. I understand," Farr replied, smoothing his tiny cornsilk mustache with one finger. "Let's see if we can locate Mr. McCurley. By the way, he likes to be called Homer."

They had only gone a few yards when Farr stopped and pointed to a stone bench beneath a live oak. The man sitting on the bench wore a dark brown fedora, white shirt, and brown dress slacks. "There he is now."

Catherine felt suddenly drawn to this man whose face she couldn't even make out beneath the shadow of his hat.

"Come on," Farr piped. "I'll introduce you." He started toward his patient.

Catherine took him by the arm. "If it's all right, Doctor, I'd like to meet him by myself."

"Certainly." Farr turned to leave. "If there's anything you need, just come back to the house. Anyone can tell you where my office is."

"Thank you." Catherine walked across the clipped lawn through a copper-colored haze of sunlight filtering around her through the trees. As she got closer, the shadowy figure on the bench turned toward her. She felt as though she were a supplicant approaching the altar.

The man stood awkwardly to his feet as Catherine got closer. He balanced himself on a heavy, mahogany-colored cane he held in his left hand. His right hand was a mass of bandages, his right foot lost in a canvas shoe-like covering that was belted above his ankle. Shadow still masked the features of his face.

"How do you do, Homer? Is it all right if I call you that?" Catherine held out her hand as she walked up to the man.

Homer found himself in an awkward position. He could only greet people with his left hand and it was now occupied with supporting his weight on the cane. "I'm afraid I'll have to sit back down to shake hands with you, Mrs. Temple."

Catherine felt the rush of warmth up her neck and into her face. "Oh, I'm so sorry. That was thoughtless of me."

Homer waved the apology off as soon as he had taken his seat. "Don't worry about it. It takes most folks a while to get comfortable around the likes of us. Come to think of it, maybe that's why they don't come to visit much. Sometimes I forget that the average person hasn't seen the things I have."

"I—I just . . ." Catherine sat on the bench next to Homer, trying to regain her composure.

"You just forget about it and let's have us a nice visit," Homer said in a reassuring tone.

Catherine smiled, feeling the almost physical presence of Homer's warmth and understanding. "All right. That's why I came down here, isn't it?"

"Yep."

Catherine gazed at Homer's face as she spoke. Several reddish lumps on his cheeks and around his eyes gave his face the appearance of an unfinished clay sculpture. His eyes were a clear hazel color beneath his white eyebrows, his nose small and straight above lips that were so softly curved, they looked almost as delicate as a child's.

Homer touched his face lightly with his bandaged right hand. "It's much better now. They're treating me with something called sulphones."

"I'm sorry," Catherine muttered, dropping her gaze. "I didn't mean to stare."

"Now we can't have you apologizing this whole visit," Homer chided gently. "It's only natural to be curious about somebody who's got leprosy."

Catherine nodded.

As though to get the inspection part behind them, Homer turned his head to the left. "The drugs are a real blessing, but I got them too late to help this."

Catherine glanced up and saw that his right ear was missing. A crusty white area around the opening was all that remained. She felt herself tremble slightly, but braced up and continued with the conversation. "Does it hurt terribly?"

"Doesn't hurt at all."

"It doesn't?"

"No. That's one of the problems," Homer explained. "You lose sensation, especially in the extremities. That's how I lost some fingers and toes."

"I'm so sorry this happened to you!" Catherine felt as though a black cloud had descended over her. She had come to minister to this man and found herself utterly miserable and unable to do anything except dwell on how horrible his condition was. *Maybe I'd just better leave this poor man alone and stick to something I can handle, like working in the church nursery or tidying up the pastor's study.*

"You've come for a visit and I'm upsetting you by all this talk. Now it's my turn to apologize." Homer reached out with his good left hand and clasped Catherine's. "There's no reason at all for you to be upset. For the first time in more than forty years I'm finally getting some rest."

Catherine smiled weakly, feeling the gentleness of Homer's work-hardened hand. "I'm afraid I don't know very much about you, Homer. When Doctor Farr came to the church, he told us there were about four hundred patients down here. With so many, he couldn't tell us anything specific."

"I was a missionary," Homer began. "I should say *we* were missionaries—my wife, Velma, and me."

"Oh, I think that's wonderful." Thoughts of Homer's condition had vanished from Catherine's mind as she found herself imagining all the exotic places he must have seen. "When I was a little girl I used to love it when the missionaries would come to speak at our church."

A twitch of nostalgia made Homer smile. "I remember a Sunday night when a missionary came to our little church in Andalusia, Alabama. When that service was over I knew what I was going to do with the rest of my life."

Remembering the little church in Eupora, Mississippi, where she had gone as a child with her mother and daddy, Catherine gazed out across the shining green lawn to a tumbledown shack. It sat in a pasture beyond a split-rail fence that marked the boundary of the hospital grounds.

Abandoned to the encroachments of innumerable summers, its rusted tin roof had dropped down on the rotted walls only two feet above the ground. Briars and weeds almost covered the remains of the structure. The thought came to her that this had once been someone's home where meals were cooked and laughter rang in the child-loud yard on summer days just like this one.

Homer followed Catherine's gaze. "I look at that old cabin a lot myself. Lived in one a lot like it."

"I think many of us who grew up in the South have—at one time or another," Catherine added, "but you were telling me about your calling."

"That's what it is, all right—a calling," Homer smiled. "A body wouldn't last long if he just picked it out in the classified ads of a newspaper."

"I imagine not," Catherine laughed.

"You sure you want to hear this?"

"Oh yes," Catherine replied quickly.

"Well, I'll try not to bore you," Homer said, shifting his weight on the bench so that he could balance himself with his good left foot touching the ground. "They sent us to Liberia. Me and my new bride. We'd only been married two weeks. There wasn't even a harbor in Monrovia in those days."

Catherine leaned back against the rough bark of the live oak, listening with wonder to this story of so many years ago. The sun was climbing steadily in the clear blue summer sky. By three o'clock it would feel like a flame held close to the skin, draining the energy from even the heartiest souls and the trees themselves would seem to hover on the brink of combustion.

"They picked us up out at the ship in a dugout canoe and paddled us thirty miles up the Cavally River." Homer's face held a serene smile as he recounted the days of his youth with his new bride and his old calling. "Trip took five days. Our first house was a mud hut with a thatched roof. The second night a leopard

34

stuck his head in the door."

"Gracious! How did your wife stand to live there?" Catherine interrupted.

"I asked myself that same question—I couldn't count the number of times," Homer replied, shaking his head slightly. "Sometimes a person can do a whole lot more than he ever thought he could."

A breeze from the river stirred the leaves of the trees and refreshed Catherine as she sat with Homer in the brief and fragile coolness of the shade. She lost herself in his story, could almost see the coconut palms along the coastal plain; the towering mahogany trees of the inland forests; the elephant, buffalo, hippopotamus, and flamingo; and the wild, dark villagers in their scanty garb.

"My goodness," Catherine cried, glancing at her watch. "I'll be late for the meeting."

"I do tend to ramble on, don't I?" Homer said, the sound of Catherine's voice pulling him back to the present.

"Oh, I could listen to your stories all day, but we've got this meeting at the church and I promised I'd be there," Catherine explained. "It's about cooking and taking meals to the families who have a death."

"Another noble calling," Homer smiled.

Catherine thought he was making a joke at first, then saw the sincere light in his eyes. "Maybe it is at that."

Homer merely nodded.

"Can I do anything for you before I go?"

"No thanks," Homer waved her offer away with his good hand. "You've done more than enough."

"I'll be back to see you next week—if that's all right." Catherine stood up, glancing again at her watch.

"It's more than all right," Homer smiled.

Catherine waved and walked away, but stopped after a few steps. "What do you like to eat?"

Homer thought on it for a moment. "Collard greens and corn bread."

Catherine smiled, nodding her head, then turned and headed toward her car.

"And ice tea," Homer called out.

Catherine waved and continued on her way. As she opened the car door, she glanced back at Homer. He still sat under his tree on the glistening green grounds of the hospital, a small man ravaged by a terrible disease—alone in the world. As she got into her car, she hoped that one day she would be as completely happy and content with her life as Homer McCurley appeared to be with his.

★ ★ ★

Located on Lakeshore Drive east of Bayou St. John, Ross Michelli's house stood on an artificially constructed mound of earth overlooking Lake Pontchartrain. Almost hidden behind the white brick wall, it held a strong resemblance to its owner: remote, austere, inaccessible.

The concrete drive led through a heavy, scrolled iron gate set into the walls. Winding through a lawn of carpet-plush St. Augustine grass, landscaped with flower beds, blooming citrus trees, crepe myrtles, and date palms, the drive ended at a five-car garage that was a part of the house.

The house itself was a low, sprawling one-story structure of white stucco with a terra cotta roof, emitting a warm burnt-orange glow at sunset. A wide gallery with heavy white columns across the front of the house afforded an unspoiled view of the lake as the

traffic along Lakeshore Drive remained hidden behind the wall at the base of the sloping lawn.

Sitting in a cushioned wrought-iron chair next to
Michelli, Lane listened to the palm fronds rustling in
the wind. Although it was a professional call, he wore
tan slacks and a blue knit shirt instead of a coat and
tie at Michelli's insistence that comfort was much
more important than style. "I don't know if I can do
that or not, Mr. Michelli."

"Sure you can." Michelli took a swallow of ice tea
from a tall, cold glass. "It's just business."

Lane glanced at a big man seated in the small alcove on the far end of the gallery. He had dark, bristly
hair and the sharp eyes of a predator. A sunken place
on his forehead looked as though he had been hit with
a piece of pipe. His bulky chest and shoulders
strained at the seams of his gray suit coat.

Lane had seen the man at the St. Louis Cathedral
when he first met Michelli, and he was also present
the two times he had met with him afterward. He was
like Michelli's atavistic shadow, but even the evil portent of his presence paled in comparison to that of his
boss.

For some time Lane had known that Michelli was
reputed to be the iron hand behind organized crime
in the New Orleans area. However, the work he had
done for Michelli in the past had always held to the
letter of the law. "I know it's just business, Mr. Michelli, but you're under investigation by the FBI and I
can't afford to get involved in something like that."

"How many times I got to tell you—call me Ross."
Michelli's dark eyes held a mica glint, but his teeth
flashed in a white smile against his olive skin. "Hey,
it's me they're after—not you. It's a part of my life I've

learned to accept and they've never pinned one thing on me in thirty-five years."

Lane knew that Michelli liked him but could never figure out why. "There are a hundred lawyers here in New Orleans you could get to do this job for you."

"I don't want a hundred lawyers. I want you."

"You're a hard man to turn down, Mr.—Ross."

"Look, I know about that oil lease business with Catelon up in Baton Rouge. He sucked you into it without telling you the truth." Michelli stared at a lone sailboat, its canvas popping loudly and its bow slapping into the water as it tacked hard in the white-caps out on the lake. "But you stood up to him, backed out of it even though he threatened to put you out of business. I know he's hurt your practice some too."

"I'll survive," Lane said flatly, thinking how right Michelli was about Catelon's effect on his law practice. "How did you find out about that anyway?"

"I know all about Andre Catelon," Michelli snorted. "Went to McDonogh No. 19 with him when we were kids. He was a punk then, and he's a punk now. I knew back in the sixth grade he'd make a good politician."

Lane continued to be amazed at Michelli's knowledge of business and political happenings. He seemed to have his finger on the pulse of the state's government and economy.

"I can understand your not wanting to do business with a politician, Lane, but I'm just a businessman."

Lane watched a storm building out on the lake. A web of white lightning flashed against a dark cloud wall. "Well, you've always been straight with me in the past."

"And that's exactly why I want you to handle this deal for me," Michelli assured him. " 'Cause I know I can trust you. There aren't many lawyers I can say that about."

"There's something else I haven't told you about that might make you change your mind."

"What?" Michelli snorted. "You got a terminal disease or something?"

"No disease," Lane answered, almost bitterly, "but it could be terminal."

Michelli waited for him to explain.

"I got a letter from the Department of Defense," Lane continued. "I'm still in the inactive reserves and they're considering calling some of them up for Korea."

"So?"

"So I might have to go back in the Marines."

"Nah."

"What are you talking about?"

"I can take care of that," Michelli remarked matter-of-factly, as though they were discussing a parking ticket. "Anything else on your mind?"

"Wait a second." Lane felt that he hadn't made himself clear. "I don't understand what you're saying, but I'm talking about the United States Marine Corps."

"So what?" Michelli answered, taking a long swallow of ice tea. "These things can be handled on a local level. Nothing to worry about."

"Ross, there's a war going on, in case you haven't heard," Lane explained slowly, a feeling of unreality coming over him. "I may have to fight."

"You're wrong."

Lane gave him a blank look.

"It's not a war—it's a police action. President Truman said so himself."

Lane shook his head slowly.

Michelli persisted with—to his way of thinking—perfect logic. "You want to fight in a police action? Join the police force. Don't go risking your neck for something halfway around the world that this country's got no business sticking its nose in anyway. It ain't the smart thing to do."

Lane saw there was no use trying to reason with Michelli. "If they call, I have to go, Ross. I don't understand the politics of it altogether, but I figure if you're going to live in this country you take the good with the bad. You don't cut and run just because you don't agree with the kind of wars we make."

"Stupid! Makes no sense at all." Michelli made a sucking sound with his teeth. "But it's your hide, Lane."

"Yes, I guess it is."

"Sure you won't reconsider?" Michelli offered. "One phone call and you're off the hook."

Lane shook his head.

"Well, you ain't gone yet. Maybe they'll call the whole thing off like sensible men."

Lane watched the gray wall of rain move across the lake toward them. The wind had risen, whipping the charcoal-colored water into a frenzy of whitecaps. Overhead the palm trees swayed, their fronds clattering now like machine gun fire. A cool spray blew in underneath the gallery, covering the tiled floor with a glistening sheen of water.

Michelli stared into the storm. "Beautiful, ain't it? More power than the atom bomb."

Lane had to agree with him. The storm held a magnificent, lethal, almost mesmerizing power. He glanced to his left toward the distant docks and slips of the New Orleans Yacht Club. Through the sweep of rain across the lake, the sailboat was little more than a small white dot in the churning waves. "I hope he makes it."

"Who?"

Lane pointed to the boat.

"Stupid," Michelli grunted. "He don't *deserve* to make it. Come on inside. We got some business to take care of."

★ ★ ★

Coley Thibodeaux was an honest politician, a state representative who looked out for the interests of the plant workers, salesclerks, carpenters, and custodians who elected him to office—not for the privileged circle of relatives, toadies, and money-proffering lobbyists that most other elected officials catered to.

This single quality should have made Coley as rare and valuable a commodity as the lost Ark of the Covenant, but he had always been that way, and people merely took his integrity for granted as a man would the comfort of an old slouch hat that he wore on weekends.

Blade-slim, with a slightly hawklike face, thin nose, long dark hair and clear gray eyes, Coley had been a marine until that part of his life ended on the war-blasted beaches of Tarawa. He still remained mobile enough in his wheelchair to handle his law practice and his duties as a representative.

Coley's district was an area of North Baton Rouge near the sprawling ESSO Standard Oil Company and other plants. Affectionately called "Dixie" by its mostly working-class population, it was comprised primarily of rednecks from Mississippi and North Louisiana as well as Cajuns from the swamps of the Atchafalaya Basin and the prairies and marshes to the west.

Hebert's Coffee Shop occupied one corner of the huge Hebert Building with the red neon sign on top depicting a bear with the letter "A" in front of it, the two symbols combining to pronounce the French name.

The building, which took up an entire block along Senic Highway across from ESSO, was the place Coley "held court" almost every weekday morning. His constituents brought their requests to his corner table where the two plate glass windows fronting the streets fitted into a massive pillar of hewn cypress. They knew he would always make time to listen to them.

Strangely enough, no one ever took advantage of Coley's accessibility. The people of his district always approached him one at a time and, as if by common agreement, saw that this daily ritual never lasted longer than an hour. They were confident that he would be there the next morning if they failed to see him in the allotted time.

By eight o'clock "court" was over. The tables, the booths along the windows, and the red-cushioned stools at the counter were filled with men and women, most of whom worked in the neighborhood. Wearing business suits, white shirts and ties, or blue jeans, khakis, and heavy work shoes, they all had the easy familiarity of people for whom class distinctions held little meaning.

Coley, dressed in his customary gray herringbone jacket, faded jeans, and brown loafers, sipped his coffee as he read the morning newspaper. Glancing up, he noticed Lane walk out the front door of the narrow office building they shared and that Coley owned. Fronting on Senic Highway, Coley's office was on the first floor with his living quarters directly behind it.

Up the single flight of stairs Lane had an office and bath.

Lane entered the noisy coffee shop through the double glass doors and walked directly over to Coley's table. Catching the eye of one of the black-and-white uniformed waitresses, he motioned for coffee.

"'Bout time you showed up," Coley grinned. "I thought all you Mississippi boys got up with the chickens."

"I think I must have picked up some of these lazy Cajun ways over the last three years," Lane shot back. "I also had to take a deposition. Some of us have work to do and some of us sit over here at Hebert's shooting the breeze."

Coley glanced back down at his newspaper. "That *is* work for politicians. How you think South Louisiana stays so warm? All that hot air blowing out of the capitol building whenever the legislature's in session."

"At least you don't pretend like it's a *real* job, like some I know." Lane thanked the waitress as she set his coffee in front of him.

"Listen to this," Coley said, folding his newspaper into a smaller square.

"I can read, Coley."

"But it sounds so sweet in my quaint Cajun accent, cher." Coley pronounced *cher* "sha," as in shack. "This fellow Daniel Marsh, he's president of Boston University—I don't expect an Ole Miss graduate like you to know who he is. Anyway, Marsh says, and I quote, 'If the television craze continues with the present level of programs, we are destined to have a nation of morons.'"

Lane gazed at the bustle of activity around him, people leaving for work and others taking their places. "Well, I certainly can't take issue with him since I don't have one."

"I saw *You Bet Your Life* with Groucho Marx over at my uncle's the other night. It was kind of funny."

Staring out the window at the seemingly endless stacks and columns and buildings of ESSO, Lane looked sadly, almost morosely preoccupied.

"I saw in Saturday's paper where Istrouma beat Warren Easton twenty-six to nothing." Coley thought he knew what was on Lane's mind, but tried to cheer him up anyway. "That made you happy didn't it?"

"Sure."

"I see where MacArthur scored a major victory at Inchon," Coley said deliberately, knowing that this would get his friend's attention.

Lane glanced up, his face clouded with concern. "If they turn him loose, he'll go all the way to the Yalu River—maybe beyond if the Chinese don't stop him first."

"MacArthur says the war'll be over by Christmas."

"It might, if he'd just recapture Seoul and be content to take back what belonged to South Korea before this thing started—but he won't. I learned something about MacArthur when I was in the South Pacific."

"What—in particular?"

"He's a great general," Lane explained, "but he loves being on center stage."

Coley folded his newspaper and laid it aside. "You don't think taking Seoul back will end the war?"

"No," Lane said flatly. "I think the general wants the whole shooting match and the Chinese aren't going to stand for it. This war's just beginning."

Coley cut to the heart of the matter. "And you think you'll have to go back in the corps?"

"Yep, that's what I think." Lane's brown eyes were thoughtful as he continued to stare out the window. "And I don't know if Catherine can handle it this time. Not to mention all the bills we've got. Can't make it on what Uncle Sam'll pay me."

"I think you might be surprised at what Catherine can handle," Coley remarked.

"What do you know about it?" Lane gave him a look of mild surprise. "I know how rough she had it when I was gone in the last war."

"Things are different now."

"How?"

"She has her faith to help her get through it."

Lane sipped his coffee, his eyes narrowed in concentration. "Well, she does seem to be a lot happier now, but things are still going to be rough if they take me."

"Paul said in his epistle to the church at Phillipi, 'I can do all things through Christ which strengtheneth me.' I believe that, Lane. So does Catherine."

Lane watched the cars of the ESSO executives pulling through the main gates. The working men walked, rode bicycles, or were dropped off by their wives.

"There's something you seem to have forgotten in all this worry about your family, Lane." Coley knew that Lane relied on his own strength, determination, and sheer guts, knew that he had been through some of the bloodiest fighting in the South Pacific and that he had stood his ground against the most powerful men in state government. He also realized there came a time in everyone's life when he discovered he couldn't make it on his own.

"What's that?"

"Yourself," Coley answered. "They might have

some problems, but if you have to go, you'll be facing death every day."

"I've been there before, Coley," Lane remarked impassively. "I can do it again."

"Just one more—"

"Coley," Lane cut him off. "I appreciate your concern, but I don't need a sermon right now. Okay?"

"Sure, Lane. It's okay."

THREE

THE SHEDDING OF BLOOD

★ ★ ★

"Well, that was a crummy movie. I should have known it *would* be, with a title like *The Asphalt Jungle*." Jessie walked along in the crowd next to Austin, past the colored posters advertising coming attractions, past the ticket booth, out under the shining marquee of the Hart Theater. She wore a red sweater over her white cotton blouse and a gray tartan-plaid skirt.

In his usual Levi's and brown penny loafers, Austin also had on his maroon and gray Istrouma "letter" jacket against the slight October chill. "That blonde sure wasn't crummy."

Jessie hit him playfully on the shoulder. "*I'd* better be the only blonde you have *your* eyes on, Austin Youngblood!"

Austin took Jessie's hand as they crossed Convention Street to the parking garage. "Oh, you are, sweetheart. I don't even remember her name."

"Marilyn Monroe," Jessie snapped. "And you can

tell *she'll* never get anywhere in the movies. Just another dumb blonde with a good figure."

Walking between the square pillars of the ground floor parking area, Austin dropped a dollar bill in the hand of the black-jacketed attendant after he roared down the ramp and stepped out of the Chevy.

With Jessie seated close beside him, Austin squealed out of the garage, the tires laying down strips of rubber on the concrete floor. "Where do you want to go?"

"I'm starving." Jessie clung to Austin's arm, leaning against him as she flicked on the radio.

Austin slowed down at the traffic light on Third Street, then zipped on through it, turning north while it was still red. "You're *always* starving."

"Did you see that light, Austin?"

"Light? What light?"

"You're going to end up in jail one day if you don't learn to obey the rules," Jessie complained. "We might have gotten into a wreck."

Austin gave her a quick peck on the cheek. "Okay, if it bothers you that much I'll never do it again," he promised as he sped through the red light at the corner of Florida Boulevard.

Jessie stared wide-eyed as a gray sedan, its driver bearing down on his horn, swerved to miss them. "Oh, you're simply impossible!"

"What? What'd I do?"

Jessie merely shook her head and leaned back, gazing down the passing side streets that led to the river two blocks away. She could see the booms and stacks of the oceangoing vessels, dimly outlined above the levee. In a few moments the Pentagon Barracks, once home to such men as Andrew Jackson and Jefferson Davis, appeared on her left. On the right, loomed the Capitol and beyond it the lake, shimmering in the city lights.

For some time now, Jessie had been riddled with doubts about her relationship with Austin. She was irresistibly attracted to him, but feared him at the same time because of his wanton unpredictability and love of danger. At times she felt that she was in too deep emotionally.

Jessie listened to the soft, warm voice of Nat King Cole singing "Autumn Leaves." She reached over and turned the volume up a little. "I just love that song, don't you?"

"It's all right, I guess." Austin leaned his left elbow on the window ledge, the night air blowing his black hair about his angular face. "My favorite, though, is Tchaikovsky's Third Movement from Sal Hepatica."

"Honestly, Austin!" Jessie sat up on the seat and stared directly at him. "Can't you ever be serious?"

"That's the problem with the world now, Jess. Too many serious people in it." Austin gave her an oblique glance. "Serious people start wars. Now, if you gave Sid Caesar command of the North Korean Army and put Milton Berle in charge of the South Koreans— why, that war'd be over in no time."

Jessie gave up on conversation at that point. She leaned her head back on the seat and gazed at the span of night she could see through the angle of the window. They were away from the downtown lights now, and she could see the clear dome of the sky salted with stars. Her mind turned to stardom—movie stars, singing stars, the stars people admire, stars that made them wish they were in their place. She dreamed of Hollywood and being chauffeured to fabulous parties at Beverly Hills mansions in the company of handsome, well-dressed actors.

★ ★ ★

Austin pulled his Chevy into the parking lot of
Hopper's Drive-In. It was packed with teenagers at the
wheels of their family cars. More kids sat inside,
jammed in the booths behind the plate glass windows
of the building. The main topic of conversation that
rang from car to car and in the small groups milling
about was the Indians' twenty-to-seven victory over
Fair Park. They had played in Shreveport and the
news had just been announced over the radio.

The carhop, a skinny, pimply-faced freshman, ran
over to the car, order pad in hand, yellow pencil
poised and ready. "What'll it be?"

"Two chocolate malts"—Austin glanced over his
shoulder at Jessie—"and a hamburger for the lady."

"Yes sir," the boy replied, scribbling furiously.

Austin leaned back against the seat so the boy
would have an unobstructed view. "Can you believe a
girl with a figure that good eats like a teamster? Eats
more than I do."

"Oh, hush, Austin! That's not funny."

The boy stared at Jessie, undecided as to what he
should say. "Uh . . ."

"That's what I thought," Austin continued. "You
hurry back now or she'll be gnawing on my arm."

"Yes sir." He hurried away toward a side door
tucked away next to the main entrance.

"You embarrassed him," Jessie admonished. "Do
you enjoy doing things like that?"

"Keeps life interesting, Jess," Austin grinned. "Besides, it's not like I stay up nights planning these
things. They just kind of—happen on their own."

"Look, there's Ellis and Janie." Jessie slid over on
the seat, waving and yelling out the window.

"Do you have to make such a scene?" Austin growled. "It's not Harry and Bess Truman, you know."

Jessie leaned back inside the car. "You talk about *me* after what *you* just did?"

"I didn't make a public spectacle of it," Austin defended himself. "You act like a thirteen-year-old instead of a high-school senior."

"I'm going to talk to them," Jessie said huffily. "You want to come along?"

"Might as well," Austin groaned. "I see Ellis is driving his ol' man's new Kaiser. Guess we'll have to listen to his speech about all its wonderful new features."

They got out of the car, Austin refusing to open Jessie's door for her, and threaded their way through the maze of parked cars and unparked people.

"Hey, look! It's Jessie and Austin," Ellis yelled out. "Whaddya think of my ol' man's new car?"

"Looks like a cereal box without the pictures," Austin replied, staring at the boxy Kaiser and hoping that his response would kill Ellis' sales pitch.

It did. Ellis' smile drooped to a straight line. "Well, it *is* a little plain, I guess."

Austin glanced over at Jessie, who was busy chatting with Janie at the other window. "Why are you so dressed up on a Friday night, Ellis? Coat, tie—the whole works."

Ellis gave him a sheepish smile. "I took Janie out to dinner."

"Dressed like that?"

"We went to Mike and Tony's."

Austin leaned on the window ledge. "This is more serious than I thought, Ellis. I certainly hope your intentions about this girl aren't honorable."

"We're getting married after graduation," Ellis blushed. "I'm going to work as bookkeeper at Daddy's body shop. Everything's all set."

Austin threw his hands up in the air, staring at the stars, lost now in the neon glare. "Where have I gone wrong? I've failed you, Ellis! Forgive me."

At that moment, Jessie gave a shriek of delight, then called through the car window to Austin. "Did you hear? They're getting married!"

"I heard," Austin replied, his hands still raised toward the heavens.

Jessie walked around the front of the car to where Austin stood. "Will you quit acting like an idiot and congratulate your friend?"

"I did," Austin replied, "in my own way."

"I think it's so romantic," Jessie said, taking Austin's arm. "A June wedding."

"We're picking out the rings after Christmas," Ellis added. "That's when all the good sales are."

Austin glanced down at Jessie. "Yes sir, ol' Ellis is just an incurable romantic, all right."

Jessie made a fist and hit Austin on the shoulder. She started to speak, then stared past Austin at something just behind him, her mouth still open.

Austin noticed that the noise level in the parking lot had dropped considerably. Puzzled, he glanced over his shoulder. Walking toward him was Warren Barbay, the meanest and toughest fighter on the east bank of the Mississippi, even though he was still a student at Baton Rouge High School. He could have held the title on the west bank also except for the "Gold Coast," an area of nightclubs along Highway 190 just over the bridge where knifings and shootings were as common as traffic tickets.

Barbay stood five-foot-ten and weighed two hundred pounds—forty pounds heavier than Austin. He had arms like fence posts, a barrel chest, and a neck as thick as his bullet-shaped, crew-cut head. Eyes like buckshot glinted from his fleshy face. He wore black, high-topped tennis shoes, jeans, and a black T-shirt that clung tightly to his bulging biceps and the corded muscles of his back.

It had to come sooner or later, Austin thought to himself. *Might as well get it over with now.* He casually took off his letter jacket and handed it to Jessie. Then he slipped out of his loafers so he wouldn't have their slippery leather soles as a handicap.

Realizing what was about to happen, Jessie took Austin by the arm. "Let's go. Please!"

Austin kept his eyes on Barbay. "Go around to the other side of the car and get in." *It should be interesting to see what he comes up with to kick this thing off.*

Jessie's eyes were bright with tears as she reluctantly let go of Austin's arm, walked around the car, and got in beside Janie. She noticed that everyone in the parking lot, and most who had been inside the building, now gathered in a ragged circle around Austin and Barbay, some of them standing on the hoods of cars to get a better view.

"I heard you think you're pretty tough," Barbay began, grinning at the crowd. He had walked to within six feet of Austin now, standing with his arms folded across his massive chest.

"You heard wrong," Austin answered calmly. He felt absolutely no fear now and this bothered him because he knew it wasn't normal.

"I think anybody that goes to Istrouma is a 'shim,'" Barbay bellowed for the crowd to hear. "That's half *she* and half *him*. Are you a 'shim,' Youngblood?"

A few giggles ran through the crowd.

"No." Austin glanced at the crowd. Even the eyes

of his close friends glittered with the frenzy of the pack, the malevolent gleaming satisfied only by the shedding of blood.

Things were not going as Barbay had expected. He wanted more of a show for his fans. "You trying to think of a way out of this, Youngblood?"

Austin knew it was inevitable now. He opened and closed his hands, balancing on the balls of his feet. "No, just curious. I've never seen a troglodyte up close before."

"What?" Barbay grunted. "What you talking about?"

One of Barbay's friends stepped over and whispered something in his ear, then melted back into the crowd.

Barbay's eyes bulged out. In his fury his beefy face now glowed like a fresh sunburn. He took two quick steps forward and swung a roundhouse right at Austin's head, whiffing at air as the force of the blow carried him half around.

Austin slid beneath the punch, came up from the waist, and pounded a straight right into Barbay's ear. He grunted in pain, staggered momentarily, then regained his balance and spun around to face his elusive opponent.

Knowing that Barbay was still stunned and trying to size up the situation, Austin stepped forward effortlessly and flicked two left jabs into his face before he could get his arms up. Blood poured from Barbay's nose with the first punch and spurted from his ruined lips with the second.

With a howl of rage and pain, Barbay charged, his arms spread outward. He caught Austin in a bear hug, running him into the side of Ellis' car. Holding on with his powerful arms, he used his spread legs to keep Austin pinned against the fender and began squeezing the life out of him.

Austin felt consciousness slipping away, felt the life-giving air leaving his lungs under the iron pressure of Barbay's massive arms. Austin relaxed, let his knees sag, and just for an instant the pressure eased. Then he came up with all the strength left in him, slamming his right knee into Barbay's groin.

As the pain hit him, air exploded from Barbay's mouth like the blowhole of a whale. He released his grip on Austin, staggering backward, bent over at the waist.

Slipping free, Austin shook his head, clearing his vision as he took three quick steps into an open part of the parking lot where he would have room to maneuver. Taking a few deep breaths, he felt his strength return as Barbay straightened up and turned to face him again.

But the advantage now belonged to Austin. He owned the fight at this point—it was bought and paid for by his agility, speed, and lightning reflexes.

Barbay moved slowly in, circling to his left, his shoulders sloping forward, his hands—the fingers thick as sausages—opening and closing as he sought a grip on his elusive opponent.

Austin feinted left, then stepped in and slammed a right hook into Barbay's chin. It rocked him back and before he could recover, Austin got in close and with blazing speed hit him with a short right to the solar plexis, two quick jabs to the ribs, taking the wind out of him, then sent him to his knees with a vicious right to the jaw.

Barbay's eyes glazed over like a poleaxed steer as he struggled to get to his feet. But he was far from finished, wading into Austin with windmill swings of both arms that caught nothing but air. Austin bobbed and weaved, throwing punch after punch into the wounded Barbay, until his face was a mass of raw flesh. Blood poured from several open cuts, his eyes were swollen almost shut, and his breath rasped in his throat. Still, he refused to go down—and stay down.

Suddenly, Austin sensed something had gone wrong. The howling mob around him had moved in much too close in their efforts to satisfy the bloodlust that was upon them. He found himself hemmed into an ever-narrowing tunnel of bodies with Barbay driving him toward a concrete wall at its end. His back hit the wall, throwing him momentarily off balance.

It was the opening Barbay had been hoping for. With the desperation of a drowning man going down for the last time, he swung one of his great, wild, looping rights that finally caught its mark.

Austin felt Barbay's rock-hard fist slam into his jaw, and his head hit the concrete with a sickening thud. Pinwheels of bright-colored lights spun inside his head and the lights were somehow the same as the pain that struck at him like knife blades. Hurricane winds seemed to fill his head as he plummeted into a thick, howling darkness.

★ ★ ★

"Austin! Austin!"

A damp coolness on his face seemed to be drawing him out of the hot darkness he had been plunged into. Gradually Austin opened his eyes. His left jawbone hurt, but nothing compared to the dull, sickening ache in his head. As his vision cleared, he saw Jessie's face close to his, her eyes narrowed in concern, slightly puffy from crying.

"Oh, Austin! I thought he killed you!" Jessie dipped

her handkerchief into a Coke glass of water and bathed his forehead again.

Sitting up slowly, Austin felt nausea sweep over him and lay back to let his head clear. He saw the blurry faces of Ellis and Janie peering at him over the backseat of the car as Jessie continued to bathe his face, urging him to lie still.

In a few moments he felt better. As he sat up, he saw that they were in Ellis' car, parked on a darkened side street of neat, white frame houses with flower beds and shade trees. "Where's my car?"

"It's still parked at Hopper's," Ellis volunteered.

The fight came back to Austin now like images from a damaged film flickering on a screen. He could see Barbay's ruined face, hear the dull roar of the crowd, and feel the jarring from his knuckles all the way up to his shoulders each time he slammed a punch into muscle or bone—then the shock of that crashing right fist. "We'd better go get it."

Ellis frowned. "Somebody called the cops. Let's wait 'til they clear out."

Austin knew that by the time the police arrived things would be back to normal and that, miraculously, no one would know anything about a fight.

"You should have seen Barbay," Ellis continued in a disgusted tone of voice, "standing over you yelling that he was still 'King of Baton Rouge.' "

"Long live the King," Austin mumbled. "Come on, let's go get my car."

Ellis turned around and started the engine. "Whatever you say."

"Runs good," Austin complimented him. "This is a real nice car your daddy bought."

"Thanks," Ellis grinned.

Austin felt bad about the way he had treated Ellis

and how he had always taken him for granted. "Hey, Ellis."

"Yeah."

"You're a real friend."

"Aw, anybody else would have done the same thing," Ellis said nonchalantly, but he grinned at Janie like a little boy with a new puppy.

Jessie touched Austin's face lightly with her fingertips. "You feel all right, baby?"

"Nothing a cold Coke won't cure quick enough." Austin laid his head back against the seat, glad for the comfort of Jessie's warm body next to his.

★ ★ ★

Austin waited in the shadows across the street from Jessie's house. He saw the light wink out behind the French doors leading out onto the upstairs gallery and knew that she would be coming out soon now. In a few minutes he saw her slipping down the driveway, keeping close to the house. Then, glancing both ways, she ran past the row of azalea bushes and across the street.

"Why do we have to go now?" she whispered. "Haven't you had enough excitement for one night?"

Austin took her hand and walked toward his car parked at the end of the block. His jaw still throbbed and the dull, sickening ache in his head haunted him with thoughts of his own fragile mortality. "I can't go to sleep now. Besides, this is something I've wanted to show you for a long time."

Soon they were spinning along beneath the towering steel superstructure of the Mississippi River Bridge and down into the gaudy neon glare of the Gold Coast.

"I hope it's not one of *these* awful places!" Jessie

stared at the rows of nightclubs on both sides of Highway 190. Older cars and mud-splattered pickups lined the gravel parking lots filled with crushed beer cans, bottles, and other assorted trash.

"Be patient," Austin replied enigmatically.

They passed through the din of nightclubs into the oak-lined four-lane, going beneath an overpass and turning left directly into a sugarcane field. The buggies and long-bed trucks continued to haul cane to the sugar mills even at night during the grinding season when the rush was on to complete the harvest before the first hard freeze sometime in December.

After threading his way along a narrow dirt road through a maze of the big-tired cane buggies drawn behind tractors that were entering and leaving the fields, Austin pulled off to the side in an open area shielded by cane on three sides. Getting out quickly, he knelt next to each tire in turn, letting air out, then got back behind the wheel.

As soon as the road was clear of traffic for a few moments, he eased the car forward to a point where a sidetrack crossed the road, pulled the car onto the tracks, and drove smoothly along them deep into the shadowy quiet of the cane fields and away from the noise of the harvest.

Gliding along on the rails between the dark walls of cane that grew almost to the edge of the crossties, Austin glanced over at Jessie. "Well, what do you think, Jess? Isn't this better than sleeping?"

"I can't see anything but sugarcane."

Austin shook his head slowly. "Women—you just can't please 'em."

"Well, the stars are nice," Jessie yawned, leaning her head out the window.

Ahead of them the tunnel-like opening between

the walls of cane widened where a main road crossed. Just before they reached it, they heard the blast of a horn as a truck, its trailer laden for the mill, rumbled across the tracks, a few stalks of cane bouncing off onto the roadbed.

"You'd better slow down," Jessie said with alarm. "There could be another one right behind it."

"Now where's the fun in that?" Austin stared straight ahead as the car gained speed through the intersection.

Jessie noticed the bright glow of the Gold Coast off to her left beyond a stand of oaks growing along the highway.

"You're going to love this." Austin grinned as the car curved smoothly out onto the main track.

The glow of the nightclubs was brighter now and the din from them through the trees sounded like radio static with the volume turned down low.

"This is it, Jess."

Jessie stared ahead as the ramp up to the bridge came into sight. "Austin, stop! That takes us across the Mississippi River!" But they had already begun the long, slow climb toward the dark, skeletal-appearing superstructure of the bridge.

Lost now in the adventure, Austin stared ahead at the headlights to his left and the taillights to his right of cars on the roadbed below, then glanced to his right at the glimmering lights of the little river town of Port Allen, its courthouse prominent even at this distance.

Jessie clutched Austin's arm. "What if a train comes along? We couldn't get off!"

Austin reached over into the backseat and dropped Ellis' Blue Horse notebook on the seat beside her. "Precise schedules, courtesy of Ellis Perry."

Jessie began fumbling through the notebook.

"Don't worry. The next train's not due for two hours."

As they continued to climb, the moon cast a silvery trail across the surface of the river far below. Beyond it lay the million glittering lights of the ESSO Standard Oil plant, stretched along the river and almost reaching the downtown section. The great deep water vessels lay at anchor out in the river or were moored along the docks, an occasional doll-like figure moving across their decks.

Jessie felt a sense of wonder replace the fear. "It's absolutely beautiful!"

Austin glanced over to his right. "Aren't you glad you came now?"

An occasional car hummed by them, beyond the lines of steel girders to their right and left that separated the railway from the traffic lanes of the bridge. As they continued on, the steeper downward angle of the highway on the opposite side took it below the level of the railway again. The superstructure of the bridge fell away and the unhampered view of the city and the great river sweeping toward the sea lay spread out below them.

Austin eased the car to a stop on the downward slope, pulling on the emergency brake. The night wind moaned high in the steel girders. Two hundred feet below, a ship churned slowly away from one of the wharves, moving out toward the center of the river for its long, winding trip down to New Orleans.

"How did you ever find out about this?" Jessie stared out the window, enthralled by the fantasy-like quality of the city at night from such a great height.

"Couldn't sleep a few weeks ago," Austin replied, caressing Jessie's hair. "Got to riding the rails and ended up here."

Jessie found herself again having to make that decision between boredom and danger. The other boys she had gone out with at school all paled in comparison to Austin, but with him it was either accept the risk whenever he decided to take it or be left at home. She knew several other girls who were dying to go out with him, so she accepted the risk.

How Austin could have turned out so differently from the way he was brought up remained a mystery to Jessie. His father was a conservative, rather stuffy banker and his mother a tall, elegant woman from one of Baton Rouge's oldest families with a lot of old money.

With a background like that, one would have imagined Austin to have turned out to be a studious, well-mannered son who was careful of his behavior and the company he kept. Austin was expected to follow in his father's footsteps along the traditional well-mapped-out route to an education at an Ivy League University and on to success in whatever field he chose.

In spite of his parents' expectations, Austin was almost the antithesis of this model. He seemed to have no direction in life except to follow whatever wild notion popped into his head. Rules to him were like red flags to fighting bulls. And if he ever had a serious thought about his future, no one was aware of it.

"You okay, Jess?" Austin continued to stroke the back of her hair, then let his fingers trail down her arm, placing the flat of his hand against her waist.

"Sure," she whispered, her back to him as she stared out the window. "I'm just enjoying the view. I'll bet nobody else in town has ever seen this before."

Austin took her by the shoulders and turned her toward him. *"This* is the sight I'm interested in."

Jessie stared into Austin's clean-featured face, with its slim nose and thoughtful curve of mouth. The fierce light in his eyes reminded her of Montgomery Clift, but then she was enamored of anything to do with Hollywood.

"There's no one but you, Jess," Austin said softly, a slight hoarseness in his voice. "There never will be."

"Austin—I, sometimes you make me afraid." Jessie tried to fight the unwelcomed affection for him that had begun welling up inside her breast. She didn't want to become attached to anyone. There was too much world out there to see; there were too many people left to meet.

"Afraid—of me?" Austin seemed shocked by the words. "How could you be afraid?"

Jessie took his face in her hands. "No—no! You don't understand. I could never be afraid of *you*. I've never felt so safe as when I'm with you." She thought of the danger they were in at that very moment, but didn't mention it.

"Well, what is it then?"

"I don't want to—to care about you, about anyone now." Jessie turned away, gazing down at the lights dancing on the dark surface of the river. Fear rose in her that this could be the night their passion got beyond her control. "And I'm afraid that we might . . ."

" 'Go all the way.' Isn't that what your girlfriends call it? I can wait, Jess. I'd never do anything to hurt you." Austin took her by the hand. "We've got right now, this moment, and maybe that's all we *do* have— all we'll ever have. I don't think about all the things waiting for me in some bright, beautiful tomorrow that may never come. Tonight is bright enough for me."

Jessie had never heard Austin talk this way. The

words sounded like something out of the movies. She brushed her fingertips lightly over the gauze dressing that bound his cut and bruised knuckles. Then she turned around, smiled dreamily at him, and fell into his arms.

FOUR

Coley's Cabin

★ ★ ★

"I think this is my favorite place in the world." Lane wore his most comfortable boots—the ones the Marines had issued him in Japan just before he witnessed the signing of the document of surrender on the *Missouri*—his oldest pair of khakis, and a blue flannel shirt. He sat in a ladder-back chair on the little tin-roofed gallery of Coley's cabin that was built on pilings out on a small, unspoiled lake deep in the Atchafalaya wilderness.

Coley sat next to him in his wheelchair. He was wearing his usual swamp outfit—faded jeans and a marine field jacket. "You *do* say something that makes sense now and again."

Smiling contentedly, Lane gazed out across the glassy surface of the lake. Above his head, stringers of Spanish moss lifted in an errant breeze. A sketch of cloud drifted across the mild November sky.

Dalton and Cassidy floated in Coley's pirogue off to the left of the cabin among the cypress knees, cane poles held in their hands as they stared intently at their red-and-white corks floating on the dark water.

Lane watched his sons, Dalton so much like himself, and Cassidy with his mother's pale blond hair, blue eyes, and slight frame, fishing in the sun-dappled shade of the cypress. Only their denim jackets and white T-shirts were similar.

He remembered the times his father had taken him fishing and hunting and hoped his own sons would have the same kind of pleasant memories when they were grown men and thought back to childhood. He also hoped that they would never have to go off to war.

"I hear the First Marines landed on the east coast of Korea." Lane needed to talk away the anxiety he felt about being called back in the corps and Coley, a marine veteran himself, was the only person he felt he could talk about it with comfortably. "That's my old outfit you know."

"Yeah, I read about it," Coley responded. "They're heading up toward the Chosin Reservoir."

Lane could still see the faces of men he had fought with—bearded, blackened with smoke and grime, eyes hollow and sunken from fear and fatigue. "I bet some of my old buddies are still with 'em."

"Wouldn't be surprised." Coley gazed at a blue heron poised on the limb of a Tupelo gum at the water's edge. Spreading his wings, the bird sailed out over the lake, his image flying below him in that other sky down in the lake.

"If they get to the Chosin, a million Chinese are going to swarm down on them." Lane kept his eyes on his sons. "I think MacArthur wants to end his career with a bang. After that landing at Inchon everybody thinks he's infallible. I don't know if even Truman will stand up to him."

Coley rubbed his thighs with both hands, encouraging the sluggish blood to feed them with oxygen. "I wouldn't concern myself too much, Lane. You've got four kids. There's a lot of marines with less than that, younger men too. They'll take them first."

"They'll take whoever they need, Coley," Lane said with no emotion showing at all. "If they need somebody with my combat and command experience, I'm a gone goose."

Coley grinned, feeling that Lane was able to handle the situation better now than in the past few weeks. "Well, if worst comes to worst, I'll look out for Catherine and the kids. You can count on it."

Lane glanced over at Coley and nodded, then gazed back toward his boys.

"I can take over most of your practice for you too," Coley continued. "I already know just about all the people. They come to me for help in the legislature anyway, so we'll just kill two birds with one stone."

Lane already knew that Coley would do everything in his power to help Lane's family if he were called back into the Marines, but it gave him a feeling of calm reassurance to hear Coley speak the words out loud.

Suddenly, Dalton's cork plunged beneath the surface of the tea-colored water. He yelled, and jerked back on the cane pole. The line cut back and forth through the water. "I got another one! He's a big 'un too!"

"Hold him, *cher*!" Coley yelled. "Keep the tip of that pole up. Don't let him get over to that brush pile. He'll get off the hook if you do."

"I got him! I got him!"

"Ease him a little closer to the boat. Catch the line with your left hand now."

Dalton lifted the fish with his left hand, his right hand holding the tip of the pole high in the air. The bluegill broke the surface in a bright shower, its yellow-white belly in stark contrast to its dark green upper body.

Cassidy stared glumly at the fish, flapping now in the bottom of the boat. Glaring at Dalton, he said disgustedly, "Shoot! I ain't caught one yet."

"You just ain't got the magic touch, boy." Dalton pulled the chain stringer with three smaller fish on it up from the side of the boat, threaded one of the hooks through the fish's gills, snapped it in place, and lowered it back into the water.

"You'll get something before long, Cass," Coley encouraged. "Just stick with it."

Dalton baited his hook with another red worm from his dirt-filled Campbell's Pork and Beans can and tossed it back out near the big stump where he had caught his last fish.

At that moment Cassidy's eyes widened as his head jerked around toward the side of the pirogue. He stared down into the water for two or three seconds, then slowly laid his cane pole down, reached into the bottom of the boat, and lifted a three-pronged frog gig out.

Lane stood up quickly to see what was happening. In a salient of yellow light angling down through the big cypress above them, he saw it—two feet beneath the surface. With a shudder, he recognized immediately the ponderous, torpedo-shaped body with its rounded snout and tapering tail. The slimy, mottled-green alligator gar was almost motionless, only its pectoral fins moving lazily to maintain its position in the water. It was almost as long as the pirogue in which Lane's two sons sat.

Cassidy had the gig raised above his head with both hands now, preparing to thrust it down into the gar.

"No, Cass! Stop!"

Too late.

Cassidy plunged the gig down with all his might, striking the creature just behind the right gill. With a thrashing of its huge tail, the fish spun violently around, sending waves rolling out on both sides of him.

Before the spear struck its mark, Lane had bounded off the top step, cleared the little pier at the foot of the stairs, and hit the water in a flat dive. With three powerful strokes, he reached the pirogue wallowing precariously now in the wake left by the gar. He grabbed the gunwale just as the small craft was tipping over, steadying it in the water.

Cassidy's face beamed with excitement. "Did you see him? He was a whopper!"

Dalton held on to the side of the pirogue, not realizing yet what had happened.

Lane saw the wooden tip of the frog gig cutting through the water's surface for a fleeting moment, then it disappeared as the creature made for deeper water.

"Shoot, Daddy! He got away." Cassidy slapped the side of the pirogue.

Shivering in the cold water, Lane towed the tiny boat back over to the pier. *What a child! If he lives to be twenty-one it'll be an absolute miracle.*

★ ★ ★

"Do I have to go?" Wearing a pair of old jeans and

a white sweatshirt, Jessie sat next to Catherine on the front seat of the Chrysler. "Couldn't I just wait in the car?"

"No, you can't wait in the car! It's enough that I let you get away with dressing like a street urchin." Catherine glanced into the backseat at Sharon, who had on her black patent leather shoes and a burgundy-colored dress. "I don't see why you can't dress decently like your sister."

Sharon smiled, her deep blue eyes soft and placid behind her eyeglasses. She smoothed her dark brown hair in place with both hands.

"Oh, you think she's just perfect because she makes straight A's."

"Jessie, I'm not going to speak to you again about your attitude. Homer doesn't have any family to come see him so it's the least we can do to bring him some Thanksgiving dinner." Catherine took the handles of the cane hamper on the seat beside her. "After all, he gave his whole life on the mission field."

"I don't care if he gave his life on the football field, this is a waste of my time!"

Catherine gave her daughter an icy stare. "You're coming with us, Jessie, and you're going to act like a lady."

Jessie knew what the look and the tone of her mother's voice meant. "All right," she moaned.

Carrying the hamper, Catherine walked with her daughters down a concrete walk bordered by crepe myrtles, their pale slick branches bereft of summer flowers. The walkway opened into a broad, round patio area floored with brick. A trickling fountain with a Greek water-bearer sculpture stood in the center. Several ancient live oaks spread their heavy limbs over the whole area, roofing it with a green canopy.

70

"Hello, Catherine." Homer waved from an alcove set back into the clipped hedge that bordered the patio. Wearing a neatly pressed black suit, white shirt, and a charcoal-colored tie, he was seated at a round concrete table with three curved benches that stood on the brick floor.

"Happy Thanksgiving, Homer," Catherine called back, ushering her two daughters toward him.

"Same to you."

Catherine placed the hamper on the table, introducing Homer to Jessie and Sharon.

"How do you do?"

Jessie took his good hand, barely able to hide her disgust at being there.

Sharon climbed up on the bench next to Homer and shook his good hand energetically. "Hi, Mr. Homer. What happened to your hand and your foot?"

Homer glanced down at his bandaged hand and his foot in its makeshift canvas boot. "I got sick over in Africa, and I just haven't gotten well yet. They're giving me some medicine here that's making me better though."

"I'm glad," Sharon beamed up at him.

Homer leaned back slightly, admiring Sharon and Jessie. "You certainly have two pretty daughters, Catherine."

"Thank you, Homer," Catherine smiled. "Why don't you show them the picture of Velma? She was so lovely."

"Would you like to see a picture of my wife?" Homer reached inside his coat.

"Oh yes!" Sharon's eyes sparkled. "Is it a picture from over in Africa?"

Jessie chewed absently on a thumbnail, glancing about at the barren flower beds.

71

Homer opened his wallet, taking a worn black-and-white snapshot carefully out of an inside pocket. He unwrapped the thin tissue paper covering and handed it to Sharon.

Sharon stared at the slim, dark-haired woman standing on the bank of a broad river. She wore a long black dress and her smile was so warm and genuine that it reached across the miles and the years, touching the heart of the child. Sharon smiled back at her. "She *is* pretty. Does she live here too?"

"No, baby," Homer explained. "She got sick over there too, but she died."

A single tear welled up in the corner of Sharon's eye, slipping down her face in a glistening trail. "I'm sorry."

"Thank you, sweetheart. But it's all right," Homer assured her. "It was a long, long time ago and besides, we had a lot of wonderful years together."

Jessie took the snapshot from Sharon, glancing down at it. Something stirred deep inside her, but she pushed the feeling and the snapshot away.

Staring at Homer, Catherine said cheerily, "Your face is *so* much better. The bumps are almost gone now."

"Medicine's working, I reckon," Homer explained. "I'm feeling some better too."

"Well, are you hungry?"

"I'm always hungry for your cooking, Catherine," Homer smiled, then whispered to Sharon. "Your mama cooks better than my Velma ever did. I hope she don't hear me say that up in heaven." He put his forefinger vertically in front of his lips and pointed upward.

Sharon put her hand over her mouth and giggled. "You think she'd be mad at you if she heard?"

"She might."

Catherine set the plate of turkey, dressing, butter beans, and cranberry sauce before Homer. Then she poured a glass of ice tea from a quart Mason jar. "There's pumpkin *and* pecan pie when you finish that."

"Aren't y'all eating?"

"We'll have ours tomorrow. You go ahead and enjoy the food while we visit."

Sharon helped Homer cut up his turkey and poured more tea for him while he ate. "Mama says you have a lot of stories, Mr. Homer. Will you tell us one?"

As Homer ate his Thanksgiving dinner, he told of a baby hippopotamus that got into Velma's garden and how she chased it back into the river with a hoe.

Sharon stared wide-eyed during the telling, asking questions the whole time. Jessie slouched on her end of the bench, sighing occasionally. She picked up a twig from the ground, began breaking it into small pieces and tossing them onto the table. A glance from Catherine stopped her.

When Homer had eaten and they had visited a while longer, Catherine began cleaning up the dishes and packing them back into the hamper.

"Never had a better Thanksgiving dinner," Homer remarked, rubbing his stomach.

Catherine gathered the rest of the things and set the hamper on the ground. "Thank you. I'm glad you enjoyed it."

"And that pecan pie was the best I've ever eaten anywhere, anytime."

"Now that *is* a compliment," Catherine beamed.

When they had said their goodbyes, Sharon kissing Homer on the cheek and Jessie taking his hand limply, he motioned for Catherine to stay behind for a moment while the girls walked away toward the car.

"Catherine, I just wanted to tell you I've had it on my heart lately to pray for your husband."

The statement caught Catherine off guard. "But you've never even met him."

"Doesn't matter," Homer shook his head. "Whenever it happens like this there's always a need."

"Well, there *has* been one thing bothering him lately," Catherine admitted.

Homer merely nodded, taking Catherine's hand as he gazed into her eyes. "You've been a real blessing to me."

"It's been my pleasure getting to know you," Catherine blushed. "I look forward to these times so much. It's kind of like having my daddy back again."

Homer's eyes grew bright with joy. He squeezed Catherine's hand as she turned and followed her girls back down the path between the crepe myrtles.

★ ★ ★

Connie Youngblood lay in her giant four-poster bed, propped up on a colorful array of pillows. She was a tall, big-boned woman with a long face and thin lips. Her jet black hair hung to the shoulders of her red silk lounging pajamas. Stacks of paperbacks covered the tops of both nightstands and a breakfast tray with leftovers sat on the floor next to the bed. "Austin, would you come in here a moment, please?"

Walking along the upstairs balcony past the partially opened door of his mother's bedroom, Austin was straight from the shower and wore only a pair of Levi's. A frown crossed his face beneath the tousled damp hair at the sound of his mother's voice. "I'm in kind of a hurry."

"You're always in a hurry," Connie called back. "Come see your mother for a moment."

Austin traded his frown in on an expression of benign tolerance as he sauntered into the room and plopped down on an antique chair by the side of the bed. "And what can I do for your ladyship tonight?"

"I just wanted to chat a minute," Connie replied, glancing at the rounded screen of the television against the opposite wall. "I just love this. It's *Your Show of Shows* with Sid Caesar and Imogene Coca. They're hilarious."

"Not as hilarious as you and Dad," Austin mumbled under his breath.

"What's that, son?"

"I said it's too *bad* I won't be able to see it." Austin stood up. "Well, I certainly enjoyed our little chat, Mother. I have to be going now."

"What's your hurry?" Connie's eyes remained riveted on the tiny black-and-white images on the glowing screen. "Sit down and visit with your mother."

"I just did." Austin headed for the door.

Connie tore her eyes away from the television. "You sit back down right now! I haven't *seen* you for days."

"Jessie's waiting for me." Austin clasped his hands together rubbing them back and forth. "I'm late as it is."

"Jessie. Always Jessie," Connie said, her voice rising to a whine. "I wish you'd stop seeing that little *tart*. Why can't you find a *decent* girl?"

Austin had been through this before. He bit his lips, determined not to react to the familiar tirade.

"Some of our friends have lovely daughters who'd be delighted to go out with you." Connie's face looked pale in the blue-white glare of the television screen.

"And why do you have to go to that awful school? Istrouma. What a horrible name."

"Horrible? It means 'red stick' in the Houmas Indian language. Grandpa told me we've got some Indian blood in our family," Austin explained, knowing his mother's feelings about the subject. "You're not ashamed of it, are you, Mother?"

Ignoring her son's remarks, Connie continued to stare at the television.

"You might also remember that it's the name of the city we live in—Baton Rouge, red stick in French," Austin continued, glad that he had won this minor victory. "Maybe you prefer the French version to the Indian."

"I don't care what anything means. How can I tell my friends you graduated from Istrouma?" Connie tried to regain her offensive position. "It's not too late to switch to University High or even Baton Rouge High. You can get your diploma from either one, although I'd prefer University."

Austin tuned his mother's voice down to a monotonous drone. He stared in silence at the screen, its images sharply elongated from the angle where he sat. The laughter sounded tinny and artificial like the laughter he heard from downstairs when his mother and father gave a party.

It suddenly occurred to Austin that he had heard Jessie complaining about the people out in "Dixie" and how she would give anything to go to Baton Rouge High. He thought she sounded exactly like he did, only in reverse. *I wonder if anyone's satisfied where they are*, he mused.

"Austin, are you listening to me?"

"Yes ma'am," he mumbled. "I'm going to stay at Istrouma. I like the people."

Connie turned toward him, her voice rising in anger. "People? A bunch of riffraff. Plant workers, mechanics, and beauticians. You have nothing in common with them."

"I'm leaving now."

"Your father would have stayed out there in 'Dixie' even *with* a Harvard education if he hadn't met me. Now he's a bank president and keeps company with the most *respected* people in town. I expect nothing less from my son." Connie's face registered a sudden thought. "Marvin! Marvin! Where are you. I declare that man is slower than molasses."

"If you don't like it, why don't you fix your own supper?" Austin volunteered.

Connie stared at her son as though he had suggested that she join the pipefitters union.

"I'm on my way."

Hearing the sound of his father's voice from downstairs, Austin stepped out the bedroom door onto the balcony. Staring over the rail, he saw his father walking across the parquet floor of the huge living room full of heavy, dark furniture, floor lamps and table lamps, and scattered rugs.

Two inches shorter than Austin, Marvin Youngblood had neat brown hair streaked with gray and fingernails that were always perfectly manicured. Wearing a white apron over his shirt and tie, he carried a tray with his and his wife's dinner on it.

Austin met his father at the top of the stairs. "Why do you let her do this to you?"

"Do what?" Marvin glanced at his son, but couldn't hold his gaze.

"You know exactly what I'm talking about." Austin blocked the top of the stairs.

Marvin took a deep breath. "Get out of the way,

Austin. I'm too tired for your foolishness." He walked around him, heading for his wife's bedroom.

"You run that bank like a general. People jump when you speak." Austin followed along after his father. "Then you come home and let mother treat you like the hired help."

"That's enough, Austin," Marvin snapped out of the side of his mouth. He entered his wife's bedroom with a smile. "Here you are, Connie. We can watch *The George Burns and Gracie Allen Show* while we have our dinner. It comes on in a minute or two. I think it aids the digestion to have a laugh or two while one eats."

Connie smiled brightly, staring at the steaming casserole and the salads positioned on the tray before her. "That'll be nice."

"Are her money and friends that important to you, Daddy?" Austin trembled with anger, the veins in his neck bulging. "Why do you let her treat you like a lap-dog?"

Marvin set the tray on top of a few scattered paperbacks on the nightstand and turned back toward his son, almost snarling as he tried to keep his voice low enough for his wife not to hear it. "Austin, I won't tell you again. You keep out of matters concerning your mother and me. When you're grown and have your own wife, you'll understand these things."

"I understand too much now!" Austin spat, bursting out of the room.

"I just can't understand that child," Connie sighed, reaching for her salad bowl.

Marvin set her glass of ice tea on the nightstand and went around to the other side of the bed. "I wouldn't worry, dear. It's just 'growing pains.' "

Austin walked along next to the railing of the bal-

cony that fronted on three sides of the living area below. His room was at the end on the opposite side
from his father's. Kicking furiously at his partially
opened bedroom door, he stormed inside and
slammed it shut.

Tall double windows framed the outside corner of
the room, affording an unobstructed view of the University Lake, Fraternity Row along Dalrymple Drive,
and the glowing Campanille rising in the distance
from the edge of the LSU parade ground. The drapes
remained open day and night.

Austin opened the doors of a tall walnut armoire,
knelt down, and pulled the bottom drawer out. Taking
out a bottle of white pills with a label bearing his
mother's name and the name of her doctor, he shook
one out into his hand. Then he rummaged toward the
back of the drawer behind a mountain of loose socks
and underwear, finding a square bottle of whiskey.

Walking over to the corner of his room, Austin sat
down on the wide ledge of the window, propping his
feet up and leaning back against the sill. He popped
the pill into his mouth and washed it down with a long
swallow of whiskey. In a few seconds he took another
swallow, then set the bottle carefully down on the
floor beside him.

As soon as the whiskey hit his stomach, Austin felt
the familiar warmth begin its slow spread outward
and upward, dulling his senses, blunting the rage that
had built up in him and the knife-edged anxiety that
always followed.

The headlights from the cars spinning along Dalrymple shimmered across the surface to the lake as
Austin stared out his window. Below him, on the path
between the street that ran in front of his house and
the lakeshore, a couple who looked to be in their sev-

enties walked along hand-in-hand. Tall and lean, the man always held to the outside between his wife and any danger that might come from passing cars. The woman was almost a foot shorter and slightly built with the same silver-gray hair as her husband. In the summer sunshine she wore a bonnet.

Austin had seen them hold to this routine for years now, sometimes walking at night, sometimes in the early morning hours, but they seldom missed. Although he knew very little about this man and wife, their ritual had somehow become a source of comfort and even security for him.

Reaching down for the whiskey bottle, he pulled the cork and took two short swallows. This time the harshness was gone from the liquor as it slid smoothly down into his stomach. He glanced back out the window, watching the couple disappear behind a row of cedars that grew along the path.

Austin felt certain from his years of watching the man and wife that they were happy beyond measure, content with each other and at peace with the world. He knew this in a way he didn't fully understand, but had come to accept as fact. *Maybe there's still hope for some of us.*

FIVE

SILENT NIGHT

★ ★ ★

"When's the play going to start, Mama?" Sharon sat swinging her legs next to Catherine in one of the wooden folding chairs that had been set up on the basketball court of the school gym.

Dalton, wearing his Philadelphia Eagles football jersey, sat on the opposite side of Catherine. He leaned forward and broke into the conversation. "What do you care, four-eyes? You was too scared to be in it."

"Was not." Sharon tilted her tiny chin upward in a rare show of defiance.

"That's enough, Dalton." Catherine patted Sharon on the leg. "It won't be long now, baby."

"I wasn't scared to be in the play, Mama," Sharon pouted, straightening her glasses. "They just didn't have any parts left for me. Sometimes I don't talk up as quick as the other boys and girls in my class."

"I know, baby," Catherine reassured her. "You just forget it and enjoy the play."

"Okay, Mama."

"We'll let Cass represent the Temple family just for tonight." Catherine crossed her fingers.

"Hey, isn't that Steve Van Buren's jersey number?" Coley leaned over in his wheelchair, parked in the aisle next to Lane's seat, as he spoke to Dalton.

"Yes sir. He's my favorite," Dalton said proudly. "I'm gonna play in college and then go to the pros and run just as good as him one day."

"I believe you'll do *just* that, Dalton," Coley smiled. "How'd you finally come out at the end of the season?"

"He had more yardage than any junior-high running back in the whole city," Lane beamed. "Didn't you, son? And all the other runners-up were eighth graders."

Dalton leaned over so he could see around his daddy, nodding proudly.

A dull roar permeated the gym with a hundred different conversations and people milling about hunting enough seats together for themselves and their families. The double doors at the back let in blasts of cold air as they were continually opened, then let go to slam shut. The PA system screeched through the speakers as someone behind the maroon-colored velvet curtains made adjustments.

Mrs. Watson, the elementary school principal, stepped through the curtains to stand in front of the heavy chrome microphone. She had her gray hair up in a bun and wore a dark polka dot dress. The microphone whined like a spoiled child as she took hold of it to adjust the height. "Good evening, parents, students, and friends. Welcome to Istrouma Elementary's annual Christmas pageant. I hope . . ."

After Mrs. Watson's usual lengthy greeting, the microphone wailed one last time as she carried it on its heavy stand off to the side of the stage.

The houselights dimmed and the curtains slowly began to part. A grade-school mural of a rocky hillside outside Bethlehem provided the backdrop for three shepherds sitting around a light-bulb campfire, glowing redly through a sheet of plastic. A small goat with cotton balls pasted to him in the failed hope of making him look like a sheep, stood placidly at the end of a clothesline tether held by one of the shepherds.

Suddenly the strains of a harp sounded from the background and Cassidy appeared on stage right, dressed in a bed-sheet angel robe with a sequin-studded cardboard halo and floppy wings. The shepherds jumped up, trembling with fright.

And waving his billowing bed sheet, Cassidy said unto them, "Fear not: for, behold, I bring you good tidings of great joy, which shall be to all people."

Out in the audience, Sharon stared wide-eyed at her little brother, hardly able to believe that he was doing such a splendid job as an angel.

The placid little goat began pawing one foot slowly on the hardwood floor of the stage.

"For unto you is born this day in the city of David a Saviour, which is Christ the Lord."

Catherine turned to Lane, whispering, "He's doing so well. He hasn't missed a single word."

The goat snorted softly.

"And this shall be a sign unto you; Ye shall find the babe wrapped in swaddling clothes," Cassidy said, projecting loudly as he had been directed to do by Mrs. Watson. With a sweeping motion of his white-robed arms toward the distant city of Bethlehem glowing in the distance on the mural, he concluded the angelic message, "lying in a manger."

The goat had had enough of the loud, white-robed

angel. With a final snort he put his little head down and charged, snatching the tether free of the shepherd's grip.

Cassidy had turned and taken one step in his elegant, carefully rehearsed walk to meet a multitude of the heavenly host, when the goat caught him dead center on his rear end.

"Ouch!" Cassidy whirled to confront his attacker.

The goat held his ground, head down, as he pawed deliberately at the stage floor.

And suddenly from stage right, the multitude of cherub-faced children—also white-robed—rushed into position.

"You dirty little . . ." Cassidy charged the goat, tackling him around the neck.

"Glory to God in the highest. . . ." the choir sang in their sweet young voices.

The goat bleated fearfully, wrapped out of sight now in the robe as the angel wrestled him down onto the stage like a cowboy bulldogging a steer.

" . . . and on earth peace, good will toward men."

"I'll kill you, you stupid goat," the angel grunted.

The curtains rushed together as the last strains of the choir died away.

The audience had mixed reactions to the first act of the Christmas pageant. Some wore expressions of mild confusion; some polite souls kept their faces blank; some snickered behind their hands. And a few, Lane and Coley among them, roared with laughter.

"Lane, you and Coley should be ashamed of yourselves!" Catherine chided.

Sharon thought it not unlike Cassidy at all and was surprised that anyone would have expected anything else of him in such circumstances.

From the door to the left of the stage, Mrs. Watson

appeared, a scowl on her face. She had Cassidy in tow, her nimble thumb and forefinger clamped on his ear. He was up on tiptoe, trying to keep up with her angry pace.

"Ow, ow, ow!" Cassidy's halo had fallen over his left eye; one wing was missing and his robe was torn and stained from his angelic ordeal.

Mrs. Watson deposited Cassidy at the end of the Temple family row.

Catherine stood up. "I'm so sorry, Mrs. Watson."

"Think nothing of it," Mrs. Watson replied, gritting her teeth. "After three years I should have known better."

Cassidy climbed onto Coley's lap, putting his arms around his friend's neck.

"Thank the Lord, I've got two glorious weeks of freedom," Mrs. Watson muttered as she returned to direct the rest of the Christmas pageant.

★ ★ ★

The winter moon had the appearance of a pale smudged wafer floating out in the darkness. Towering above the dark green sedan, the skeletal superstructure of the bridge cast a wet sheen in the dim light, its steel beams drenched with the night mist. Far below, a foghorn's lonely wail sounded from a tugboat as it felt its way downriver.

"Why did we have to come up here?" Janie asked disconsolately. "And on Christmas Eve of all times! This place really gives me the creeps!"

"Oh, come on, baby," Ellis encouraged. "Just give it a chance. I think it's kind of romantic."

"It's romantic all right," Janie mumbled, pulling her brown wool coat closer around her as she stared out into the gloom. "About as romantic as a Dracula movie."

"This is our secret place, Janie," Jessie joined in. "Austin and I thought you'd be happy we showed it to you. It's the prettiest view in six parishes."

Janie stared out the window. Fog completely shrouded the river, a fog that seemed to be rising steadily, growing heavier as the night wore on. "What view? All I see is this stupid bridge and a lot of fog."

"But the lights are still pretty from up here," Jessie offered, trying to be cheerful.

The ESSO refinery and the city beyond it glowed softly through the mist that thinned out beyond the banks and levees of the great river.

Austin merely grunted and took another swallow from the square, black-labeled bottle.

"Let me see your ring again, Janie." Jessie knew this would get her mind off their being high over the river on the railroad trestle in the cold, damp car.

Janie's face brightened as she held her left hand over the backseat.

Jessie took her finger, gazing closely at the tiny diamond on its thin gold band.

"I'm so glad I got my ring on Christmas Eve, Ellis!" Janie exclaimed breathlessly, leaning over to kiss him on the cheek. "I'll remember this night for the rest of my life!"

"Well, a man only gets married once," Ellis proclaimed in the manner of a sage imparting his wisdom. "That is, if he picks the right girl—like I did."

Janie smiled and took his hand across the seat. Then she shivered slightly as the wind moaned high up in the cold steel beams above them.

"Here, Janie, this'll warm you up," Austin offered, handing his bottle to her.

"Oh no, I couldn't."

"It's okay, baby," Ellis assured her, taking the bottle from Austin and gulping at it. "Brrr!" he shuddered. "Maybe it *will* take the chill off."

Janie took a taste of the whiskey while Ellis held the bottle for her. Making a face, she shivered again, but motioned for him to give her another swallow.

Austin reached for the bottle, gave it to Jessie, and took it back after she had turned it up twice. "I sure appreciate your picking me up down at the Heidelberg tonight, Ellis."

"Always glad to help a stranded friend."

"You didn't tell me you were stranded, Austin." Jessie gave him a surprised glance. "What's he talking about?"

"I had to go to that party at the hotel with my parents tonight," Austin said disgustedly.

"Why didn't you just leave if you didn't like it there?" Jessie had never known Austin to stay anywhere he didn't want to.

Austin's eyes held a steady, unblinking light as he spoke. "My sainted mother hid my car keys. She's determined to expose me to the finer things in life like formal parties at expensive hotels where I can find the perfect wife who'll lounge around in bed all day and take pills at night just to get a few hours sleep."

Jessie felt a thick uneasiness in the car. Ellis and Janie gazed at each other with troubled expressions, and Austin turned his bottle up again.

"Maybe we should go home now." Janie slid across the seat toward Ellis.

"No! It's Christmas Eve and we've all spent our allotted times with our families—haven't we?" Jessie thought fondly of how they had exchanged presents around the tree earlier that evening. Tomorrow would bring more presents for all the children, even though they all knew about Santa Claus. A part of her, even at seventeen, cherished this tradition and thrilled at the thought of coming downstairs to a surprise gift under the shining tree on Christmas morning.

"I have," Ellis answered, "and I gave Janie her ring over at her parents' house."

"I know *you* had your usual Norman Rockwell celebration, Jessie."

"Let's hear some music," Jessie suggested. "We'll all be graduated in five months. No telling what will happen to us then or where we'll be."

Ellis kissed Janie on the lips. "I know where *I'll* be. With my pretty new bride in our *own* little house."

Janie reached over and flicked the knob on the radio. The dial began to glow as the tubes warmed up. "Did I tell you about the little place Ellis and I found riding around last week, Jess? It's on Wenonah Street."

"No!" Jessie was glad to have the mood in the car changing. "You mean you're already looking for a place to live? That's wonderful!"

"Oh yes! It's white with green shutters and a cute little picket fence in front and big shade trees." Janie had forgotten all about the cold and the high trestle where they were perched above the river. "And it's only three blocks from Plank Road where Mr. Perry's body shop is."

"*Frosty, the snowman, was a jolly, happy soul.*" The comforting voice of Gene Autry sounded faint at first, then louder as the radio warmed up.

Jessie listened to Janie's excited monologue about her future home and the plans she and Ellis had made for their wedding, but the Gene Autry song kept forcing itself inexplicably to the forefront of her mind.

She could almost see Cassidy in his Gene Autry outfit with all its fringes and the shining cap pistols strapped to his hips.

The more Janie talked, the less Jessie seemed to be able to keep her mind on what she was saying. Thoughts of Christmas and her family inserted themselves between her and the friend she was trying to listen to. She had a sudden almost irresistible desire to leap from the car and run all the way back home, just to hug her brothers and sister, to tell her mother and father how very much she loved them. *I must be losing my mind! I just saw them all less than three hours ago.*

Jessie found herself remembering her mother's words earlier in the evening. Catherine had come into her bedroom just as she was putting the finishing touches on her makeup.

"I wish you wouldn't go out tonight, sweetheart." Catherine sat down on her daughter's bed. *"You'll be out on your own soon enough. Wouldn't you like to spend Christmas Eve with your family? We'll sing some carols and everyone will get to open one of their presents like we've always done."*

"Oh, Mama, that's so square!" Jessie capped her lipstick, took a Kleenex from a box on her dressing table and blotted it, leaving the bright outline of her lips on the white tissue. *"Besides, I've spent some time with y'all already and Austin's counting on me to be with him."*

Catherine shivered slightly and stood up. "Well, I'm going to pray for you. Surely you'll allow your mother that one concession."

Feeling her mother's hand on her shoulder, Jessie sighed deeply, then relented, "Oh, all right! If it makes you feel better, go ahead."

In the thick darkness above the river, Jessie could almost hear her mother's fervent prayer for her safety. *"For he shall give his angels charge over thee, to keep thee in all thy ways."*

Austin rejoiced that Jessie had taken Janie's mind off her surroundings. "You're really going to do it, huh? Lock up with the ol' ball and chain."

Ellis took the bottle from Austin, swallowed twice, and passed it on. "Yep. Best decision I ever made in my life. I just can't wait for June to get here."

"Well, here's to you, ol' pal, if that's what you really want." Austin toasted the happy couple.

The music played softly, the bottle was passed around until it was empty, and the conversation gradually died away. Ellis' Blue Horse notebook lay unopened beneath his seat. Janie slipped down on the seat of the car, her head pillowed on Ellis' lap as he dozed off against the backrest.

In the backseat, Jessie lay cradled in Austin's arms, breathing softly in a dream of singing on a sound stage, her figure draped in silk as she smiled into the camera.

A hundred feet below the sleepers, the fog churned off the river like thick smoke, spreading outward across the banks and up onto the approaches of the road and the railway as they led onto the bridge.

The radio played softly.

Sleep in heavenly peace.

Austin awakened with a start. He thought the sun had come up while he slept, then suddenly realized that the intense brightness was a single beam of light shining through the windshield of the Kaiser.

Struggling to sit up, Austin pushed Jessie off him and stared over the backrest. Through the fog, he could see the glaring white headlight of the locomotive. The rails vibrated beneath the Kaiser as the heavy rumbling engine struggled to haul its long line of boxcars up the incline of the bridge.

"Wake up!" Austin grasped Jessie beneath her armpits, hauling her toward the door on his side of the car. "Ellis—Janie, we've got to get out!"

Mumbling to himself, Ellis pushed up on his elbows, then used one hand, trying to rub the sleep out of his face. "What—what's the matter?"

The locomotive thundered ahead, shaking the trestle as it used all its awesome power to clear the final section of the incline. A sudden blast from its whistle slashed through the night like a giant scythe.

Jessie pushed against Austin. "What are you doing? Leave me alone."

Ignoring her, Austin jerked the door handle frantically. It wouldn't budge. Grabbing it with both hands, he strained against it with all his strength. It snapped off in his hand. With a curse, he saw that he had forgotten to unlock the car door.

In the front seat, Ellis was fumbling inside his jacket for his car keys.

Finally and fully awake, Jessie screamed hysterically as she saw the blinding light of the locomotive.

Austin pulled the lock up, rolled down the window of the back door, reached out, and opened it from the outside.

Ellis had found his keys and was grinding the starter, pumping the accelerator wildly in his panic to get his father's car started and back down the tracks away from the roaring train.

Janie clutched frantically at Ellis' arm. "Hurry! Hurry! Oh, God! Oh, God!"

"The engine's flooded, Ellis!" Austin yelled, pulling Jessie around the waist as he stepped out onto the crossties. "Get out of there!"

Jessie fought against Austin. "We can't leave them in the car! Help them!"

"Oh, God! Oh, God!"

Bracing his right foot against the edge of the car's floorboard, Austin pulled Jessie free of the backseat. "We've got to get away from this car!"

Austin saw that it was no use trying to get Ellis out: his left hand was frozen to the steering wheel; his right continued to grind the key. He stared straight ahead in a stupor-like trance at the huge locomotive coming right at him.

"Get out, Ellis! Get out!" Austin lifted Jessie bodily, his arms still around her waist.

Janie threw both arms around Ellis, burying her head against his chest.

Austin spotted a six-inch girder spanning the distance from the railroad to the highway. With Jessie still screaming and fighting him, he backed out across it, dragging her along with him. Eight feet out, the girder tied into a second, perpendicular girder, then to a vertical beam. He stopped and braced himself against the cold, wet steel wall, clutching to Jessie as she continued to scream for Janie and Ellis.

A deafening crash shattered the night as the locomotive plowed into the Kaiser. Ellis' and Janie's screams were lost in the sound of shrieking metal as the huge engine ripped through the car, crushing it like tin foil as it plowed it down and under and along the tracks in front of it.

Austin held Jessie tightly against his chest so she couldn't see what was happening. Through the heavy mist, he watched the mangled car skidding and twisting in front of the massive locomotive. Five seconds later he heard a heavy WHUMP! that sent hot air rushing past his face as a bright yellow-orange ball of flame exploded against the night.

★   ★   ★

Our Lady of the Lake Hospital stood on the north shore directly across the lake from the Capitol, whose windows on that side as well as the south side facing the business district were lighted during the Christmas season to form an enormous cross that could be seen for miles around.

Austin sat on a concrete bench at the top of the steps to the main entrance of the hospital that led up a slope from the parking lot. He stared out at the dark surface of the lake bearing a bright reflection of the cross.

"Austin . . ." Marvin Youngblood walked quietly up behind his son.

Austin appeared not to have heard his father.

Marvin sat down next to him, placing his hand on his son's shoulder. "I know it's a terrible tragedy, but you can't blame yourself for it. Even the police said it wasn't your fault."

Again Austin made no response whatsoever.

"Jessie's all right now. The doctor gave her a shot and let her parents take her on home."

"It *was* my fault." Standing up slowly, as though it was a great effort for him, Austin glanced back at the entrance to the emergency room where the black hearse waited, his expression as dead and dry as December flowers. "They were our best friends—and I killed them."

Drawn to the light, Austin walked down the steps toward the lake. When he reached the shore, he stared out at the huge gleaming cross reaching out toward him on the dark surface of the water. He thought of

93

the sick and dying in all the hospital rooms behind him, and he thought of his friends lying pale and cold in the white glare of one of those rooms. He had come to realize how much Ellis' friendship had meant to him—too late!

PART TWO

★ ★ ★

THE HOUSE NEVER LIVED IN

SIX

TEARS

★ ★ ★

Sitting on the bleachers at the morning assembly, Jessie felt herself filling up with tears. This sort of thing had been happening since that terrible night on the bridge, and she had come to believe there would be no end to it. These moments would descend on her at odd times and places—she could never predict their comings and goings.

"Well, y'all have been back from your Christmas vacation three days now and I hope you've gotten down to work." Charlie Garrett, his brown wavy hair precisely cut and combed, stood on the stage in front of the heavy floor microphone, his crinkly smile turned on his audience.

Jessie knew she would have to leave the gymnasium. The feeling was growing strong now. Over the past few days he had felt as fragile and brittle and cold inside as a crystal vase. She knew that soon she would shatter and the tears would spill over in spite of anything she could do to prevent it.

"I want to remind all of you to be extremely careful walking around the campus as you change classes because of the construction that's still going on. We've got a school we can really be proud of now." The microphone hissed and popped. Garrett smiled and continued. "They tell me the architectural style is contemporary conservative-modern and that it's the first large school in the South to have radiant heating."

Slipping quickly into Austin's maroon and gray letter jacket, Jessie grabbed her books, stood up, and began threading her way down the bleachers through her classmates. Austin, carrying his books and leather jacket, followed her.

"Personally I miss the old school over in the Istrouma neighborhood with all the streets named for Indian tribes. But don't forget that we brought with us our namesake and the same ol' fighting spirit. This nation is built on change and progress so my opinions—" Noticing Jessie and Austin leaving, Garrett stopped momentarily, then continued, making no effort to stop them. It was the only time in his recollection he had given such a dispensation—and it would be for this one time only. "Let's all do our part to make 1951 a great year here at Istrouma."

An undertone of whisperings and murmurings ran through the gym as Jessie and Austin left. By now, everyone knew about the Christmas Eve tragedy. On the first day back from vacation, all their friends expressed their sympathy and encouragement in all the right words.

That accomplished, however, an invisible barrier seemed to fall between Jessie and Austin, and the rest of their classmates. Awkward smiles and glances kept them at a distance as though their proximity to death that foggy night had produced in them some sort of contagious disease.

Jessie hurried along the edge of the hardwood basketball floor, through the double doors, down the short corridor, and out into the cold winter day. She headed along the concrete walk of the portico, past the cafeteria, and toward the main building, but didn't quite make it.

Dropping her books on a wooden bench, Jessie sat down and buried her face in her hands. Great sobs racked her body. She could almost feel the breaking deep inside her breast, could almost feel shards of glass piercing her as tears poured down her cheeks. Next came the darkness and the cold, flowing out of her along with the hot tears, giving her a brief release from the grief that now seemed an eternal part of her being.

Austin sat down next to her, putting his arm gently around her shoulders, feeling her trembling beneath it. He knew there were no words that would make things different, nothing he could say to make her feel any better.

A sky sealed with clouds curved above the young couple as they sat together on the bench. All about them the lead-colored day was torn by gusts of wind.

A small black-and-white terrier trotted down the walk beneath the portico, stopped briefly, stared directly into Austin's eyes and, sensing no danger, headed out across the raw dirt of the schoolyard toward the baseball diamond.

"Take me away from here." Wiping her face with a lace-trimmed handkerchief, Jessie gazed at Austin, her eyes red and swollen and dark with sorrow.

"Where?"

"Anywhere."

"But we've—"

"Austin, please!"

"Are we coming back today?"

"No! I'm going to put my books back in my locker while everyone's still at assembly."

"I'll wait for you next to the music building."

★ ★ ★

Austin noticed that Jessie had washed her face and put on fresh lipstick. It bothered him more than he would have imagined to see her so distraught. Taking her by the arm, he led her down the sidewalk to the chainlink gate and out into the parking lot. He opened the car door, noticing that even though Jessie seemed to have gotten control of her emotions, she was moving slowly and woodenly as though in a trance. Muted by brick walls and distance, the sound of their classmates singing "God Bless America" rose on the wind like a ray of hope.

Austin walked back around the car, opening the door as he gazed at the new construction. Suddenly, the girders and beams of the unfinished buildings became in his mind the superstructure of the bridge, rising into the misty night. He could almost feel the shuddering thunder of the locomotive as it barreled toward the Kaiser.

Forcing himself to block the horrible scene out of his mind, Austin leaped behind the wheel of his car and slammed the door. With the engine racing, he sped out of the school parking lot to the cry of rubber tires on pavement, headed north on 38th, and screeched to a stop at the red light at Winbourne a half block away.

Jessie reached over and turned the car's heater on, feeling the air flow out cold at her feet. "Please don't drive that way! I'm just not up to it."

Austin turned the heater off. "You have to let it warm up first. I've told you a hundred times!"

Giving him a look of hurt mingled with mild shock, Jessie turned away and stared out the window.

Taking a deep breath, Austin said as gently as he could, "I'm sorry, Jess. Where do you want to go?"

"I think I want to see their house," she mumbled to the gray day outside the window.

"Whose house?"

Jessie turned back around, gazing directly into Austin's eyes as though surprised that he had to ask. "Why, Ellis and Janie's, of course."

A horn blew behind them. Austin restrained himself from an outburst at the driver and turned left, heading toward the old Istrouma neighborhood. "I don't think that's such a good idea, Jess. Not this soon, anyway."

"I want to see it, Austin," Jessie replied defiantly. "If you won't take me, I'll walk."

Realizing that she would do just that, Austin continued on toward the little house that Janie had so lovingly described for them on the night of her engagement to Ellis.

Stopping at the traffic light on Plank Road, Austin turned the heater back on.

Jessie felt the warm, soft flow of air against her legs. She held her hands down, rubbing them together as the heater began to drive the damp January cold out of the car.

Keeping his eye on the light this time, Austin crossed Plank Road, turning right at the fourth street, just as Ellis had described. Five houses down on the left, he pulled over to the side of the street and parked in front of a picket fence.

Jessie gazed out the window, biting her lower lip. The house was just as Janie had described it—small and neat and white with green shutters and a green-trimmed garage at the rear, down the two strips of concrete that served as the driveway.

A walk, flanked by freshly planted cedar trees, led through the gate and up to a front porch where a cypress swing hung from chains attached to the ceiling. A brick-bordered flower bed ran along the porch and down the left side of the house. To the right, next to the driveway, a single old sycamore stood winter-barren and etched darkly against the gray sky.

Watching the tiny cedars shudder in the wind, Jessie spoke softly. "I'd like to live here someday."

Austin thought it a morbid thing to say, but didn't tell Jessie. He had learned that her thinking processes had been altered dramatically since the accident. She could be tender and affectionate and the next moment flare into anger. "I'd think this would be the last place you'd want to live."

Immersed in the somber residue of that night on the bridge, Jessie thought on her own statement, turning it over in her mind as she searched for its source. "Maybe it's because we took this away from them— the life they would have had together here in this house."

Recalling that he had persuaded Ellis to drive his father's car that night against his protests about the danger, Austin was shaken by a spasm of remorse. He longed to escape the implacable consequences of his actions, but felt that he had somehow stepped beyond redemption. "There's nothing we can do to make things the way they were, Jess."

Lost now in her fantasy, Jessie opened the door, got out, and headed around the car toward the house.

Austin stopped her at the gate, taking her by the shoulders. "Wait! We can't go in there."

Jessie stared at Austin as though he had spoken in a foreign language. "I want to go see it up close."

Shaking his head, Austin opened the gate and followed Jessie up the walk.

"It's so homey looking." Jessie stepped up onto the porch, peeking through the half-glass door into the living room. "Such beautiful hardwood floors!"

"Maybe we'd better leave now."

Jessie had a wistful expression on her face as she turned and looked out on the front yard, then down at the flower beds. "We'll plant wisteria and you can make a trellis for it to climb. And maybe some marigolds right here."

Austin gazed at the faraway look in Jessie's eyes. "Jess, we don't live here. Nobody does."

"I know that!" Jessie walked to the end of the porch and sat down in the swing, a serene look in her eyes. "I think pansies and impatiens would give us plenty of color. Don't you?"

Austin followed, sitting next to her as they moved slowly back and forth in the swing.

The January wind moaned in the eaves of the house. A battered pickup with wooden sawhorses and lumber and toolboxes in the back rattled by out on the street. The driver, wearing overalls and a coarse work jacket, turned his weathered face toward the couple on the porch of the vacant house. Then he said something to the man in a felt hat sitting next to him. They both laughed as the engine coughed, almost died, then sputtered back into life. The truck disappeared behind the corner of the neighboring house.

"Can we stay here for a little while?" Jessie's voice was almost carried away by the wind.

"You're not too cold?"

"No."

"All right." Austin put his arm around Jessie, pulling her close to him for warmth.

Jessie took Austin's hand in both of hers, receiving great comfort in his touch and in simply being close to him. She felt almost as though they shared some remarkable and unbearably sad knowledge that none of their family or friends could ever understand; almost as though they lived in a separate world, depending on each other for their very existence.

★ ★ ★

"What are you doing here?" Gordon Perry stood at the foot of the steps, holding a "For Sale" sign in his left hand and a small sledgehammer in his right. He wore gray twill trousers and a matching work jacket with a *Perry's Body Shop* patch sewn to the left breast and *Gordon* stitched across the right. His heavy black oxfords were stained with grease.

Startled out of his chilly reverie, Austin took his arm from Jessie's shoulder and sat up straight in the swing. He stared at Gordon Perry with his gold-rimmed glasses and thinning sandy hair and knew exactly what Ellis would have looked like in twenty years. "I—uh, we were just looking at the house."

Jessie shook her head slightly and stared at Mr. Perry, her eyes dull and uncomprehending.

"I bought this house for my *son*," Perry continued, his voice rising, "and I won't have *you* coming here for *any* reason you—you *murderer*!"

Austin had thought himself dead inside, but now felt a stab of pain in his chest at the sound of the name Perry branded him with. "We're leaving, Mr. Perry."

Jessie stared blankly at the man as though still not

realizing what was going on.

Austin took her gently by the arm. "C'mon, Jess. It's time to go."

As they passed Mr. Perry, still standing on the front walk at the foot of the steps, he dropped his sign and grabbed Austin by the arm. "My son thought you were some kind of *hero*. He looked up to you!"

"Go on to the car, Jess." Austin gazed into Perry's eyes, blazing with anger, then stared at the sidewalk. A crack ran diagonally across it with dry winter grass showing through. *That'll need some weed killer in the spring.*

"Austin—I . . ."

"Go on, Jess. It's all right."

Jessie turned and walked slowly toward the front gate, glancing back only once.

"I tried to tell Ellis to leave you alone, but he wouldn't listen." Perry's grip tightened on Austin's arm, his voice cold and controlled now. "I told him you were nothing but trouble."

"I'm sorry, Mr. Perry," Austin almost whispered. "It was all my fault."

"Sorry doesn't bring my son back to life! Sorry doesn't give him the wife and home and family you robbed him of! He was just a boy!" Perry shouted. "Sorry doesn't give me any grandchildren!"

Austin stared at the crack in the sidewalk. The wind seemed suddenly like a frozen blade, knifing right through him. "I don't know what else to say."

"He was our only child." Perry raised the heavy blunt hammer above his head, his body trembling with rage. "He was my son! My *son!*"

Austin glanced up at the hammer. He felt no fear at all. Something deep inside him wanted its heavy steel head to come crashing down through his skull.

Suddenly Mr. Perry let Austin's arm go, turned, and with a howl of grief and loss, hurled the hammer at the front of the house. It crashed through the living room window, scattering glass fragments across the porch.

Austin glanced at the twisted mask of pain that Perry's face had become. Then he turned and walked slowly out the front gate and got into his car.

Gordon Perry slumped down on the walk, sitting with his face in his hands, paralyzed by his terrible sorrow.

★ ★ ★

"I've got to get out of this town." Jessie stared out the window of Austin's car.

Turning right on Plank Road, Austin headed south. "Your parents would never let you go any-where, Jess. You've got to finish school."

"I can't take it anymore."

"You can't let what Mr. Perry said bother you. He's just so upset over what happened, he doesn't know what he's saying."

Austin felt that his own words were hollow and meaningless while Perry's still lay on his soul like a mantle of darkness. "Things'll get better."

"It's not just him." Jessie gazed at the C. L. Adams automobile dealership with its huge letters proclaiming *KAISER-FRAZER Is Here to Stay*. All our friends treat us so—so differently. It's like we don't belong here anymore."

"That's all in your mind, Jess," Austin said, feeling exactly the same way himself. "They just don't know what to say to make us feel better. They're *still* our friends."

Jessie pulled Austin's jacket closer around her,

shivering slightly as she turned on the radio.

"They try to tell us we're too young . . ." The mellow and distinctive voice of Nat King Cole filled the inside of the coupe as Jessie forced herself to sing along, trying to rid her mind of the unrelenting memory of Christmas Eve that seemed now like an eternal nightmare.

"Hey, you want some hot chocolate?" Austin tried to sound cheerful.

"Why not?"

Turning into the parking lot of Sitman's Drug Store, Austin parked near the main entrance, waiting for the song to end. He had loved Jessie's voice since the first time he had heard her sing for morning assembly. "You really ought to think about singing with a band or something, Jess."

Jessie gave him a thoughtful glance as the song ended. "I just might do that—someday."

The wind whipped their hair about their faces as they hurried inside. Rubbing their hands together for warmth, they walked along the main aisle of the store past the glass counters stacked with jars of Jergens Face Cream and bottles of Old Spice After Shave and the floor display of Kleenex Tissues, on to the fountain area. Jessie slid into a booth as Austin walked over to the counter.

"Two hot chocolates, Billy."

Billy Whitaker, in his first year out of high school, grabbed two heavy mugs and began filling them with the steaming brown chocolate. Vaseline Hair Tonic stained his white paper hat and his black bowtie wriggled beneath his Adam's apple as he talked. "Why aren't you in school?"

"Holiday."

"Holiday? What holiday?"

107

"Washington's birthday."

"Washington's birthday?" Billy had known Austin for years, but played along anyway. "That's next month."

"It is?" Austin shrugged, reaching for the mugs. He felt like an actor playing a particularly distasteful part for the first time as he made small talk with his friend. "Guess the joke's on me."

"It will be if Mr. Garrett catches you," Billy warned. "I can *still* feel that paddle of his."

Austin fished a quarter out of his blue jeans pocket and dropped it on the counter. "Hey, Billy. You wanna try to figure out a riddle?"

Billy glanced around the almost empty store. "Why not? I got nothing else to do."

"What do Attila the Hun, Winnie the Pooh, and Smokey the Bear have in common?"

Billy wrinkled his brow in concentration. "Beats me. Nothing *I* can think of."

"They all have the same *middle* name." Austin turned and carried the chocolate over to the booth. As he placed them on the formica-topped table, he heard Billy call out behind him.

"Hey, I get it! That's a good one, Austin." Billy rang up the twenty cents in the register, took the nickel Austin had tipped him, and walked over to the juke-box at the far end of the soda fountain area. He dropped the nickel in, studied the selections for a few seconds, then punched two buttons.

The records in their shiny metal frames spun around pinwheel fashion until the proper one came into alignment. Then the arm moved forward, placing the record on the turntable. Billy smiled, always fascinated by the technology of the jukebox, and returned to his glass-washing duties behind the counter.

108

Austin sipped his chocolate in silence, wondering if Jessie was serious about wanting to leave. He was surprised that the news had bothered him as it did. Before Jessie, one girl had been as good as another as far as he was concerned, but the thought of not being able to see her whenever he wanted to had begun to give him an empty feeling in his chest.

From the jukebox came the sound of Gene Autry singing "Frosty the Snowman."

Shaking his head in disgust, Austin glanced over where Billy attended to his dishwashing chores.

"Call me a kid," Billy shrugged. "I like it."

"Jess, did you really mean it when you said you had to get out of here?"

Jessie looked up from her chocolate, a thin, brown line following the curve of her lips. "Yes."

"But where would you go? What would you do?" Austin reached over, taking her hand. "We've got to stick together in this thing, Jess."

"I saw an ad in Sunday's paper," Jessie mumbled, looking back at her mug. "The USO's sponsoring a national talent competition that starts next month. All forty-eight states will have one winner who gets a trip to Hollywood."

Austin relaxed, knowing that Jessie's chances of winning were practically nonexistent. "What in the world would you do in Hollywood, even if you *did* make it out there?"

"There's a chance to go on one of the USO tours with Bob Hope. Maybe even a screen test."

Austin watched a woman with a red scarf tied around her head push a grocery cart through the open double-glass doors that connected Sitman's with the A&P next door. Stopping at the perfume counter, she chatted with the salesclerk.

"I thought we were going to LSU together, Jess. What about your degree in music?"

Jessie sipped from her mug, the chocolate line along her top lip growing thicker.

Austin smiled, thinking that she looked like a little girl trying to play grown-up.

"What are you grinning at?"

Austin pointed to his lip.

Snatching a napkin from its shiny chrome holder, Jessie wiped the chocolate off. "I don't think I'm cut out to teach a bunch of snotty-nosed kids their music scales! What kind of life would that be?" Her voice rose in defiance.

Austin considered how their relationship was changing since the tragedy. Before, he had always decided what they would do, where they would go and when, with Jessie conceding to his wishes except for those rare times when she asserted herself for no reason that he could ever figure out. Now when they seemed so distant from everyone else, when they needed each other more than ever, she went spinning off on a flight of fancy.

"I can't figure you, Jess."

Jessie stared at Austin, her brown eyes shiny and full of light. "You know I've always wanted to try show business. College was just something to do until I figured out how to get a break. Well, now I just might have that chance."

"Not much of a chance if you ask me," Austin mumbled, both hands gripping the warm mug.

"Nobody's asking you!"

"That movie star business is for kids. You'll be eighteen this year."

"You're just jealous!"

"Jealous of what?"

"Of my talent, that's what!"

Austin could see one of Jessie's mood swings happening, but the anger flaring in his chest wouldn't let him remain silent until she settled down. "Talent? You call winning a few local contests or singing a couple of solos in church talent?"

"What can *you* do—besides beat people up, that is?" Jessie banged her mug down, chocolate spilling over its sides. "A *gorilla* can do that!"

Austin took a deep breath, letting it out slowly. "Jessie, I know you've been upset lately, but you're acting like a child."

Jessie glared at Austin, then slid out of the booth and walked away.

Following her, Austin called out, "Where do you think you're going?"

Jessie walked briskly through the entrance into the A&P and on through the doors that led out to the parking lot of the little shopping center, where she whirled around to face him. "Down to Morgan and Lindsey's to buy a Betsy Wetsy doll! I'm a child—remember?"

SEVEN

THE CONTEST

★ ★ ★

A few leftover winter leaves, dry and brown and brittle, rustled in the March wind and scraped along the sidewalk as Austin walked down the slope from his house. Crossing Lakeshore Drive, he sat down and leaned back against the trunk of a thick willow on the bank of University Lake.

The day was falling away in the purple distance. A faint rose-colored glow, all that remained of the sun, tinted a narrow band of clouds hanging motionless above the horizon. A snowy egret lifted from a slim cypress, sailing low across the water's surface toward the dark shoreline. In the shallows, minnows darted among the shadows.

Austin had been running three miles almost every day, hoping that disciplining his body would help him hold together the fragile integrity of his mind. Still, he felt passing spasms of guilt that would leave him troubled and physically weak. It had been two months since that raw January day at the little green-and-white house when Ellis' father had confronted him.

In the hard hours before dawn, Austin would awaken from the same dream, the sound of Gordon Perry's voice still ringing in his ears.

"You murderer!"

"I'm sorry, Mr. Perry. It was all my fault."

"Sorry doesn't bring my son back to life! Sorry doesn't give him the wife and home and family you robbed him of!"

Staring at the cattails moving slowly in the breeze, Austin didn't notice the couple walking along the path behind him.

"Hello. Lovely evening, isn't it?"

Startled, Austin turned around and stood up. Standing before him were the man and woman that he had seen walking together countless times from his bedroom window.

"Sorry. Didn't mean to disturb you." Over six feet tall, the man wore gray sweatpants and a dark red jacket over his blade-slim frame. The failing light glinted on his silver-gray hair, touching his ears and his collar.

"Oh, that's all right." Austin glanced at the man's tiny wife in her pink sweater and long gray skirt. Her soft, delicate features gave her a childlike, almost elfin quality and her face seemed suffused with immeasurable serenity.

"We're forgetting our manners," she said in a musical little voice. "I'm Sarah Edmonson and this shady-looking character here is my husband, Tom."

"Austin Youngblood." He shook hands with both of them. "You've been walking a long time, haven't you?"

"Almost seventy-five years," Tom grinned. "Since I was two years old."

"You'll have to forgive Tom." Sarah patted her husband on the arm. "He always thinks of himself as a comedian instead of a college professor. And to answer your question, yes, we've been walking along here for about eight or nine years now."

"I've seen you a lot of times from up there." Austin pointed to his bedroom window.

Sarah gazed up the slope. "That's a lovely house. You have brothers or sisters?"

Austin shook his head. "Just me."

"I'll bet you've got a girlfriend."

"I'm not sure right now," Austin replied, watching a boy in a cowboy hat and fringed shirt whiz by on his bicycle. "Seems like we argue a lot lately. I haven't seen her in almost a week."

"Do you love her?"

"Sarah, you're meddling again." Tom squatted down next to Austin, pulled out a long stem of grass growing next to the willow, and began chewing on it. "You'll have to excuse her, Austin. Ever since we lost our own son, Sarah sort of adopts every young man we meet."

Austin found himself accepting and enjoying the straightforward openness and honesty of the Edmonsons. He thought it strange, however, that there seemed to be no hint of sadness in Tom's speaking of the loss of their son. "It's okay. I don't mind."

Sarah sat down on the grass, curling her legs beneath her skirt in girl-like fashion.

"Yes, Mrs. Edmonson. I *do* love her." Austin thought it stranger still that he would tell Sarah Edmonson these words before he ever said them to Jessie.

"Then things will work out for you—if she feels the same way." Sarah's pale blue eyes darkened momentarily. "You may have some rough times, but don't give up."

"No ma'am, I won't."

"We'd better be going, Sarah." Tom held his hand down toward his wife. "We've disturbed this young man's meditations long enough."

"No! You don't have to go." Austin blurted it out without thinking. Simply talking with the Edmonsons made him feel better than he had in months. "You're a professor? You teach over at the university?"

"Taught. I retired at sixty-five." Tom sat down on the grass next to his wife. "Figured that thirty-eight years of inflicting students with worthless information was enough."

"What'd you teach?" Austin had become intrigued with the man.

"Philosophy."

"That's something I don't know a thing in the world about," Austin confessed.

"And you're a better man for it. Goethe, Nietzsche, Schopenhauer. All of them morbidly unhappy men who did their best to make everybody else just as unhappy," Tom remarked offhandedly. "Men with powerful intellects who used beautifully crafted language to promote their dusty, dead philosophies on the rest of the world. Pretty words, but dead words, my boy—words with no hope in them."

Slightly stunned by Tom's reply, Austin asked, "If you feel like that—why'd you teach it?"

"Didn't know any better 'til nine years ago." Tom smiled at his wife. "Then I met a man who taught nothing *but* hope—and faith and love."

"Who's that?"

"Jesus Christ."

Somewhat stunned, Austin had expected Tom to mention some renowned lecturer he had heard at the university. "I thought you meant somebody you *know*—somebody alive."

"Oh, He's very *much* alive, son! Make no doubt about that," Tom assured him. "And I *do* know Him."

Austin could see the absolute certainty in Tom's intense blue eyes as he spoke the words. For some reason this brought a chilling fear to Austin and he had a strange, almost overwhelming desire to get up and run away.

"In fact, He's the Author of life." Tom took a slim brown New Testament from his jacket pocket and began thumbing through its worn pages. "It says here in the first chapter of John, 'All things were made by him; and without him was not any thing made that was made.' And over in chapter six, Peter said to Jesus, 'Lord, to whom shall we go? thou hast the words of eternal life.' "

Finding himself unable to respond, Austin stared out over the dark water.

Sarah's voice sounded as soft as the small waves lapping gently against the bank of the glistening lake. "Austin, I don't mean to pry, but I have the feeling you're deeply disturbed about something."

Austin picked up a small willow branch from the ground and flipped it end-over-end into the water. The urge to run came again, but the sound of Sarah's voice seemed to hold onto him, the sound of a mother concerned for her own.

"Yes ma'am."

"You don't have to tell me what it is, but there's

Someone who already knows and cares more than
you could ever imagine."

Remembering that night on the bridge, the sound
of Gordon Perry's condemnation, the long, bitter
nights, Austin felt a sharp pain rising in his chest. He
gazed at Sarah, his eyes bright with unshed tears. "I
sure need somebody."

"Jesus loves you, Austin. He died for you." Tom
laid his hand on Austin's shoulder.

At that moment, Austin knew beyond any doubt
that Jesus was who He said He was—and that He
had lived and died and risen from the grave on this
earth. He could see Him in the face of Tom and
Sarah Edmonson and hear Him in the unfathom-
able truth of their words. Still he felt that nothing
could take away his responsibility for the deaths of
his friends.

"Let me give you a very simple truth, Austin."

Austin turned and stared into Tom's eyes. They
were clear and unfaltering.

Tom grinned with wry amusement. "And remember, this comes from a man who spent his life taking
simple things and making them as complicated and
as obscure as possible."

Feeling a slight hope rising through the dark, Austin's smile came from deep inside him.

Turning the pages of the little Testament, Tom
found his place and began to read. " 'Whosoever
believeth that Jesus is the Christ is born of God.'
Christ meaning God's anointed one, the One who
made salvation possible, made it possible for man to
be reconciled with God—God's Son. That's simple
enough, isn't it?"

"Yes sir."

Tom continued in his calm, deliberate fashion.

"He that hath the Son hath life; and he that hath not the Son of God hath not life. These things have I written unto you that believe on the name of the Son of God; that ye may know that ye have eternal life, and that ye may believe on the name of the son of God."

Austin found himself nodding as Tom read on. He remembered the times he had sat in church services, hearing the same words with a deaf ear. "I do believe that, Mr. Edmonson. I always *thought* I did before."

Closing his book, Tom added, "It all takes place in the heart, Austin." He pointed to his chest. "You believe in here." Then pointed to his head. "Not in here."

Austin shook his head slowly back and forth. He had no doubt whatsoever that the words Tom Edmonson read were true, but the guilt he felt seemed a permanent part of his life. "But you don't know what I've done."

"Doesn't matter what you've done, son," Tom grinned. "The Bible says that if you confess with your mouth the Lord Jesus and believe in your heart that God raised Him from the dead, why then you're saved."

Austin merely nodded. He still felt a bright hope glimmering in the darkness, but couldn't seem to find the words to say or the voice to speak them out.

"I almost envy you, son. You've got your whole life ahead of you to live it as it was meant to be lived." Tom shook his head slowly. "The years I've wasted! To paraphrase the apostle Paul, I count them all but dung."

The three of them stood up, brushing off the dry grass and bits of leaves.

Sarah put her arm around her husband's waist, gazing up at him. "Don't fret about those years, Tom. Look how happy we are now."

The old professor seemed to lapse into a state of slight confusion. He made a fist and brandished it, raising his arm high above his head. " 'Forgetting those things which are behind . . . I press toward the mark. . . . ' Can't seem to remember the rest of it, Sarah," he concluded, turning toward his wife.

Austin stared at him in mild surprise. He was beginning to become accustomed to Tom's harmless idiosyncrasies.

Putting his arm down, Tom gave him a sheepish grin. "You'll have to indulge an old man's flights of fancy, Austin. I tend to get carried away sometimes." He touched his temple with a bony forefinger. "And my mental faculties flit about like a spring butterfly."

"His other love was the stage." Sarah took her husband's arm. "Come, Mr. Barrymore. It's time we finished our walk."

"To be sure, my dear."

Sarah took Austin's hand. "You've just received the most wonderful news a person could ever get, Austin. Just lay your burdens at the foot of the cross and join the family."

Tom shook his hand by way of farewell. "Sharing the faith—there's nothing quite like it!"

Still holding Tom's hand as though not wanting to let him go, Austin said hesitantly, "I—I don't think I feel any different. It's hard to say."

Tom wished that Austin would have the courage to profess Jesus out loud, but had learned that people could not be intellectualized or coerced into the kingdom of God. He had seen people pressed to make a public stand for Jesus before they were ready in their hearts—and had seen them fall away. "This gift of God—this salvation—doesn't depend at *all* on feelings, my boy. It's by God's grace and our faith."

"What do I do now?"

"Read your Bible—the Book of John would be a good place to start," Tom replied. "And get into a church, a body of believers who live by this Book." He patted his coat pocket where his New Testament rested.

"Could I ask you a few more questions?" Austin hated the thought of Tom and Sarah leaving him.

"Why, certainly."

As the lavender afterglow faded gradually through shades of night, Austin and his new friends talked for ten more minutes beneath the willow at the edge of the lake. Laughter punctuated their conversation from time to time as a chorus of tree frogs sang background music.

When Sarah and Tom returned to their walk, Austin watched them until they disappeared around a curve in the path. A quarter moon rose beyond the distant shoreline, casting a thin line of silver across the wind-rippled surface of the lake.

Austin stared up at the night sky. Then, remembering the promise behind the words he had heard spoken, he bounded across the street, did a somersault on his front lawn, and ran up the slope toward his house.

Entering through the kitchen door, Austin turned on lights in the empty, darkened house. Singing "Frosty the Snowman" in an off-key baritone, he took a leftover pot roast out of the refrigerator and made two thick sandwiches. He wolfed them down with a tall glass of milk, then cleaned up his mess.

Heading directly to his father's study, Austin searched through all the bookshelves and cabinets, and finally at the back of a bottom drawer in the massive teakwood desk he found the Bible, covered in black leather. Sitting down in the brass-studded swivel chair, he turned on the desk lamp and opened the heavy Book to the presentation page.

> Presented to: Marvin Youngblood
> From: Mother
> Christmas 1923

Opening to the table of contents, Austin found the Book of John and turned to it. He began to read and when he got to the twelfth verse he read it a second time aloud, "But as many as received him, to them gave he power to become the sons of God, even to them that believe on his name."

Austin read until his eyes grew blurry and tired and he took the Bible to his room and read by his own lamp until he drifted off to sleep.

★ ★ ★

Late afternoon sunshine fell through the canopy of oaks, bathing the curving concrete benches of the Greek Theater in soft amber light. Shadows flickered in the haze as the April breeze swayed the limbs. Beyond the stage, rigged with lights and sound equipment, light winked off the reflection pool set in the midst of a small grove of pines. Spring's warmth had touched the air that day and the chill of evening had not yet begun.

A crowd had gathered for the state finals of the national USO Talent Competition. The women wore their new spring outfits of soft pastel colors and their men had grudgingly knotted ties around their necks and put on sport coats.

"I'm so nervous!" Catherine took Lane by his forearm, leaning close to him. "I hate the thought of her going all the way to Hollywood, but I'm simply dying for her to win! Does that seem so very strange?"

Lane gazed at his wife, thinking how much like a girl she looked in her pale blue dress with its scalloped neck and white lace trim. "For a man maybe. Not for a woman. You belong to a strange and wondrous breed."

"My, how poetic," Catherine replied, straightening Lane's print tie she had picked out to match his tan jacket. "It must be the spring weather."

"Our little girl's a young woman now, Cath." Lane remembered that time almost eighteen years ago when he had first seen Jessie nursing at her mother's breast in the little hospital in Oxford, Mississippi. "She'll be graduating from high school in a couple of months."

"I expect I'd better get used to her being away from home," Catherine admitted. "Maybe this trip out to California—if she wins tonight—won't be so bad. After all, it'll only be for three or four weeks."

"Yep, then she'll be here for at least four more years getting her degree at LSU."

"Daddy, I want some popcorn." Sitting next to Lane, Dalton was swinging his legs, wriggling uncomfortably, and poking his finger inside his buttoned shirt collar.

Catherine leaned forward to see him better. "This isn't a football game, young man. You just sit up straight and act like a little gentleman."

"Yes ma'am."

Coley had parked his wheelchair next to the bench in the aisle that sloped down to the stage and had to lean back slightly, bracing himself on the chair's arms to keep from gradually sliding forward. "Maybe we'll go out for malts after this shindig's over, Dalton. How'd you like that?"

"Yeah, boy!"

"I like this, Mama," Sharon said softly, straightening her flowered skirt. "When's Jessie going to sing?"

"It won't be long now, baby. Three or four more contestants and she'll be on." Catherine brushed her daughter's shiny brown hair back from her face, thinking what an obedient and well-mannered child she had always been.

Catherine had been greatly relieved when Mrs. LeJeune, a neighbor and friend, had said that she would baby-sit for Cassidy. She dearly loved the child and, being a widow, she was glad for the company.

Onstage, a slightly overweight girl with flaming red hair and a purple jumpsuit sparkling with sequins, launched into the finale of her tap number. She finished with a flourish and arms outstretched toward her audience. A smattering of applause left her with a downcast expression as she walked off the stage.

Jessie stood at the edge of the stage behind a roughly built set that had been painted to resemble a swamp scene for the occasion of the contest. She wore a lavender sheath with a neckline that Catherine had had a fit over, but had finally relented because it was such a special occasion and because she promised to put on a sweater as soon as her number was over.

A dark-haired girl from St. Martinville had just finished singing "Shrimp Boats." Peeking out at the audience, Jessie spotted her family and glanced quickly about the theater trying to find Austin, who promised that he would come.

Suddenly, the open-air houselights, rigged on hastily erected poles, went out. Taking a deep breath and expelling it slowly, Jessie made her way carefully over to the microphone in the center of the stage. The piano began a soulful introduction and a soft white spot winked on, casting Jessie in a dazzle of light. An involuntary murmuring ran through the audience among the men who stared at Jessie's trim figure and soft blond hair, gleaming like spun gold in the narrow beam of light.

Jessie had practiced her song endlessly, or so it seemed to her. She felt that she had every note, every intonation, every inflection of voice down perfectly. With a slight toss of her shining hair, she grasped the microphone with a practiced, graceful motion, stared directly out at her audience, and tried to sing the song exactly like her mother's record by Dinah Shore. A hush fell over the audience until she sang the last lines.

These golden days I'll spend with you.

Jessie finished her song to applause and a few loud rebel yells and whistles. She basked in the mild adulation of her fans, and then, as she had planned it, the spot winked out and she disappeared from the stage.

Having been momentarily blinded by the bright light, Jessie stumbled and almost fell to the rough concrete, when she felt strong arms around her waist, lifting her up. She turned around, the houselights on now, and stared into Austin's smiling face.

"You've certainly got a way with a song, lady," he grinned, "and with an audience."

"Oh, Austin!" Jessie threw her arms around his neck. "I was so afraid you wouldn't come!"

"You didn't think I'd let one little spat keep me away, now, did you?"

Jessie stepped back and took his face in her hands. "I'm afraid there's been more than one lately."

"My fault," Austin said magnanimously. "We'll do better from now on."

"Oh, Austin. . . !" She kissed him tenderly on the lips. "I was thinking of you the whole time I was singing. These may really be 'precious days' for us! Let's make the most of them."

Jessie felt a sense of relief, seeing that Austin truly meant what he said. "Did you see my family?" She stood on tiptoe, peeking over a part of the temporary scenery. "They're all here except for Cass. I think Mama believed that if they brought him he'd steal the whole show before the night was out."

"I spoke to them earlier. Some of our classmates were out there cheering you on too." Austin stared raptly at Jessie, thinking how she already looked like a Hollywood star in her new dress and high heels—to him anyway.

Suddenly Jessie could almost see the faces of Ellis and Janie out there with the others, rooting for her to make it to Hollywood. She knew that she would have given even this dream up if they could actually have been there with her. "I saw—" Trying to speak, her words caught in her throat, turning into a sob that she tried to choke back.

Austin stepped close to her as she laid her head against his chest. "I was thinking about them too, Jess. But we can't go on blaming ourselves forever."

In a few moments Jessie stepped back, then nodded her head in agreement.

Austin took his handkerchief and carefully wiped the tears from her cheeks. "We can't have you accepting this award with mascara on your cheeks, can we?"

Jessie felt that she would never love anyone as much as she did Austin, but the urge to get away from the memory of what happened in this city would not go away.

Ten minutes later, the master of ceremonies stepped to center stage.

Jessie put her finger to her lips as Austin started to speak. "Shhh!"

EIGHT

THE CRASH OF DRUMS

★ ★ ★

"Well, it looks like our little girl's Hollywood bound." Lane pulled into the garage, turned off the lights and then the engine of his '39 Ford coupe.

Catherine leaned back against the seat, sighing deeply. "I always thought she had a good voice, but then I felt that all mothers tend to exaggerate the abilities of their own children. And look what happened! She won the state competition. I've never heard her sing so well."

"The way she looked didn't hurt anything either," Lane added. "Did you see those judges?"

"Would you let me out of this backseat?" Dalton leaned forward, his head next to Lane's. "I'm hungry."

"Hungry? Already? You just had a hamburger and a two-gallon malt."

"Aw, Daddy. It wasn't *that* big."

Catherine laughed and ran her hand through Dalton's already rumpled hair. "I think all thirteen-year-old boys are bottomless pits."

"Let's go inside then," Lane agreed, opening the car door. "I could use a cup of coffee."

Sharon got out next to Catherine, following her toward the house. "Mama, I'm tired."

"Okay, baby." Catherine picked her up, knowing that on occasion she still liked to be treated like a small child, although she was almost eleven. "You just hug your mother and we'll get you upstairs and into bed right now."

"I'll bet I can beat you to the back porch," Lane challenged Dalton, bending down in a three-point stance.

"You won't stand a chance," Dalton bragged, getting into position.

"Take your marks, get set . . ." Lane sprinted off down the brick walk, five yards ahead of Dalton before he shouted, "Go!"

"Hey, wait a minute!" Dalton bolted after his father, but couldn't make up the difference.

Lane stood on the wide porch, unlocking the back door when Dalton ran up the steps. "Where you been, slowpoke? You stop off for another malt?"

"That's not fair," Dalton complained.

"I don't remember saying anything about *fair*," Lane grinned. "I said I'd *beat* you."

Dalton turned to Catherine carrying Sharon up the steps. "Mama, did you see what Daddy did?"

"Yes, I *sure* did," Catherine replied, trying to keep from laughing. "You should have seen the tricks your father played on *me* when we were dating."

"What did he do?"

Catherine walked past Lane, who bowed as he held the door open for her. "I'll tell you when you're a little older."

While Catherine was upstairs putting Sharon to

bed, Dalton got a box of Sugar Frosted Flakes down
from the cabinet and a full quart of Lily milk and the
cream pitcher out of the refrigerator. Sitting down at
the table, he flicked up the tab with his fingernail and
pulled the cardboard top out of the milk bottle. Using
a spoon, he dipped the heavy cream at the top of the
bottle into the pitcher until only the milk was left.

Lane set the white enameled pot on the burner to
heat, while he got two cups down for him and Catherine. When the coffee was hot, he poured a cup,
added a spoon of sugar, and sat down at the table with
his son.

Dalton was already halfway through his second
bowl of cereal. "Boy, these are good!"

"Looks like you're eating the right cereal." Lane
picked up the box, staring at the picture of Tony the
Tiger. "You'll be playing for the Tigers one day—I
hope."

"Yep," Dalton mumbled through a mouthful of cereal, a thin line of milk running down the corner of
his mouth. "I wanna be all-American."

Lane sipped his coffee, gazing at his son who, even
in this gawky and clumsy adolescent stage, exhibited
speed and balance far beyond his years. He felt that
Dalton probably could be an all-American if he continued to develop to his full potential—and didn't get
injured. "Dalton . . ."

"Yeah, Dad."

"You think you could take care of your mother and
the girls if I had to go away for a while?"

Dalton stopped a spoonful of cereal halfway to his
mouth. "Why would you do that?"

"I don't want to, son, but I don't have any choice
about it." Lane spoke somberly, staring into his cup,
then looked directly into his son's eyes. "I've been

called back into the Marines. They want me to leave next week."

"Why don't they make somebody else go for a change?" Dalton complained, dropping his spoon into the cereal. "You've already been in a war."

"That's exactly why they want me now." Lane forced a smile. "Because I've been to war and I know what to do."

"It's not *fair!*"

"Yes, it *is* fair." Lane held his son's eyes. "This country's *worth* a few sacrifices, son. I guess you could say it wasn't *fair* that I made it back home after World War II. A lot of good men I fought with didn't. But thinking like that doesn't do *anybody* any good. It's just a fact of life that sometimes we have to fight to keep the things we believe in."

Dalton stood up, trudged across the kitchen, and put his bowl into the sink. When he turned around, his brown eyes were shining with tears.

Lane went over and put his arms around him. "It's okay, son. Everything's going to be just fine."

"I don't want you to go, Daddy." Dalton's voice was hoarse and full of grief. "I'm scared. What if you're one of the ones that don't come back this time?"

Lane held him out at arm's length. "Now don't you go talking like that," he said with a tenderness he seldom used with Dalton. "You're going to be the man of the house when I'm gone. You've got to be brave for your mother."

Dalton sniffed and wiped his eyes with the back of his hand. "I will, Daddy. You can count on me."

"I know I can, son. Now let's go on up and we'll talk awhile before you go to sleep."

"Okay, Daddy."

Lane put his arm around Dalton's shoulder and they started up the stairs.

"Daddy?"

"Yeah."

"Would you tell me about the time you and Papaw were out squirrel hunting and you ran across that bear?"

Lane gazed down and, in the face of his son, could almost see himself as a boy. "Sure thing."

★ ★ ★

Catherine sat with Lane on the scrolled iron bench next to the fountain, listening to the music it made as water flowed from one sculptured tier to another. The mild, katydid-shrill evening was full of stars, glittering through the spreading limbs of the ancient live oak.

"It's not fair!" Catherine had put away her tears in favor of a righteous anger. "You're almost thirty-eight years old and you've got four children."

Lane remembered that Dalton had said much the same thing. "I don't think it can last much longer anyway, the way we're pouring men and supplies in."

"Well, why are they taking you, then?"

"They need officers with combat experience."

Catherine thought of the noisy and crowded train station in Birmingham, Alabama, the last time Lane had gone off to war. She remembered the passionate urgency in his kiss and the feel of his arms around her as they stood on the platform near the engine, billowing with clouds of steam.

But this time she knew somehow that there would be no desperate fear holding her on the brink of midnight sleep; no hopeless plunge into a dark and unrelenting despair. "Catherine, are you all right?"

Taking Lane's hand, she leaned her head on his shoulder. "Guess I just had to blow off a little steam. But I'm not going to waste the time we have left worrying or letting my anger get the best of me."

"Well, you'll have Jess here with you." Lane pulled Catherine closer. "She'll be a big help. Except for those three or four weeks when she's on her trip to Hollywood."

"You know there's still a chance that she could be going on that USO tour."

Lane glanced down at Catherine, shaking his head slightly. "Not *much* of a chance. She'll be competing against the best in the whole country."

Catherine let her mind wander back to a few hours earlier when Jessie had had such an effect on the audience at the Greek Theater. "She's very good, Lane. I didn't really think she had such potential until tonight."

Lane remembered the faces of some of the men in the audience when Jessie was singing. "She's always had a good voice, but the effect she had on—well, I guess I'm amazed that my little girl has grown up so much."

"She was our first," Catherine said wistfully, gazing at a moonlit cloudbank rolling in from the southeast. "I guess part of us will always think of her as a child." She remembered dressing Jessie in her ribbons and lace for Sunday morning services. "I surely wish she'd get back in church though."

"Ah, she'll be all right," Lane assured Catherine. "She's just going through a phase."

Catherine sat up, staring at Lane, her blue eyes filled with a hopeful light. "If you'd go to church with us more—maybe that would help."

Lane gave Catherine a crooked smile. "I've got one

more Sunday before I belong to the corps. You think that's going to make a difference?"

"Goodness! It's slipped my mind already." Catherine determined then that she would make the next few days happy ones for both of them. She punched Lane playfully in the stomach. "You're too old to be playing soldier. That's why I forgot."

"Maybe you could convince President Truman of that. I'd just as soon let the young stallions handle this one."

A sudden breeze sprayed them with water from the fountain. The limbs of the trees began bending as stronger gusts followed, rustling through the leaves. A metal pan blew off the back porch and clattered along the walk. Then the first heavy drops hit them with a stinging coldness.

Lane grabbed Catherine by the hand, running down the walk toward the back porch. Stepping inside the washroom, she handed Lane a towel and took one for herself. They walked over to the porch swing and sat down, drying off and shaking their heads like wet puppies.

Then Catherine slid over close to him, lying back against his chest as they watched the rain sweep through the trees and pound the tender young plants in the freshly turned earth of the flower beds. They remained like that through the storm, taking joy in the warmth and comfort of simply being together while the rain slackened.

The air grew heavy and cool, filling with a fine mist. Still without the need for words, they watched the plop-plopping of rainwater dripping from the eaves of the house onto the banana leaves, glistening in the wet, yellow light from the windows. The distant muted wail of a tugboat sounded from the river.

The sad and lovely strains of "September Song" floated from a neighbor's open window.

"Oh, listen," Catherine whispered. "How beautiful!"

"Reminds me of that first fall up at Ole Miss after we got married," Lane remarked, his voice carrying a poignant sound as though part of him had traveled back to that faraway time and place.

Catherine listened to the last words of the song. "I remember when you'd come in on Sunday afternoons after a road trip, completely exhausted and hungry as a bear. We'd have dinner out back under the big pecan tree and afterward just lay there talking and resting on that old quilt your mother made for you when you were just a little boy. And you'd usually drop off to sleep with your head in my lap."

"Boy, do I remember those meals! Fried chicken and okra and fresh corn and string beans and tomatoes and those cobblers you'd make from the blackberries you canned back in the summer. I can put on five pounds just thinking about it."

"We had time for other things besides eating too," Catherine whispered, stroking the back of his hand.

Listening to the wind sighing high in the crowns of the trees, Lane thought of Catherine on those Sunday evenings fresh from her bath, fragrant with the scent of gardenia and the smell of the sun still in her hair.

"I wonder what happened to it?"

"Huh? Happened to what?"

"The quilt, of course."

"Quilt?"

"Yes, silly. The one your mother made. I haven't seen it in ages."

"Oh, *that* quilt. Who knows?" Lane replied, thinking how he would never understand the mind of a woman. "Cass probably traded it off for a Hershey bar."

Catherine laughed softly. "You ever wonder what he'll grow up to be?"

"Sure I do," Lane answered quickly. "I just hope they'll have reasonable visiting hours."

Catherine sat up in the swing. "Lane Temple! That's your own flesh and blood you're talking about."

"You know I love him dearly, my good and precious wife." Lane put his arms around her, drawing her close again. "Right now though, you're the only flesh and blood I've got on my mind—and what lovely flesh it is too."

"You should be ashamed of yourself," Catherine chastised good-naturedly. "Talking like that out here in the open! What if the neighbors heard you?"

"Oh, I'm ashamed all right," Lane grinned. "I'm purely mortified."

Suddenly Lane scooped Catherine up in his arms, hurrying across the porch and into the house. As he carried her up the dimly lighted staircase, she laid her head on his shoulder, brushing her lips against his neck.

Later they lay on their poster bed, dozing among the cool and rumpled sheets. Lane awakened, tucked the bedspread up around Catherine's shoulders, and sat up on the side of the bed. Staring at the long white curtains blowing into the room from the open French doors, he reached for the pack of Camels on the nightstand and shook one out of the pack. Picking up his lighter, he glanced at the marine emblem on it and flicked it into flame.

Lane drew the smoke deeply into his lungs, feeling its harsh dry pain, wondering after years of smoking what attraction it held for people like himself. He had awakened with a half-formed thought at the edge of his mind. As it began to form he spoke it out loud. "The bugle . . ."

Hearing Lane's voice, Catherine stirred, beginning to come awake.

"The crash of drums . . ." Lane tried to remember where he had heard the phrases and who had spoken or written them.

Awake now, Catherine sat up in bed.

"The rattle of musketry. . ."

Catherine placed her hand on Lane's shoulder. "What are you talking about, darling?"

Lane stared out the window beyond the billowing curtains into the night, his voice unfamiliar and distant. "The strange, mournful mutter of the battlefield."

Catherine moved close and slipped her arms around him from behind, laying her head on his shoulder. "Where did you hear something like that?"

Lane took another deep draw on his cigarette, the tip glowing brightly in the shadowed room, and let the smoke curl from his nostrils. "I can't remember who said it. Someone in love with war, I suppose."

★ ★ ★

"It's like a dream!" Jessie felt the excitement of winning the USO contest still swirling and dancing inside her. "I'm actually going to Hollywood!"

Austin glanced over at her. The breeze through the car window blew her hair about her face in a soft, bright cloud. "I'm proud of you, Jess."

"Hollywood!" She stared at the little ice cream parlor located in the front of the dark bulk of the Louisiana Creamery as they hummed along Plank Road, wondering if they sold ice cream that good in California. As they crossed Choctaw, she saw the lighted show windows of Ourso's Department Store, and imagined herself attending some gala opening night in the formal gown worn by one of the mannequins.

"Guess you'll forget all about your old friends when you start running around with the Hollywood crowd," Austin remarked casually, trying to hide his uneasiness at the thought of actually losing Jessie to the Hollywood lifestyle. "Yes sir, brunch at Malibu with Doris Day—dinners at the Brown Derby with Gary Cooper or maybe Dean Martin."

"Oh, don't be silly!" Jessie tried to make light of his humor, but just the sound of the names excited her. "Why would *they* be interested in a nobody like me?"

"*I* think you're pretty interesting."

"Sure, but you're just . . ." Jessie stopped herself before she spoke the word *ordinary*, thinking that was not like her at all. "Oh, you know what I mean."

Austin could already feel Jessie leaving him in a way that was perhaps even more real than physical separation. "Yeah, I'm afraid I *do* know what you mean."

"Come on, now. Don't be that way." Jessie slid over in the seat, curling her fingers in the back of Austin's hair. "We've got more than a month before I have to leave. Let's make the most of the time we have."

"Sure."

Jessie laid her head on Austin's shoulder, gazing out at Blake and Bowles Office Supply. *They sure did treat me good when I worked there last summer. I hope the people out in Hollywood are that nice.*

"Did they give you a date to leave yet?" Austin turned left on Evangeline Street.

"The first week in June," Jessie replied. "That's all I know so far."

Austin pulled the coupe over to the side of the street, parking in the shadow of the huge live oak in the front yard of the Temple home.

"I had a great time tonight," Jessie said softly, kissing him on the cheek.

"Me too." He turned the engine off, listening to the ticking sounds it made.

"Dinner at Mike and Tony's. That's a real treat for a little country girl like me."

Austin turned to face her. "You certainly don't look like a country girl in that outfit. I noticed the men in the audience tonight didn't seem to think so either."

"Forget about them. You're the only man in my life." Jessie put her arms around Austin's neck, pressing against him, kissing him warmly on the mouth.

Austin eased over from beneath the steering wheel, his left arm circling Jessie's waist as he responded to her kiss. In a few seconds he pulled back.

"What's wrong?" Jessie stared into his eyes, surprised by his reaction.

Again it seemed to Austin that a battle was raging inside him. He had experienced this feeling many times since that evening down by the lake with Tom and Sarah Edmonson that had changed his life. Desire for Jessie was just as strong in him as it ever was, but he knew that he couldn't allow himself to give in to it.

"Nothing."

"Something's different about you, Austin. You haven't acted like yourself in two or three weeks."

Austin felt like a hypocrite. *Maybe this being a Christian is something I just can't do. Why do I still have feelings like this about Jessie? I should be able to just love her and let that be enough. And why can't I just come out and tell her about Jesus? Why can't I tell anybody?*

"Did you hear what I said, Austin?"

Austin felt he should tell Jessie about the change in his life but couldn't bring himself to do it. "Nothing's wrong with me. I'm still the same ol' mixed-up, but remarkably loveable kid you've always been so crazy about."

Jessie gave him a skeptical look. "Is there somebody else, Austin?"

Austin smiled, amused at Jessie's choice of words. *There is somebody else. But how can I tell you how much He's changed my life?* "You're the only girl I've ever really cared about, Jess. You oughta know that by now."

"Well, come on over here and show me, then." Jessie smiled at him dreamily, turning her head slightly to one side. "You certainly never had any trouble before."

"I guess I'm just kinda tired. That final term paper in English is wearing me out." Austin could feel the phoniness of his words, feel their fragile facade cracking under Jessie's steady gaze. "Look, there's your daddy."

Jessie gazed at the upstairs gallery beyond the trailing edge of a spreading oak limb. She watched her father walking slowly back and forth behind the railing, smoke from his cigarette rising in a white plume against the shadows.

"You think he wants you to come in?"

Jessie's face reflected her sagging spirits. "I don't think he's even noticed that we're down here. The tree blocks the view from up there. That's why you always parked here, remember?"

141

"I remember," Austin admitted, his passion for Jessie relentless now. "Why's he up so late, then?"

"He's probably worried about Mama—and the rest of us," Jessie sighed.

Concerned at the sadness that had crept into Jessie's eyes, Austin slid over in the seat and put his arm around her. "What's wrong, Jess? He's not sick, is he?"

"No. He's not sick." Jessie didn't want to think about the war in Korea, where her father would have to go and risk his life again, anymore than she wanted to think about what had happened to Ellis and Janie.

"Well, what is it then?"

"The Marines have called him back in." Jessie pressed against Austin, laying her head on his shoulder. "He's leaving next week. I think he just told Mama tonight."

PART THREE

★ ★ ★

HEARTBREAK

NINE

DREAMY

★ ★ ★

"Oh, Mama, I did it! I won!" Jessie almost shouted into the phone.

Catherine had dreaded the possibility of hearing those words since the night Jessie had won the state competition at LSU. She knew it meant that her daughter wouldn't be coming home now, but tried her best to sound happy anyway. "That's wonderful, Jess. I'm so proud of you!"

"I'm going to get some free acting lessons and they're giving me a screen test sometime next month—and, Mama, I actually met Bob Hope!"

"Oh, my goodness!" Catherine could almost see the look of wonder on Jessie's face. "What's he like? Is he as funny and nice as he seems in the movies?"

"I just saw him for a minute or two, Mama. I'm not his best friend yet."

Catherine gazed out the kitchen window into the backyard where Dalton was cutting the grass. The blades of the push mower were spinning in the sunlight beneath the small green flurry of grass clippings.

"Mama, are you still there?"

"Yes, baby. I'm here."

"You should see the place they rented for me now that I'm going to be here for a while." Jessie looked over the railing of the terrace built out over the side of a cliff. "It's a little house and it's way up almost on top of a big hill."

"Are you sure it's safe?"

"Oh, Mama! Don't be so silly." When Jessie had first seen the bungalow on its stilts overlooking the Pacific Coast Highway, the same question had entered her mind.

"What does it look like out there, Jess?" Catherine wanted some kind of background to picture her daughter in so she would have a firmer hold on her in her mind. She longed desperately to catch the next airplane for Los Angeles.

Jessie gazed far below and beyond the highway at the morning mist covering the ocean like a white blanket. Even at that distance, she could hear the waves crashing against the shore. In the opposite direction she could see the shadowed crests of the Santa Monica Mountains. The whole scene was bathed in the cool pink light of sunrise.

"Did you hear me, Jess?" Catherine wondered if the long distance lines were harder to hear on.

"Yes, Mama. It's just beautiful."

"Jess . . ."

After living eighteen years with her mother, Jessie knew the tone well. "No, Mother."

"What do you mean?"

"No, I'm not going out with anybody."

"You think you know me so well, don't you?" Catherine made a face at the telephone.

"Yes, I do," Jessie laughed. "And you don't have to worry. I'm a big girl now."

"You mean none of those movie stars have asked you for a date?"

"They don't ask nobodies like me out. This whole town is full of beautiful actresses."

Catherine felt a deep sense of relief. "It's just as well, I think, Jess. I imagine the lifestyle out there isn't something that would suit a girl like you."

"I'm going to be much too busy to get involved in the social scene, Mama." Jessie longed to see the glitter and glamour of Hollywood, but felt that there would be little chance of that in the short time she had. "I did see some movie stars though. Not up close or anything."

"Who?"

Jessie felt a sense of pride in telling about her experiences in the famed movie capital. "Well, we did our rehearsing for the contest on a sound stage and we took this bus through the studio lots every day."

"Did you see Gary Cooper?" He had long been Catherine's favorite.

"No, but I did see William Holden."

"Never heard of him."

"Well, how about Betty Grable," Jessie bragged. "Did you ever hear of her?"

"Oh yes," Catherine replied, remembering her from movies during the war. "She was the most famous pinup girl in World War II. I even found a picture of her in your father's duffel bag when I unpacked it."

"Have you heard from Daddy lately?" The question was out before Jessie could stop herself, and she regretted it immediately. Lane had been stationed temporarily in San Diego and she still hadn't been down to see him.

Catherine's initial emotion was anger, followed quickly by the sharp pang of disappointment. Struggling to keep her temper in check, she chose her words carefully and spoke them calmly. "Jessie. . . . You haven't been down to see your father yet?" She wanted to shout that it might be the last time she would ever see him alive, but put her hand over the receiver instead.

"No, Mama."

"You know he's not allowed off the base now and he could be going overseas at a moment's notice."

Jessie frowned at a car looking like a toy as it moved slowly along the early deserted highway far below. "It's just that we've been so busy and—"

"Too busy to take *one* day off?"

"Mama, you just don't know—"

"For your own *father*?"

"I'll go down to see him just as soon as I can get away." Jessie held her hand over the phone's receiver and took a deep breath. "I'll take a bus. It's only three hours."

"See that you do." Catherine felt a failure as a mother because of Jessie's attitude, having forgotten as most mothers do what it's like to be eighteen.

Jessie wanted to say something that would get her mother's mind off the trip down to San Diego. "Mama, you know I said I wasn't dating anyone?"

"Yes." Judging from the tone of her daughter's voice, Catherine felt that she was about to have something else besides Jessie's not visiting Lane to worry about.

"Well . . ."

"Does that mean you *are* dating someone?" Catherine stepped over to the stove, lifted the lid off a heavy pot and stirred her butter beans, seasoned with salt, pepper, and a little bacon fat. She thought how much Lane liked them and wished he could be there to have supper.

"Not exactly." Jessie changed it quickly. "I mean not at all, but. . . . Oh, Mama, he's so *dreamy!*"

Catherine hadn't heard Jessie use the word since she was fourteen. "*Who,* for goodness sakes?"

"Tony Vale."

Running through the abbreviated list of movie stars filed in her mind, Catherine couldn't find a Tony Vale. "I don't believe I ever heard of him."

"Maybe not, but you will soon," Jessie assured her. "He's got a starring role."

"If he's starting off with a starring role, he must be a very good actor."

"He's had a few minor parts, but his singing is what really landed him the role. His voice is absolutely the most *marvelous* thing you've ever heard in your life."

"I know who you're talking about now. He made a record or two. And he does have a very fine voice." There was another word, *marvelous,* added to Jessie's working vocabulary. Catherine was beginning to think of them as Hollywood words.

"He's been singing all over the East Coast for years." Jessie didn't mention that it was in nightclubs and that Vale called himself a saloon singer. She thought of having lunch the previous day with Vale and several other crew members who would be going on the USO tour. "Mother, are you still there?"

"Yes, dear."

"And he's got the most beautiful brown eyes and long dark lashes—almost like a girl's."

"He sounds very pretty."

"Not pretty!" Jessie was incensed that Tony would be labeled that way. "Handsome."

"Sorry."

Jessie glanced at the notepad next to the telephone. "By the way, how're the children? I bet you thought I'd forget to ask, didn't you?"

"Maybe." Catherine was mildly surprised that Jessie had remembered. "Dalton's cutting the grass right now. He's such a big help around here. Dependable and solid as a rock—just like his daddy."

"Well, let's try the other extreme, then," Jessie teased. "How's Cass?"

"Cass is—Cass," Catherine sighed. "And, as usual, I hardly know Sharon's on the place."

"Give them a big kiss for me."

"Okay, baby." Catherine wanted to keep Jessie on the phone to hear the sound of her voice awhile longer, but could already sense the impatience in her tone.

"I have to go now, Mama." Jessie watched the red sun flare as it topped the mountains. "Someone from the studio's coming by for me and I haven't even started to get ready yet."

"I understand. And, Jess . . ."

"Yes, Mother."

"You've been raised right, so don't do anything you'd be ashamed of later."

"Oh, Mama! You worry too much."

"I'm a mother. That's my job," Catherine reminded her. "And don't forget about your father."

"I won't."

"Well, bye for now. I love you, baby."

"I love you too, Mama."

Catherine poured a cup of tea from the pot that

had been brewing on the counter and sat down at the table. Taking Lane's last letter from the pocket of her apron, she brushed a few strands back from her forehead and read the last paragraphs:

> One thing for sure, I'm sleeping good at night. Trying to keep up with these young bucks is tough. They call me the "ol' man," but I've stayed with 'em so far.

"I'm sure you have, Lane, my darling. You never were one for giving up—on anything." Catherine spoke the words out loud as though trying to reassure Lane that she was behind him.

> Sometimes when we have a little free time they'll come to the "ol' man" to find out what it's really like in combat. How do you tell someone about it? I haven't figured it out yet. All I can do is tell them that they'll be fine if they obey orders because they're fighting with the best there is— and that's the gospel.
>
> The colonel talked about keeping me here as an instructor, but I think they need experienced men in Korea too badly. I think I like practicing law better than soldiering—I know I like sleeping with you more than in a barracks full of hairy men. I dream of you a lot, Catherine.
>
> Time to go. Lights out in five minutes.
>
> I love you more than I ever have. All my love to the children.
>
> Lane
>
> Oh yes. Don't pester Jessie about coming down here to see me. She's got her own life and this may be her one big chance to make it as a singer.

★ ★ ★

151

At five-nine and one hundred and thirty-five pounds, Tony Vale looked lost in the baggy army fatigues and combat boots as he stood near the edge of the set. He ran a comb through his dark, wavy hair, took a deep breath, and walked over to the microphone. Smiling out at his imaginary audience, he held on to the heavy mike stand, launching directly into the song with the band taking their cue from him.

"Hello, young lovers, wherever you are. . . ."

Wearing fatigues that duplicated Vale's, except that her trousers had been cut off to become shorts, Jessie sat on a tall stool next to a light stand, a rapt expression on her face. She hung on every note, every syllable.

Vale's rich baritone seemed to flow through her as he caressed the lyrics of the song. The voice was a gift. It could be improved through practice and breath control, but never had she heard a singer with such perfect diction. She knew that came from the years of concentrated effort that most singers would not subject themselves to.

The song ended to applause from the performers in the troupe, most of whom were veterans of years in show business. Even they knew a talent like Vale came along very rarely.

Vale took an exaggerated bow, flashed his third-best smile to his makeshift audience and walked over to Jessie, still sitting on her stool. "Well, how was I? Think I might have a future in this business?"

"You know the answer to that question, Tony." Astonished that with all the beautiful starlets in Hollywood Vale found time for her, Jessie was nevertheless intimidated in his presence. "You're better than Bing Crosby."

Vale flashed his white teeth in a laugh that was as

smooth as his singing style. "I don't think I'll ever be as good as the old crooner, but it's nice of you to think so."

"When do you think we'll be leaving for Korea?"

"You in a hurry to get shot at?"

"No, just wondering."

Vale glanced around him at the rest of the troupe, minus Bob Hope, who would only practice with them for the last week before the trip. "We could probably have the show ready in a month. But we've got all that military red tape to deal with, so it'll probably be September—maybe even October."

Jessie relished the thought of two or three months in Hollywood in the company of Vale and the other performers. "That gives us plenty of time to get it right, then."

"You've got it right already, dollface." Vale gazed directly into Jessie's eyes. "Your songs, I mean."

For the first time, Jessie felt uneasy under Vale's steady gaze, but it passed quickly. "I don't think I'll ever sing the way I'd really like to. But it's my dance numbers that are simply awful; I feel like an old mule clomping about."

"I can't get enough of those southern ways of yours, Jessie," Vale laughed again. "It's so easy being around you. I don't feel I have to keep my guard up like I do with most other women—maybe *all* other women."

Jessie blushed. During the week they had been rehearsing together, a question hung at the back of Jessie's mind. She decided this was as good a time as any to ask it. "Tony, there's something I've been wanting to ask you."

"Not anymore."

"I don't understand."

"I'm not married anymore. Jessie, you'd better close your mouth. It ruins your looks."

Jessie quickly put her hand over her mouth, then took it away and smiled. "How did you know that was the question?"

"It's *always* the question." Vale gazed off into the past. "We were just kids. Right out of high school."

Jessie breathed a sigh of relief that Vale was single, although she realized that it may not affect their relationship one way or the other. Still, it seemed that he was the most real thing in her world now. Her love for Austin and that terrible Christmas Eve both seemed like things that happened long, long ago—if at all. She felt that her life hinged on Tony Vale and the things that his world could offer her now.

"I was about your age," Vale continued. "By the way, how old are you?"

"Eighteen."

"Exactly your age. Anyway, we had a kid nine months after the wedding and separated on his first birthday. What a way to celebrate, huh?"

"Boy or girl?"

Vale seemed distracted and distanced, as though he was looking at pictures in a scrapbook he carried around in his head. "Huh? Oh, a boy. I see him at Christmas and on his birthday."

"I'm sorry it didn't work out."

Vale took her hand. "Don't be. Nobody really knows what they want at that age. I'm a decade older and wiser now and I still sometimes wonder what the whole thing's all about."

Jessie nodded.

"Besides," Vale brightened. "If I was still married, I wouldn't have met you."

Jessie smiled again and squeezed his hand.

"Let's get some lunch."

★ ★ ★

The huge stucco mansion, with its Spanish arches and blue-tiled floors, stood high up on one of the dry hills that overlooked the ocean. Chaparral, mesquite, and scrub oak covered the land outside the white walls. Inside them the terraced lawn was landscaped with oleander, yucca plants, and slim palms swaying in the sea breeze. Passion vine and bougainvillea hung in bright cascades from white trellises.

A Roman porch, complete with ivory-colored Corinthian columns, fronted three sides of the enormous pool. Lighting in its tiled walls gave the water a smoky-blue appearance as it shined on pastel flowers floating on the surface.

"Drink up, Jessie." Tony Vale, his olive complexion in marked contrast to the white dinner jacket, waved his hand at one of the waiters weaving through the crowd carrying silver trays filled with drinks.

The boy, no more than sixteen and obviously of Spanish descent, carefully placed two full champagne glasses on the marble-topped table, bowed slightly, and walked back into the crowd.

"I think one's my limit, Tony." Jessie had bought a pale green gown and worn her hair up for the occasion. Still, she felt like a child among these people who epitomized the power and glamour of the movie capital.

Vale shook his head. "No one drinks just one glass of champagne."

"Well, all right, then. Just one more." Jessie's first glass had left her light-headed and slightly dizzy. She couldn't bring herself to tell Vale she had never tasted champagne before. It went down so easily, tickling all the way, that she felt like giggling with each swallow she took.

"I'm so glad you could come." Vale waved to a short bald man in a black tuxedo as he hurried past them. "One of the most talented directors in the business."

Jessie was awestruck by the opulence of her surroundings and by the people who occupied them. In her slightly giddy state, she felt that the night was more of a dream than something that was actually happening to her.

"Are you having fun?"

Staring toward the opposite side of the terrace, Jessie hadn't heard Vale at all. A striking woman with hair almost the same color as hers walked along the poolside with a tall, elegant man wearing a tan silk jacket. Her pale skin looked almost translucent against the black strapless gown. "Isn't that Marilyn Monroe?"

"Why, yes," Vale replied as though Jessie had committed a minor blasphemy by not recognizing her immediately. "In a year's time she'll be the hottest property in town—or so I'm told by people in the know."

"She's so lovely." Jessie remembered seeing her in *The Asphalt Jungle* on one of her dates with Austin. Then suddenly she couldn't get him off her mind. She could almost feel his lips against hers and the comfort of his arms. *What's wrong with me? I'm with someone as wonderful as Tony Vale and I start thinking about Austin. I must be losing my mind.*

Jessie's reaction was lost on Vale. "The champagne bothering you, Jessie?"

"What? Oh no." She pushed Austin's memory aside. "I was just thinking how much prettier Marilyn Monroe is in person than she is on the screen."

"Well, she's no Vivien Leigh when it comes to talent, but she certainly does have a certain—presence, I guess you'd call it, about her."

As the evening wore on to the sound of popping corks and tinkling glasses, the conversations grew more animated, the laughter more unrestrained, and the personal contact more intimate. Soon, a young woman in a silver gown let out a shriek of panic as she splashed into the pool. Her date, who had thrown her in and who had also graced the cover of the previous month's *Photoplay* magazine, jumped in behind her.

Jessie watched in shock as a dozen or more of the elegant Hollywood crowd shed their inhibitions along with most of their clothes and joined the first couple in the pool. She stared at the faces around her. Gone were the practiced graces and exquisite mannerisms that had masked them in the early stages of the party. Now she saw faces gone slack with drink and jaded by excesses of power and money and the myriad pleasures that they could demand.

Suddenly, Austin's face appeared in Jessie's mind almost as though he stood before her. He was so real, she nearly reached out for him. Then she glanced at Vale and all thoughts of Austin vanished. The champagne coursed warmly through her veins and she let it take her to a world where the cutting edges of doubt and worry were softly rounded off.

"Why don't we—"

"Can you take me home now, Tony?" Jessie drifted in a drowsy land of muted noises and blurred colors. "I'm getting kind of tired and we've got rehearsals tomorrow."

Vale was about to complete his sentence with "—join them in the pool," when Jessie interrupted him.

"Ah—I was just about to suggest that."

★ ★ ★

Jessie sat on a chaise lounge on her terrace, listening to the waves crashing against the rocks far below. Away from the lights of the city now, she could see the gossamer moonlight falling on the pewter-colored surface of the sea.

"Here we are. Just like Mama used to make." Tony stepped through the opening in the curtained glass wall and out onto the terrace. He had stopped at a small grocery store on the way to Jessie's and bought coffee and two small cups.

"This is so nice of you, Tony," Jessie said with mild disbelief that a real Hollywood star would do something as mundane as make coffee for her.

"In case you haven't noticed, I'm a nice fellow." Vale handed her the demitasse and sat down in a chair next to her. "Just what we need to cap off a perfect evening."

Basking in the pleasant afterglow of the champagne and the charm of Tony Vale, Jessie thought that the party somehow didn't seem nearly so shocking or offensive. *After all, the people, especially Tony, were all so nice and well-mannered.* It occurred to her that perhaps she was just being a prude, thinking herself better than they were.

Jessie recalled from her years of going to Sunday school the parable of the Pharisee who entered the temple, thanking God that he was not as other men. *I certainly don't want to be like that, now, do I?*

Jessie sipped her coffee carefully. "Oh, that's perfectly delicious!" She had noticed that the custom among the movie crowd was to exclaim about the smallest pleasures and found herself falling into the habit.

"Glad you like it." Tony gave Jessie a reflective glance. "My daddy used to sell this kind of coffee in his little grocery store in Brooklyn."

Jessie thought of baseball, the *Dead End Kids*, and the massive bridge spanning the Hudson that had become a national treasure. "You were born in Brooklyn?"

"Yep. Born and raised." Tony sipped his coffee and sighed deeply. "I almost feel like a kid again every time I drink a cup of this stuff. Mama used to bring it to me in bed on winter mornings. Sometimes I think I can still feel her hand on my cheek—she had the softest hands—and smell that coffee.

"She'd always sit and talk for a while, tell me about how her life was when she was growing up in Naples, what the buildings and the little narrow streets looked like, about the trip over to America—I loved to hear her say *America*—on a tramp steamer, things like that. It was always the best part of the day."

Jessie slipped out of her high heels and leaned back, delighting in the sound of Vale's voice and deliciously comfortable on the chaise lounge.

"Yeah, those were the good ol' days, all right." Vale held his cup cradled in both hands as though it contained the memories he was trying to preserve. "I remember we used to have stick ball games in the streets and in the summertime we'd get a fireman to open a hydrant so we could play in the water. It came gushing out like Niagara Falls. Sure felt good on those hot days."

Jessie thought she could still see the child that Vale used to be in the sad sort of smile he wore now and in the different kind of light that filled his eyes.

"Sounds like you had a pretty good time growing up in Brooklyn."

Vale glanced away toward the gleaming surface of the ocean. In the pale moonlight it had the appearance of wet slate. "I did until Mama died. Then my old man—Daddy kind of went crazy, I guess you'd say."

"How old were you when she died?"

"Nine. I couldn't please him no matter how hard I tried after that."

Jessie noticed Vale's jaw muscles working beneath his smooth skin as though grinding away the painful memories.

"I'd get up in the morning and stock shelves in the store before I went to school." Vale set his cup down, leaned back in his chair, and ran both hands through his thick hair. "Then when I got home in the afternoons I'd make deliveries for him 'til eight, nine o'clock. Didn't matter though. He'd just as soon backhand me across the mouth as look at me."

"I'm so sorry, Tony. I didn't know."

"Not your fault, sweetheart." Vale stood up and walked over to the rail and gazed down at the rocky shoreline. "When I was thirteen, I got out of that hellhole. Took a job waiting tables at a restaurant in the neighborhood. Mr. Canjelosi, the owner, let me sleep on a cot in the back. He knew how my ol' man was treatin' me. I guess he saved my life.

"A year later I started singing in the restaurant while I waited tables. People seemed to like it all right and Canjelosi did too 'cause it brought in the customers. After that I sang at a few local joints, then at some of the fancy ones in Manhattan and before I knew it, I was on my way."

Jessie was moved by the story of Vale's unhappy childhood and felt that his telling her of it had brought them closer. She got up and walked over to him.

Vale turned around at the sound of her steps, then took her in his arms.

Jessie noticed how small and delicate Vale appeared as he moved toward her, his arms going around her waist, one hand pressed against the small of her back. For a fleeting moment, she thought of Austin's hard, muscular body. Then Vale's lips were on hers and his hand trailed softly and with a practiced touch over her pale skin.

TEN

HEARTBREAK RIDGE

★ ★ ★

In the spring of 1951, the Chinese launched two major offensives: the first in April, another in May. Both failed miserably with hundreds of thousands of Chinese and North Korean troops killed by United Nations infantry, artillery, and air strikes. Sensing that their superior numbers no longer held a strategic advantage for them, the Chinese and North Koreans agreed in July to begin talks about a possible armistice.

Two more years of fighting lay ahead, but the character of the war had changed for good. Neither side would again mount a major offensive. It had become a war of "limited objectives," a war designed to take a hill here or a ridgeline there. All along the front that roughly coincided with the 38th parallel, men began digging in permanently.

To the ordinary soldiers fighting the war, however, the term "limited objectives" held little meaning. They never sat in the paneled rooms where men with scented cheeks in immaculate uniforms made the strategic decisions. To them the fighting in a war of "limited objectives" was just as bitter, and an enemy bullet or mortar shell killed you just as thoroughly as in a major offensive.

★ ★ ★

Lane saw that the command post—nothing more than a bunker made of logs with sandbagged walls and roof—was located on the ridgeline of one of the thousands of nameless or numbered hills that men fought and bled and died for and that afterward warranted not even a punctuation mark in the history books. It was hot that August day he arrived in Korea.

Lane stepped into the dimness of the bunker and reported to the battalion commander. Fishing his orders out of his field jacket pocket, he laid them on the makeshift plywood desk.

"Hate to see 'em calling men back in as old as you are." The battalion commander handed the orders back.

"I'm not crazy about it myself." Lane felt much better now that he was out of the sun.

The colonel, swarthy and with three days' dark stubble on his broad face, smiled thinly, handing Lane his binoculars. "Take a look over there, Captain, and you'll see what the men are up against in this war. You're lucky that you're just passing through my sector of the fighting."

Without speaking, Lane took the heavy glasses, training them across the valley. Men scrambled among the rocky outcrops of the opposite slope that rose steeply toward the ridgeline. Mortar rounds and artillery exploded among them as they fought their way slowly upward.

Lane watched a marine leap from behind a boulder, sprinting toward the next cover. Soundlessly in the mock closeness of the glass, he dropped suddenly, throwing his arms outward, sliding backward down the steep slope.

Two more men ran from behind the same boulder, leaving their weapons and their safety to grab their fallen comrade and drag him back along the last ground he had covered in this life. A drifting cloud of smoke obscured the one dead and two living marines, and when it was gone so were the men. Lane hoped that they had made it to safety.

"It's heartbreaking to watch, isn't it, son?" The colonel's voice sounded like an elegy.

Lane knew the question was purely academic and made no attempt at a reply. Below him he could see the fighting closeup and safely through the colonel's glasses.

Lane could tell when the men got near an enemy bunker. They'd begin moving sideways, looking for cover, any kind of cover, circling around as they tried to close in for the kill among the harmless-looking little black puffs of smoke made by the exploding grenades the North Koreans were lobbing out at them from inside their bunkers.

Lane handed the colonel's glasses back to him. "Same men—different terrain."

"That doesn't surprise you, does it? Marines are *all* the same, Captain—" The colonel paused in his conversation, squinting in the sudden light of the bunker door opening.

A corporal with a thin face and buck teeth stepped in and sat down at his radio over in one corner of the bunker. Slipping the headphones on, he began relaying a message to one of the company commanders.

"Sameness. It's the source of our strength—simply stated, of course."

"Yes sir."

Opening a file, grimed and scarred by travel, the colonel thumbed quickly through a few sheaves of forms. "You've got quite a record, Temple."

Lane knew he had been formally accepted into the war when the colonel dropped "Captain" in favor of his name. "That was a long time ago, Colonel—in another war."

The colonel gazed back into the past. "Guadalcanal, Tarawa, Iwo Jima."

For Lane, the names rang with shellfire and the roar of invasion craft.

Closing the file, the colonel stared directly at Lane, a gunmetal glint in his eyes. "Now it's the Frozen Chosin. God help us, with another winter coming on."

Lane knew he referred to the fighting at the Chosin Reservoir the previous winter when the Chinese had sent hundreds of thousands of soldiers across the Yalu River to attack the Marines. Lane had seen the David Duncan pictures in *Life* magazine of the men fighting and dying in the mountains of North Korea, their bodies frozen stiff, arms and legs straight out and rigid. Their friends had stacked them like so much cordwood on the trucks grinding down the narrow mountain roads on the long, bitter retreat to the sea.

He had heard the stories about how mortar tubes would shrink in the cold, too small for the shells to fit in them; how men's hands would freeze to any exposed metal with the flesh peeling off when they pulled them away; how the grenades froze so solidly that you couldn't pull the pins.

"You still with me, Temple?"

"Yes sir. Everybody's heard about the Frozen Chosin." Lane almost longed for the blazing sun of the South Pacific.

"It was worse than you heard."

Lane stared at him, the unasked questions still in his narrowed eyes.

The colonel fished a cigarette out of his breast pocket, sticking it in the side of his mouth.

Lane held out his lighter and flicked it into flame, wondering if it would survive this war.

As the colonel lit his cigarette, his eyes squinting in the smoke, he noticed the marine emblem. "From the last war?"

"Yes sir."

"I had one just like it. No idea now what happened to it. May be up at the Chosin." The colonel inhaled deeply, letting the smoke curl from his mouth.

Lane knew that he wasn't talking just to hear the sound of his own voice or to spin marine yarns, that there was a purpose to this conversation.

"They come at you in waves. Don't seem to have much training, but there's so many of them it doesn't matter. A lot of hand-to-hand fighting up there—shovels, bayonets, rifle butts, and when you run out of something to hit them with you use your fists. Never had to do that before."

Lane was remembering stories he had heard on the way over. "What about the bugles, Colonel?"

"Creepy. Never heard anything like it. And some of the officers still rode those little Mongol ponies."

"Ponies? In *this* war? I know the Polish cavalry still rode horses when Hitler's Blitzkrieg hit them in '39, but I thought that was the end of it."

The colonel squinted into the stream of blue-white smoke, rising toward a small cloud floating at the top of the bunker. "You'd think they were part of Ghengis Khan's hordes, the way they still fight."

Lane smiled bitterly. "Ponies in a time of jet airplanes and nuclear bombs."

"They blow those bugles at the beginning of an attack," the colonel continued, his left eye twitching slightly. "Then it's the mortar and artillery fire for a while—and you think you're back to normal fighting."

Lane waited for the punchline.

"Then the next thing you know, it's Ghengis Khan time again. They come at you in hordes."

"'Scuse me, Colonel." The corporal had taken his headphones off, letting them dangle around his neck. "It's Lieutenant Coxe, sir. Says they're almost out of ammo."

The colonel leaned back in his chair, gazing out a narrow slit in the bunker wall at the yellow sun dropping toward the ridgeline. "Two more hours—maybe less." Then he turned back to his radioman. "Tell the lieutenant to hang on 'til dark. We'll resupply him then."

"Yes sir." The corporal put his headphones back on, muttering into the handset.

"Now where was I?" The colonel stubbed out his cigarette in an ashtray made from the base of a 105 artillery shell. "Oh yeah—bugles and ponies."

Lane sat down on an ammo crate next to the desk.

"We were near a little village named Hagaru the first time it happened. We dug in for the night on a ridgeline. You could barely see the Chosin way down below us. Then it got dark and started to snow and you couldn't see anything."

Lighting a Camel, Lane leaned his elbow on a firing port, listening to the colonel's story and judging the kind of enemy he would be facing.

As the colonel continued his narrative, a shadow crossed his face. "We thought we were still headed for the Yalu River and when we got there, the war would be over. Didn't have any idea that the Chinese were slaughtering our army on the other side of the mountains from us.

"It was the day after Thanksgiving and everybody thought we'd all be home by Christmas." He took out another crumpled cigarette and lit it from Lane's. "Well, about nine o'clock we heard the bugles."

The colonel stared at Lane. "Yep, that was the first time I ever heard 'em. Gives me the creeps just thinking about it."

Suddenly Lane felt the cold chill of fear in his gut as he heard the *whir-whir-whir* of an incoming mortar shell. He dove for the floor, both arms covering his head. The shell exploded off to the right, followed by another and then a third. Glancing up, he said, "Sorry, sir. Guess old habits die hard."

The colonel never budged from his chair. "Be glad you still got 'em. Might save your life one day." Then he looked at the low ceiling of the bunker. "Nothing but a direct hit from a bomb would come through that."

Lane stood up with a sheepish smile, brushing the grit from his fatigues.

Continuing as though nothing had happened, the colonel stared at the distant hills. "Next thing they did was light up the whole place with searchlights. Then you could see the Chinese swarming up the hill like sheep. We put everything we had into them: heavy machine guns, BAR's, rifles, grenades, artillery, mortars. Then it got down to gun butts, knives—I saw one guy laying into them with his helmet, swinging it by the strap."

The colonel's eyes held a hard, distant light. "They just kept coming. Hitting us in waves about six or seven hundred yards apart. Then they'd stop for an hour or two and you could tend to the wounded, bring up some more ammo, and maybe get a little rest. Then the whole thing would start all over."

Lane knew now that there was more to the colonel's story than just letting him know the mind and tactics and the suicidal nature of the enemy.

"I had two hundred and nineteen men in my company." The colonel ran his hands through his cropped hair. "Forty-three of us were alive the next morning."

Thinking of Catherine and his children, Lane watched the sun touch the opposite ridgeline.

"Sorry you had to be the one, Captain."

"Sir?"

"I've been needing to get this out of my system for nine months." He smiled genuinely at Lane. "I can tell you about it since you're not going to be in my command. Besides, you've been through enough to understand."

"Yes sir."

★ ★ ★

Thanksgiving had come around again and nothing even remotely on the magnitude of the Chosin Reservoir had happened. The First Marine Division manned the high ridges of the coastal range from the Sea of Japan on their right flank, tying in with the Republic of Korea's army on their left. With its own artillery regiment, its Marine Air Wing and supporting naval gunfire, it was as powerful an infantry division as had ever seen combat. It had to be. North Korea had massed a million Chinese soldiers, forty divisions, and nine divisions of their own army above the 38th parallel.

Lane commanded a rifle company. He sat now in his bunker, dark stubble on his face and a Camel dangling unlit from the corner of his mouth, briefing a new rifle platoon leader who had just come up with a supply train. The Chinese carried huge loads up the mountain paths on A-frames: rations, ammo, oil, rolls of barbed wire, shovels, tents—all the things required in the occupation of men killing other men.

The young officer, slim and dark and eager, saluted, his orders gripped tightly in his left hand. "Lieutenant Morales, Herman A, reporting for duty, sir."

Lane gave him a casual salute, took his orders, glanced at them and tossed them on his company clerk's desk near the opposite wall. "Have a seat, Morales."

Morales sat on a rough stool made from a ration crate.

"This won't take long. Then we'll take you out on the company line."

"Yes sir."

"Where you from, Morales?"

"Salt Flat, Texas, sir."

Lane shrugged with his eyebrows.

"I know, sir," Morales explained. "No one else has ever heard of it either. It's a little ways east of El Paso in the Guadalupe Mountains."

Letting the new men talk about themselves for a few minutes when they first arrived had become a ritual with Lane. They were in rightful awe of war and their surroundings, confused and usually completely open and ready to talk about home and themselves. He had found it a good way to learn what a man was like on the inside, rather than having only access to the inside of his personnel file. "Married?"

"No sir."

Lane thought it refreshing that a marine could still show some shyness about women as Morales was doing. "Got a girl waiting for you back in Salt Flat, Texas?"

Morales gazed out the narrow opening in the bunker at the sunlight on the freshly fallen snow. Then he nodded. "Juanita. She's only seventeen though. Just a kid."

Lane knew from Morales' file that he was twenty.

"She's real pretty and makes the best corn tortillas and beans in the whole county."

Lane smiled, hoping Morales could see that he was genuinely interested in the conversation.

"We used to ride up into the mountains on Saturday mornings and spend the whole day. There was this lake we found in a little valley and we'd hobble the horses and let them graze while we had a picnic. And—I'm sorry, sir. Here I am, rambling on like an old woman."

"No one's shooting at us, not right now anyway, so don't worry about it." Lane then asked the question he knew Morales was waiting for, that all the new young officers wanted him to ask. "You going to marry this girl, Morales?"

"Yes sir," he beamed. "Just as soon as we whip these Chinese and I get back home."

"How you going to support her?" Lane sounded more like the girl's father than Morales' commanding officer.

"I'm staying in the corps, sir. I've wanted to be a marine as long as I can remember."

"Well, you've come to the right place to find out

whether you can handle combat or not. Most men never get that chance, fortunately."

Morales sat up straighter and said flatly, "I'll do what I'm ordered to, sir."

Lane gazed into the steady dark eyes. "I believe you just might at that, Morales."

Morales nodded slightly.

"With the peace talks still alive and winter on us, there's not going to be any major action for a while." Lane had decided that he knew enough about his new officer for the time being. "But, as I'm sure you already know, the worst thing that can happen to a bunch of marines is to let them just sit around."

"Yes sir."

"We're going to keep prodding away at the enemy, hit and run, ambushes, taking prisoners—keeping them as nervous and as jittery as we can."

"Yes sir."

"Sometimes you'll take out combat patrols; sometimes recon patrols when you just get information without firing a shot."

Lane noticed Morales looking at a snapshot tacked to the wall next to his desk. "My daughter," he growled.

"Sorry, sir." Morales stared directly at a spot one foot above Lane's head. "It's just that I—I didn't mean any offense, sir."

"She *is* pretty, isn't she?"

Morales grinned, his teeth white against his dark skin. "Yes sir. She sure is."

Lane stood up and grabbed his web belt from a peg in the log wall of the bunker. It held the holstered .45 he had used in the South Pacific. "C'mon. Let's take a walk."

"Yes sir."

Lane walked next to the edge of the chest-high trench that followed the company's line of defense along the ridgeline. Located just down the reverse slope, the trench linked together the network of bunkers located twenty-five to fifty yards apart. The bunkers themselves were dug directly on top of the ridge or slightly down the forward slope and were connected to the main trenchline by shallow crawling trenches.

Morales stared at the motley assortment of dress that the marines had collected: a turtleneck sweater, a plaid work coat, a navy blue ankle-length overcoat, field jackets, fur hats and hunting caps with ear muffs, a Red Sox baseball cap, a few stolen army jackets, overseas caps. One especially independent soul wore cowboy boots, jeans, and a cowboy hat with an *FDR for President* button pinned to it.

Lane noticed the shock on Morales' face. "Think they'd pass inspection at Quantico, Morales?"

Morales merely shook his head.

Stopping next to a small bunker, Lane spoke to a very large red-headed marine. His beefy face was covered with freckles and his shoulders and arms, bulging beneath his green sweater, looked as though they would turn the point of an icepick. "How's it going, Alexander?"

Alexander spat a brown stream of tobacco juice down the front slope and grinned up at Morales. "Jes' fine, sir."

"Any sign of enemy activity over there?" Lane pointed to the ridgeline on the opposite side of the valley.

"No sir. Not this morning."

Morales followed Lane along the line as he talked to his men. They seemed at ease in his presence and he called them by their last names, but he didn't make small talk, and to Morales' surprise, he didn't make any introductions. Instead he asked about the results of an ambush sent out the night before or the chances of getting some mortar fire laid in on a small grove of trees that seemed ideal cover for the Chinese.

As they walked the line, marines continued the routine of waging war: shifting sandbags around to provide better cover, cooking their rations over the small primus stoves, cleaning their weapons—one was giving his buddy a haircut.

Morales noticed several blackened areas in the snow where incoming rounds had hit. They seemed invisible to everyone else on the line.

"I think I'll give you the second platoon, Morales." Lane walked in the trench now, Morales close behind him, in a section where the enemy lines meandered in too close to their own to stand out in the open.

"Yes sir."

"They're a good bunch of men. Two of the sergeants fought in the last war."

"That's good to know since the sergeants run the corps anyway." Morales glanced at everything around him, taking the information down in a small notebook with a stub of a pencil, filing it for further reference, studying the rules of the game as any good leader would do.

Lane gave him a reflective glance. "You learn quick, Morales."

Except for an occasional can or cardboard carton lying in the snow, the line was well policed. Down the front slope, several strands of barbed wire stretched darkly against the snow. Beyond the wire, the shadowy woods began and in the gray distance the ridges stairstepped toward the higher mountains where the spring offensive would take them.

"You seen enough for now, Morales?"

"Yes sir."

As they walked back along the edge of the trench, Lane noticed Morales nodding to some men, making a comment to others, feeling out the troops. The sun was a dull red glow now, hanging above the far-off peaks as the evening chill began to settle in. White plumes formed when the men spoke.

Noticing the field of fire of one of the light machine guns was slightly off, Morales stopped and began scribbling in his black notebook.

Whir-whir-whir.

Hearing the sound of the 82-mm mortars, Lane found himself already stretched out in a dive toward the trench when he shouted, "Incoming!"

A deafening explosion ripped the evening apart, sending jagged fragments of hot metal thunking into the logs and sandbags and spanging off ammo boxes stacked next to a bunker wall waiting to be stored inside.

Lane waited for more explosions, but none came. In the sudden silence, he rose slowly from the frozen bottom of the trench and stared over the edge.

The black notebook lay thirty feet away, torn almost in two, several pages fluttering in the light breeze. Lane forced himself to look where Morales had been standing, then jerked his head away and slid back down until he sat on the hard-packed snow, his back against the trench wall.

Lane knew there was no need to call for a corpsman. It had been a direct hit. He had seen little more than a red-stained and blackened scattering of rags against the snow.

★ ★ ★

Lane picked up a writing tablet from the desk, turned the lantern up, and crawled into his sleeping bag. Taking a pencil from his inside jacket pocket, he began to write. Near the far wall, his first sergeant snored softly.

Cath,
Another day gone by—that makes one more closer to home. Things are pretty quiet up here now. Winter's coming on and the Chinese aren't stirring around much. Hope they sit by their fires and drink tea 'til July.
Had good weather today—sun sparkling on the snow like the diamonds I could never afford to buy for you. Oh, well, maybe someday.

Suddenly the sound of firing erupted down the line. Lane listened to the ripping noise of a Chinese burp gun followed by the clattering of a heavy machine gun and the sharp crack of rifle fire. From his mortar section came the thunking sound of outgoing 61-mm rounds. The firefight lasted two minutes, ending with a few sporadic bursts from the machine guns.

Chinese patrol keeping us on our toes, probing for weaknesses. Sounds like they didn't find any.

Got a new man in today. His name is Morales. A good-looking kid from Salt Flat, Texas. I never heard of it either. Probably the size of Sweetwater, Mississippi. They're sending a lot of these boys like Morales over here now—young, clean-cut, all-American types who believe in their country and think it's the right thing to do to fight for it.

I feel like a father to some of them, Cath. But, of course, I can't show them that side because they have to take orders from me and it would interfere with the discipline. When that happens people can get hurt. Listen to me, will you? I'm beginning to sound like a Marine Corps training manual.

I miss you, Cath. More than the last war, I think. Maybe I'm getting old—or maybe I love you more. Give the kids a big hug and a kiss for me. We'll try to wrap things up over here real soon if we can just get a little help from the Chinese—like maybe packing their rice bowls and going back across the Yalu River where they belong.

> All my love,
> Lane

Lane folded the letter carefully and sealed it inside an envelope. Then he reached over and turned the lantern out. In ten minutes he was asleep and he dreamed of clean sheets, fresh from the clothesline with the smell of the sun still in them, and of Catherine lying next to him, her arm across his chest, and the slow, rhythmic warmth of her breath against his neck.

★ ★ ★

Standing outside his bunker in the freshly fallen snow, Lane sipped the strong coffee, carrying the slightly metallic taste of the cup. Five miles off to the east and far below him lay the Sea of Japan, bright blue and glittering in the morning sunlight. In front of him, to the north, the evergreen forest stretched across the valleys and ridgelines.

"Morning, Captain."

Lane turned and faced Alexander, a wad of to-bacco the size of a golf ball bulging the side of his jaw. He could have just walked up or he could have been there for several minutes. For a big man he moved very quietly. "Morning. Any of the men hurt down there last night?"

"No sir." Alexander spat a stream of brown juice into the pristine snow.

"How about the other side?"

Alexander gazed at the distant sea. "We kilt two of them heathens, sir."

"Any papers on them?"

"No sir." Alexander reached into his mouth with a thick forefinger, took out the tobacco, and flung it down the forward slope past the barbed wire. Slip-ping his utility knife from its sheath, he cut another plug and inserted it into his mouth. "Terrible thing about that new man, sir."

"Yeah." Lane saw again the aftermath of the mor-tar shell. "You never know when one's got your name on it. They probably didn't even have a target sighted. Just some harassing fire."

"He was a mite slow."

Lane knew Alexander was a career marine who had little sympathy for men who didn't measure up.

Lane felt anger smoldering in his chest, but knew Alexander meant nothing by his remark. It was just the way he saw the world—divided into two camps. There were some, like him, who were professionals and others who were civilians in uniform. "Maybe if he'd had a few more days on the line, he would have reacted quick enough."

Alexander shrugged noncommittally, wiping his knife on the sole of his boot.

"I want a combat patrol out tonight, Alexander."

Lane tried to convince himself that revenge had nothing to do with his decision. "Take out some of their bunkers and get me a prisoner. We're going to make 'em squirm a little."

"Yes sir." Alexander gave his captain a thin smile. This was his kind of war.

"Pick the men and have them down here at ten hundred hours for a briefing."

"Yes sir," Alexander mumbled around his plug of tobacco, "and, Captain . . ."

Lane turned around.

"Happy Thanksgiving."

ELEVEN

OLD FAMILIAR
PLACES

★ ★ ★

The DC–3 banked westward over the Sea of Japan, gliding smoothly in toward the narrow coastal plain. Beyond it hills rose abruptly and in the distance the snow-covered mountains gleamed brightly in the clear morning air.

"It's all so lovely! Look how blue the water is." Jessie stared out the window, wondering how there could be fighting and dying in a land that looked so shining and peaceful.

Vale leaned closer to her, glancing down toward the miniature valley where several crude buildings stood near a brown, dusty-looking runway. "After what I saw in Seoul, you can have this country."

"You complain too much," Jessie chastened him. "We're here to cheer our boys up."

Vale kissed her on the cheek. "I guess you're right. Maybe you're what I've needed all along, Jessie. Somebody to keep me on the right track—make me think about other people instead of myself all the time."

Jessie patted his hand. "You're not so bad—for a kid from Brooklyn, that is."

Snowflakes blew past the window as they came in low over the hills. Snow covered everything but the frozen, brown flat of the valley where the runway lay. The DC–3 taxied to a stop near a corrugated tin building with a windsock attached to its sharp-peaked roof. A deuce-and-a-half as well as a Jeep stood idling in front of it, their exhausts blowing clouds of gray-white smoke into the wind.

"Well, boys and girls—here we are. The garden spot of the Orient." Bob Hope, his head half-hidden by the big fur collar of his army cold-weather gear, stood at the front of the plane. "And remember, the beaches are closed."

The troupe clambered down the steps of the airplane and toward the waiting vehicles. Bob Hope and Frances Langford climbed into the Jeep and the rest into the canvas-covered truck. The tiny convoy followed the narrow dirt roads up into the hills, meandering along valleys and through snow-covered pine forests that looked like postcards from New England.

Two hours later they reached Regimental Reserve, located in a valley nine miles behind the front lines. A mountain stream running too fast to freeze, even in the sub-zero temperatures, gurgled over rocks and boulders along the edge of the camp. Three thousand men lived in tents and crude buildings in this reserve area where they took a break from their daily regimen of war.

The trucks pulled up in front of a long quonset hut with dark gray smoke boiling out of a black pipe that had been punched through the roof. Several men stood in the snow outside the door beneath a hand-lettered *Commanding Officer* sign. They shifted from one foot to the other and beat their gloved hands together to keep warm.

Jessie climbed down from the truck, squinting into the glare of the late morning sunshine. The general, short and stocky and jut-jawed, stepped forward, greeting Bob Hope and welcoming the troupe to his camp. Then they were all ushered inside, out of the cold.

Jessie entered the building on Vale's arm. Marine officers had packed the large front room, eager to greet the performers who had come all the way from Hollywood to entertain them. A babble of conversations filled the air along with clouds of cigarette smoke as introductions were made. Jessie found herself surrounded by young uniformed men, all trying to talk to her at the same time. Some of them offered her coffee, others held out crusty-looking donuts on brown paper towels.

Jessie tried to talk to as many of the men as possible, shaking hands, asking where they were from, and smiling at their remarks about how pretty she was.

"Looks like you've got a fan club before you even make a movie." Vale stood at her shoulder, trying to keep from getting pushed aside by the jostling marines.

"I think movies are the last thing on their minds right now." Jessie smiled at him, then turned back to the young men, basking in their affection and near adulation. "You're from Houston? Why, that makes us next-door neighbors almost."

Vale glanced over at Frances Langford, mobbed by three times as many marines as Jessie, many of them older men who remembered her from the last war. After becoming weary of his role of Jessie's unwilling and unofficial bodyguard, Vale pushed his way through the crowd, sat down in a chair against the wall, and lit a cigarette.

Turning to speak with a short, acne-cratered officer who had been trying to get her attention, Jessie glanced at a man seated at a desk beyond a low wooden railing on the opposite side of the large room. He was sorting through a stack of forms with a balding clerk. Turning his face at an oblique angle to her, he reached for a pencil in a tin can on the corner of the desk.

Without a word, Jessie began pushing her way through the young group of officers toward the far side of the room. Surprised by the sudden change in her demeanor, they stepped back, making a path for her to get through.

Jessie climbed the low railing and ran to the officer seated at the desk, throwing her arms around him. "Oh, Daddy, Daddy! I'm so glad to see you!"

"Jess!" Lane stood up as Jessie came into his arms, hugging him tightly and kissing him on the cheek.

Across the room, the group of men stood open-mouthed, wishing they could trade places with the older marine across the room who was getting all the attention.

Jessie hadn't seen any of her family in five months. She almost felt like a child again, the way she did when her father would come home from work years before he went to war the first time. She would run across the yard and feel the almost palpable rush of love from him as he took her up in his arms. She remembered that he called her his "Little Princess" and that there was always candy or gum waiting in the depths of his coat pockets.

Overwhelmed as well as surprised by this outpouring of affection that she felt for her father, Jessie brushed away the tears that had suddenly filled her eyes. "You look kind of skinny, Daddy. You're not hurt, are you?"

"A tough ol' marine like me?" Lane stared into his daughter's upturned face, thinking what a lovely young woman she had grown into and how much she looked like her mother. "You must be kidding."

The clerk, who had daughters of his own, was thoroughly enjoying this reunion. He moved a scarred wooden chair over for Jessie to sit in.

"Thank you," Jessie smiled, her face glowing with the joy of being with her father.

"How did you know where I'd be?" Lane had known from Catherine's letters that Jessie was going on the USO tour, but it had never occurred to him that he would actually see her.

"I didn't. Not for sure anyway," Jessie confessed. "I found out what part of the country you were in. Actually, Mr. Hope found out for me."

Lane reached over and took his daughter's hand as though she might not be real.

"He's such a nice man, Daddy. We had two or three places we could have gone in this part of the tour and when he found out you might be in this reserve area, he said we'd come here." Jessie took out a handkerchief and wiped her eyes, unable to control the tears that continued to well up inside her along with the unexpected outpouring of love.

"It's all right, sweetheart. I'm fine." Lane leaned over and gave her a quick hug.

Across the room, the young uniformed men milled

about restlessly, smoking and drinking coffee. With Jessie gone, most had turned their attention to Frances Langford, who still had a throng gathered around her.

"There was no way to find out exactly where you were," Jessie continued, sniffing slightly. "We didn't know if you'd be up at the front lines or not."

"I just got down here this morning." Lane glanced over at the clerk. "We were just going over some paperwork. War or not, the paperwork goes on."

"Mind if I join you?"

Jessie glanced around and waved Vale over to where they sat. "Daddy, this is Tony Vale. He's a singer and a movie star and a good friend of mine."

Lane knew at once that Vale was more than just a friend. He could see it in his daughter's eyes. Taking in Vale's easy manner and smooth smile, Lane took an instant dislike to the man—something that probably wouldn't have happened if Vale had been with someone else's daughter.

Vale put on his down-home smile and stuck his hand out. "Pleased to meet you, Mr. Temple."

"Lane's fine, Tony," Lane told him. "Besides, you're not *young* enough to be calling me Mister."

Lane's choice of words wasn't wasted on Vale. He had met fathers before.

"By the way, how old are you, anyway?" Lane regretted the question immediately, thinking that it made him sound like a father out of a Victorian novel, then just as quickly felt justified in asking it. *After all, any father's got a right to know these things.*

"Daddy, that's rude!"

"It's all right, Jessie." Vale shifted uncomfortably on the plywood floor. "I'm twenty-nine, Lane."

"Jessie's eighteen."

"Yes, I know."

"She looks older." Lane glanced at Jessie. "I just wanted you to know how young she is."

"Daddy, for goodness sakes!"

"No, he's right, Jessie." Vale took a cigarette out, offering one to Lane, who shook his head. "I have nothing but respect for your daughter, Mr.—Lane. You've obviously done a good job of raising her properly."

"That's her mother's doing," Lane insisted, his eyes narrowed at Vale. "I'm only about half-civilized myself. I think it's all the killing I've seen in two wars."

Vale gazed at the flinty light in Lane's eyes and the hollow, gaunt appearance of his face. Growing up in New York, he had run across men as lethal as cobras, but he somehow felt that Jessie's father could make them whine for their mamas. "Well, you don't have a thing to worry about with me."

Jessie stepped between them. "Okay, that's enough for now. I'm sure you'll be good friends before we leave."

Vale nodded, glancing at Lane.

★ ★ ★

By 2:00 P.M. the day was at its warmest. A yellow and red RC Cola thermometer tacked to a stunted oak outside the headquarters building registered thirteen degrees. Boulders in the stream wore a thin sheath of ice and icicles hung from the eaves of buildings and the limbs of the trees.

The entire camp had turned out for the USO performance, in addition to all those on reserve stationed nearby who could manage transportation. Almost four thousand marines filed onto the drill field, gathering around a wooden platform that had been set up at one end.

At 2:30, Bob Hope walked out onto the stage to thunderous applause. He wore an enormous fur hat with earmuffs, a heavy cold-weather jacket, and carried a golf club. Smiling out at his audience, he went right into his act, pausing briefly for laughs between his numerous one-liners. "It's nice to be here in Palm Springs East," he began, twirling his golf club. "And this is *some* wind you've got. One of the local farmers told me his chickens lay the same egg three or four times."

After his ten minutes with the boys, poking fun at Korea and the military in general, Hope welcomed Frances Langford on to a tremendous ovation. Following the usual light banter with Hope, she sang "I'm in the Mood for Love," the song that had endeared her to the fighting men in North Africa during World War II.

Two dance numbers, one juggler, and a comedy routine later, the sun had begun dropping behind the trees and the temperature had started to plummet.

Sergeant Alexander sat on the ground next to Lane in six inches of snow. "When's your daughter coming on, Captain? I wanna see if she sings as good as you say."

Lane shrugged. "They didn't ask me to help plan the show, Alexander."

As if in answer to Alexander's question, Hope brought Jessie on next. She wore a red frilly dress over flesh-colored long johns. The late sun glistened in her pale blond hair. She got a riotous welcome from the men as they applauded, whistled, stomped their feet on the frozen ground, and gave a few healthy yells.

Hope took her hand and had her do a pirouette.

"Just wanted you marines to see what you're fighting for."

This set off another exuberant show of appreciation out in the audience.

Alexander whistled through his teeth and clapped his gloved hands loudly. "She's the best-looking woman I've seen on or off a movie screen. But can she sing?"

"You're just about to find out." Lane felt a father's joy in seeing his daughter on stage with one of the world's best-known entertainers and in knowing of the hardships and dangers she had chosen to endure to bring a little bit of America to men who were homesick and lonely and, much of the time, afraid.

As Hope walked to the side of the stage, Jessie nodded to the band, cradled the mike in her hands, and began to speak, a little nervously at first, from the heart. "I've never seen so many handsome men in my life!"

The men responded with cheers and applause.

"I wish all of your wives and girlfriends could be here, but I'll just have to try and give their love to you in my own small way. We're all so proud of you!"

More cheers and whistles and clapping followed from smiling marines who acted as though they didn't have a worry in the world—marines who had, just days before, been staring into the teeth of the Chinese and North Korean armies.

Jessie took the microphone in both hands, staring out over the sea of faces. "A lot of you fought in the last war. It hardly seems fair that we'd ask you to lay your lives on the line again for us so soon, but we have. You're the best of us: the best Americans, the best fathers and sons and brothers, the best fighting men in the whole world—marines!"

This set off a thunderous applause with every man standing to his feet, cheering wildly.

After they had settled down and taken their places on the frozen, snow-covered ground, Jessie paused, smiling at them a few seconds before she continued.

During her brief pause, Hope turned to Vale, who stood next to him just offstage behind a makeshift curtain, and said, "You know, I helped her with this little speech, but you can't teach someone to make an audience react like that—even men away from home and at war. This kid's a natural. She'll be taking over for me if I don't watch it."

"Those men can tell she means every word, Bob." Vale gazed out at Jessie. "That's why they're going wild over her. They know it's coming from inside here." Vale pointed to his chest.

"The package ain't bad either," Hope quipped.

Jessie continued, her voice taking on a more solemn tone. "There's a marine out there who's very special to me. He fought in the hot South Pacific in the last war and here he is again, in cold Korea."

Out in the crowd, Alexander punched Lane on the shoulder. "That's you, Captain."

"He's my daddy and I'm dedicating this song to him—and to my mother. It was their song when he went off to war for the first time and I think it might bring back memories for a lot of you too." Jessie made a slight gesture toward the band, gazed out over the upturned faces, and began to sing:

"I'll be seeing you, in all the old familiar places . . ."

And as she sang, her voice clear and pure, caressing the bittersweet lyrics, the men responded as marines almost never do. They remained perfectly still and silent, mesmerized by this eighteen-year-old girl who had come halfway around the world to sing to them.

The song did indeed bring back memories of other times and other places when love affairs were young and the world was bright and all the nights were something to remember. Not a few of the battle-hardened marines self-consciously brushed away tears from their eyes.

When Jessie finished her song, she smiled and nodded slightly to the men as though it had been worth the trip over just to see them and to sing for them. Their reaction was total silence. She left the microphone, headed to the side of the platform where Vale waited for her. Still there was nothing but silence.

Hope took her by the arm as she reached the edge of the stage, standing with her out of sight behind the curtain. "Where are *you* going?"

Jessie was dumbfounded, thinking she had ruined the song. "I don't understand."

"I never in my life got a reaction like that!" Hope exclaimed. "'Course I never looked that good either."

All Jessie could do was give him a confused stare.

Hope put his arm around her shoulder. "Little girl, you captured four thousand marines all by yourself. No army in the world's ever done that."

Jessie was beginning to understand that the performance had been all right.

"Watch this." Hope ambled out to the microphone, turning his infectious smile on his audience, still half-lost in their individual reveries brought on by Jessie's song. He glanced back at Jessie with a quick wink.

"What's he up to?" Jessie asked Vale.

"Watch."

Hope took the microphone, gazing out over the

191

still-enraptured faces of the marines. "Well, that's all for Miss Jessie Temple—unless, of course, you men want to hear some more."

Pandemonium broke loose—cheering and whistles and shouts of "We want Jessie! We want Jessie!"

Jessie had three curtain calls that day, all for the same song, and when they were over, the men wanted still more. Nightfall was upon them by then and heavy, wet snowflakes had begun to blow across the drill field.

"I think the Siberians are sending us a little sample of their weather. Guess ol' Joe Stalin's boys want to see what we're made of." Hope stood again at the microphone, grinning out through the gloom at the men who were all standing by then. "We've got to shut it down, fellas. If we don't get inside, we'll all be USO popsicles up here."

Laughter and a few halfhearted boos ran through the crowd as the men milled about now to keep warm.

Hope raised his hands to the men. "You're a great bunch of guys. God bless you all."

★ ★ ★

"She's my daughter, Vale. I don't want her getting hurt." Lane, staring across at Vale, sat at the end of a rough wooden table in the nearly deserted officers' mess. A thin stream of smoke wavered upward in the stale air from the Camel, stuck between his fingers.

A blizzard had descended on the camp, making travel on the narrow mountain roads impossible and requiring the troupe to stay over. After bidding Jessie good-night, Lane had mentioned to Vale that he would like to have a talk with him and Vale had reluctantly agreed.

192

Vale tried but couldn't hold Lane's steady gaze. "You don't have to worry."

"Somehow, that doesn't make me feel any better." Lane took a draw from the cigarette and stubbed it out in the congealed clump of mashed potatoes and gravy on his plate. "Maybe you could try again."

"I don't know what you want me to say, Lane. I like Jessie very much." Vale shifted uneasily in his chair. "She's a decent girl. I haven't been around that many, not for a long time now, so I know how special she really is."

Lane pinched the bridge of his nose with his thumb and forefinger. He could tell when he first saw Jessie with Vale that she was infatuated with him. "What have you got in mind for my daughter, Vale?"

"Friendship. I like being with her, that's all." Vale, used to being catered to and having his whims satisfied by the people around him, found the company of Lane Temple disturbing. The man seemed singularly unimpressed by Vale's Hollywood movie contract and his stature as a rising star.

"You're eleven years older than Jess and you've been married three times. That makes me very uneasy."

Vale was taken off guard. "One of them was annulled! How did you find out about my marital status anyway?"

"I talked to a few other people in the troupe," Lane replied flatly. "They didn't think it was that unusual at all. Maybe it's the thing to do in the circles you travel in, Vale, but it's not what I want for my daughter."

Vale felt a hot flame of anger burning in his stomach. He had become weary of being treated like a kid from the wrong side of the tracks by this unwashed marine. "I've had about enough of your interrogation,

Temple. Jessie's eighteen years old—she can make her own decisions."

Lane's lips grew thin and white. A cold anger glowed in his eyes and his voice held an iron edge when he spoke. "I came to you as a concerned father, Vale. Now I'm telling you man to man. If you hurt my daughter—in any way—the day will come when you'll pray for the earth to open up so you can crawl inside it."

Vale steeled himself in the face of this man who had seen too much death in one war too many. He hoped that it was only the months of combat taking their toll on Lane making him speak the way he was and he took the chance. "I grew up hard, Temple. Threats don't work on me."

"I don't make threats, Vale." Lane realized he had gone as far as he could—maybe too far. He was locked into the Marines now, into a war that might hold him for months or years. Vale had the upper hand.

"What are you gonna do?" Vale tried to control his anger, but felt safe that Lane wouldn't try anything under the circumstances. He knew a marine officer assaulting a USO entertainer who had come to a war zone to perform for the troops could cause Lane some virtually insurmountable problems.

"She trusts people now, Vale. Don't take that away from her." Lane stood up and turned to leave.

"Temple . . ."

Lane turned around.

Vale smiled at him, calm and relaxed now that the confrontation had ended. "Someday we'll have a big laugh together about all this."

Lane's only reply was an icy stare. He walked quickly across the darkened mess hall while he still had control of his temper, wondering if Vale's parting comment was made out of sincerity or arrogance.

★ ★ ★

"Daddy..." Jessie stood with Lane outside the door of the headquarters building. Beyond the dark line of the forest, the morning sky was streaked with shades of pink. "I just want you to know how sorry I am that I didn't come down to see you when you were in San Diego."

Lane smiled at his daughter, proud of the courage that had brought her to Korea to give something back to her country. He also felt a heavy sadness lying like a stone in his chest in the knowledge that he may not see her for a long, long while. "You just put that out of your mind right now. I know how busy you must have been up there getting ready to come over here."

Jessie took her father's hands, noticing the small scrapes and cuts and the grime from life on the front lines. They told her the story of hardship that she knew she would never hear from his lips. "Oh, Daddy, I love you so much!"

Lane took Jessie in his arms, patting her gently on the back.

"I didn't realize *how* much until I saw you yesterday." Jessie stared up into his eyes. Seeing her father in the grim and uncertain reality of the war for the first time the day before had burdened her with sharp pangs of guilt that she had always taken him for granted, had never imagined that someday she might lose him. It had suddenly hit her with the force of a physical blow that her father lived on the front steps of death every day. "I think sometimes we get so busy with our lives, we forget about the things that really matter."

"That's a pretty grown-up thing for an eighteen-year-old to say, Jess." Lane could see Catherine in the face of his daughter. "I think I'm still trying to learn *that* lesson."

A horn blew. Jessie glanced down the frozen, brown walk that had been cleared through the blanket of fresh snow. The Jeep had begun slowly pulling away while the truck still idled at the side of the rutted road, waiting to take her away from her father and from the war.

"You'd better get going, Jess." Lane kissed her on the cheek, remembering other times when war had torn him and Catherine apart. *Now it's come to the next generation.* "Kiss your mama and the kids for me."

"I will." Jessie threw herself against Lane, hugging him tightly. Then she ran down the frozen path toward the waiting truck, its driver fidgeting nervously while he watched the Jeep disappear down the road into the forest.

At the bottom of the path, Jessie turned, gazing back at her father. She stood that way for five seconds as though trying to burn his image into her memory. Then with a quick wave she turned and climbed into the canvas-covered rear of the truck.

Lane lit a cigarette, changed his mind, and trampled it into the snow. The olive drab-colored truck carrying his daughter skidded slightly on an icy spot in the road, straightened out, then vanished into the gloom of the forest.

TWELVE

THE ENDLESS DARK

★ ★ ★

A stunted pine, strung with tinsel made from tin foil, and decorated with a few bits of glass and pieces of C-ration cans cut in rough shapes of angels and reindeer served as a Christmas tree. Standing at the end of a long row of tents, it resembled a bedraggled street urchin straight out of a Dickens novel.

Out on the drill field a few men played football in the ten-degree weather. Wearing no protective pads or helmets, they grunted in pain when a defensive player drove his shoulder into a runner's flying legs or a lineman made a solid block on a charging linebacker.

The sky looked like a gray wool blanket stretched from horizon to horizon, laden with the threat of another heavy snowfall before the day was out.

Lane stood at the edge of the drill field, the red wool scarf Catherine had sent him wrapped around his neck. He chewed on the last piece of fruitcake that had been in another package. All the rest of it had disappeared in a flurry of reaching hands as soon as he walked over and offered some to a few of his men who were busy singing Christmas carols around a fire.

"That was some show last night, wasn't it?" Alexander, his face flushed from whiskey, stained the snow with a stream of tobacco juice and walked over to where Lane stood watching the mayhem out on the field.

"The Chinese must have made a mighty big push up on the line to make that much noise," Lane replied. "Woke me out of a sound sleep about midnight."

"Wudn't even no attack."

Lane gave him a puzzled look. "That much artillery fire and no attack?"

"Yep," Alexander mumbled around his tobacco. "Just a bunch of the boys whooping it up to celebrate Christmas."

"I'll bet the general thinks that's real amusing." Lane admired the resourcefulness of the men in their unique celebration of the season, but kept it to himself.

"They say it was some show, all right," Alexander continued. "They shot off red and green flares and a whole lot of star clusters. Bet it was real purty up close."

"The Chinese must have thought we were launching a full-scale offensive."

Alexander smiled, nodding his big shaggy head. "They did. They let us have it with everything they had for about an hour. Wish I coulda been there."

"You'll get back quick enough."

"I 'spect I will," Alexander admitted.

A foggy memory drifted at the back of Lane's mind with the mention of the action up on the front lines. "You know, I thought I heard another shot on the other side of the camp just as I was getting back to sleep last night. Must have been around two or three this morning."

"You did," Alexander replied cryptically. In keeping with his taciturn nature, he volunteered little information.

"You want to tell me what happened?" Lane stared directly at his big sergeant. "Maybe you'd like me to have the company clerk send you a memo."

"Naw. I don't read that good anyway." Alexander squatted down, took a handful of snow and rubbed it on his face, blowing air through his loose lips like a horse. Then he took a stained green handkerchief from his back pocket and wiped his cheeks, eyes, and dug in his ears.

Lane waited patiently while Alexander finished his morning toilet.

"Couple of boys over in Dog Company," Alexander began, blowing his nose and stuffing the handkerchief back in his pocket. "Playing Russian roulette."

The war in the Pacific had had its boredom and tedium and hopelessness just as Korea did—just as every war has. Lane had seen this kind of thing before, men going past the point of caring, but it never failed to arouse in him a sickening dread that he, too, might one day succumb. He didn't ask the obvious question, knowing that Alexander would get to it in his own time.

"They got ahold of a bottle."

They got to drinking and . . . These words comprised the prologue to countless tragedies in the Marine Corps—in war and during peace.

"I reckon they'd been drinking all night. You 'member that ol' boy from North Carolina, the one got his right ear half shot off back in September?" Alexander touched his own right ear as though assuring himself that it was still intact. "Well, it's *all* shot off now—along with most of his head."

Lane knew that would be the end of it. There might be an occasional joke about the incident, but it would soon die of its own weight. A death in combat was considered a suitable topic for conversation, but not one like this.

"Yessir." Alexander spoke the word as a solemn pronouncement. "If you're lookin' for a way out, a .45's 'bout as sure as they come."

Lane heard a sickening thud out on the field and glanced around. One of the men lay unconscious, stretched flat on his back in the snow. Two of his team-mates dragged him off to the side of the field, propped his head on somebody's field jacket, and returned to the game.

"One of them boys is gonna git kilt before that's over," Alexander prophesied, punctuating his words with his tobacco-stained pocketknife.

"Guess they have to let off a little steam one way or another," Lane replied. He was glad the man from North Carolina wasn't from his company. It made his death much easier to forget and he believed he probably wouldn't dream about it. "We'll be going back on the line in a week or two, I imagine."

"Nope."

"You heard different?"

"Yep," Alexander said flatly. "Buddy of mine over in Admin. We're leavin' first thing in the morning."

Lane never ceased to be in awe of sergeants like Alexander—career marines who, because of their years of contacts, always knew ahead of time exactly what was going on in the tight-lipped world of the military. "How long have you known about this?"

"Purty good while."

Turning back to the game, Lane watched a pass spiral high against the gray clouds, arcing over the defender's outstretched hands. The lanky end snagged it with one hand, tucked it under his arm, and ran it into the end zone marked on either side by fallen tree trunks.

"He's a good 'un." Alexander nodded toward the player who had just scored. "Used to catch passes from Norm Van Brocklin before he come over here."

Lane grunted his approval. "Guess I'd better get ready to head out tomorrow. Maybe we'd better let the rest of the men in the company know, Alexander—unofficially, of course."

"Most of 'em know already, sir," Alexander said matter-of-factly. "I'll catch the rest of 'em in the chow hall when they go to Christmas dinner."

Lane nodded at Alexander's efficiency and walked away, his boots crunching in the snow. Turning around, he called back, "You're a good man, Alexander. You oughta be running the company—maybe the battalion."

"Don't I know it," Alexander grinned, then turned back to the football game.

As Lane walked past the scrawny little Christmas tree with its make-do ornaments, he thought how sad it looked in the white and olive-drab expanse of the camp. Nothing in sight carried any semblance to things soft and gentle and feminine. The camp, the war, the corps consisted of nothing but things hard, bland, colorless, and utilitarian.

It suddenly occurred to him that it could be no other way. The men themselves must be permeated with these qualities for their very survival. Still, he longed for something bright and soft and fragrant.

Thinking of the first Christmas he and Catherine

had spent in Baton Rouge in their little garage apartment, Lane could almost feel her lying next to him on the sofa, almost smell the fragrance of her skin as they watched the colored liquid lights bubble and shimmer on the tree.

Lane looked again at the little pine, leaning sideways under the weight of metal and glass, fashioned by hands more accustomed to digging trenches and pulling triggers. *That surely is a pitiful little tree. But they tried. God bless their hearts—they tried.*

★ ★ ★

The clatter of helicopters drowned out all other sounds as they rose slowly against the cobalt sky in their angled turnings back toward the south. The entire company was now moving across the fresh snow of the reverse slope toward their new positions on a different ridgeline in the same old war.

Lane stared across a valley three thousand feet deep when he reached the top of the ridgeline. The mountains, white and cold and remote, ran northward, each one a little taller than the one before until they reached the final peak more than a mile high.

Carrying his Thompson sub-machine gun, Alexander walked over to Lane and pointed to the tallest mountain. "Is that the one we got to go against in the spring?"

"I believe that's it, Alexander," Lane answered casually, although he knew a campaign like that would be anything but casual. "Nothing definite yet though."

Alexander squinted at the tall peak.

"I wouldn't worry about it yet," Lane said, regretting his words the moment he spoke them. If Alexander ever worried about anything, no one ever knew it. "We've still got three or four months of winter facing us."

"I ain't worried, Captain," Alexander muttered, "but it shore will make things simple if we do."

Lane seldom bothered to ask Alexander to explain his cryptic comments anymore—sometimes his big sergeant chose to and sometimes not.

"Yep, we won't even need to worry about a hotel. If we try to take that big rascal we can hold the next reunion for the First Marine Division in my living room."

"You're a real comfort, Alexander," Lane snorted. "Get the men settled in."

"Yes sir!"

Lane found the bunker he and Alexander would share. It was cut into the ridgeline twenty feet behind the main trench and slightly above the rest of the bunkers on the forward slope. Completely covered now with snow, it was constructed of logs with a double layer of sandbags on the roof. A side door and a narrow slit for a firing port in the north side were the only openings. Glancing inside, he saw that it looked as clean and as comfortable as accommodations on the front lines get.

Night was falling fast as the men settled into their new positions. A full moon rose, shining brightly on the snow-covered ridge and the open areas of the valley below. Lane walked the line with Alexander, seeing that the mortar section was in position, that the fields of fire for the machine gun sections were properly overlaid, and that the watch had been set.

Stopping in an open spot between bunkers, Lane noticed a shadowy figure emerge from the tree line fifty yards beyond the wire. Dropping into a crouch, he pulled his .45 and aimed it toward the man, now moving silently in toward the wire.

"Hold it, Captain."

Lane felt Alexander's hand on his arm, pushing it down. He managed to control his anger, keeping his voice down. "This better be good, Alexander."

"That's Tenkiller out there, sir."

"Who?"

"You ain't met him yet." Alexander squatted next to Lane. "He come into the company three or four days ago."

"What's he doing out there?" Lane recalled the name as he watched the man cross through the wire and run silently, graceful as a deer, across the snow toward his own position farther down the line.

"Settin' rabbit snares."

Lane merely glared at Alexander.

"He growed up on a farm. Says he can ketch a few rabbits, make a stew—you know, kinda liven up these C-rations. You gotta admit they taste like something the dog drug in."

"I'm going to say this one time, Alexander." Lane stood up and holstered his .45. "You keep that man inside the wire unless he's on a combat or recon mission."

"Yes sir." Alexander watched Tenkiller vanish into the growing gloom. "But you know how them Indians are, sir. They're mighty independent."

"You going to have a problem with this?"

"No sir. I can handle it."

As they continued along the line, Lane noticed how the front slope dropped off steeply and that there was plenty of wire out, two things which were essential in making the line more easily defensible and which gave Lane a moderate sense of well-being about their new positions. He knew they were too

204

high for the 61-mm mortars to reach them so their threat came from the 82's and the 105 Howitzers—and the Chinese infantry if they allowed them to get close enough.

After Lane had finished making the rounds, satisfied that his company was in place, he heard a distant drumming roar in the sky just as he prepared to step down into the bunker. He knew it was a flight of B–29's coming back from a bombing run far to the north near the Chinese border.

Alexander stepped outside, staring up into the night sky. "A purty sight, ain't it?"

Lane watched along with him. Moonlight silvered the long tapering wings of the bombers, giving them an ethereal appearance against their background of stars. Other marines were out now, seemingly awestruck as the flight passed over, engines thundering with a high, hard hammering precision.

Lane was about to step down into his bunker, when he heard another sound from the north. It was a lone B–29, and by the sound of its engines, he knew it was in trouble. He saw a spark on its wing, then as it drew closer, crossing over the Chinese positions, he could see flames.

All along the lines, marines were out cheering the crippled aircraft home. In a few seconds, however, it became obvious that it wasn't going to make it. The fires grew, engulfing both wings; then the sound of the engines died out altogether as the '29 went into a glide, wobbling silently over the snowy hills and valleys. The marines grew silent.

Suddenly the glare of an explosion blew out the light of the stars and the moon with its intensity. The plane began tumbling over and over, parts breaking away from the fuselage, bits and pieces of flaming wreckage in the night sky. It hit far down to the right toward the Sea of Japan.

Lane turned to Alexander. "Get on the radio. Tell the men to keep a watch for flyers coming in, some of 'em might have had time to bail out."

"I didn't see no chutes."

"Just make sure everybody knows."

"Yes sir."

Gradually the men returned to their bunkers as a sense of desolation settled over the line. Occasionally, someone would step outside and glance at the wreckage, still burning out in the night like a distant, dismal portent.

★ ★ ★

Lane awakened at sunrise. Light filtered like smoke through the gunport, tinting the soot-caked sandbags and logs and earth a faint lavender color. A candle, impaled on a stump of a limb protruding from the top log, flickered from Alexander's side of the bunker. He sat hunched over, stirring a can of pork and beans that sat on the Coleman stove.

"Want some?"

Lane glanced at the proferred can of beans. "Not just yet. How 'bout some coffee?"

Alexander lifted the pot from the other burner, poured the coffee—thick and brown and steaming—into a metal cup, and handed it to Lane.

Lane grunted his thanks.

After wolfing down the beans, Alexander threw his field jacket on and walked to the narrow door. "I'm gonna make sure everything went okay last night."

"Fine," Lane mumbled.

After Alexander had gone, Lane finished his coffee, slipped into his boots and jacket, and went to see to

the final settling-in of his company into a new piece
of the front line. He surveyed the ground of the forward slope, the fields of fire and the dead spaces;
checked the mortar concentrations; made sure the
telephone lines were intact and tended to a thousand
other details that could turn the balance when the
fighting started.

In the middle of the afternoon, Lane returned to
the bunker. He ate a can of peaches, then took Catherine's last letter from the breast pocket of his fatigues. It had been handed to him just before he
climbed into the helicopter back in battalion reserve
the day before. He had only read it once and would
probably read it a dozen more times before the next
mail call.

> My dearest Lane,
> The world seems so dreary without you. I
> don't mean to worry you—we're all just fine, but
> there's been such an emptiness inside me since
> you went away, almost as though I'm only half a
> person. Maybe that's as it should be. I pray that
> we'll be together again soon.

Lane stared at the thin strip of afternoon sky he
could see through the gunport, speaking out loud to
the empty bunker. "I know exactly how you feel, Catherine."

> As I write this, Jess is somewhere in Korea. I
> hope you get to see her, although I guess that's not
> very likely. Dalton's playing basketball for the jun-
> ior high team now. Made nine points in his last
> game. Sharon's still making straight A's, which is
> nothing new, and Cassidy's been behaving him-
> self all week—now, that's something to write
> about!

207

I started working part time in the office at the high school last week. You should see the new school. They've almost finished it now and it's so modern.

It's been cold (got down to 38 degrees last night) and rainy for days now. Sure wish you were here to snuggle with me at night. We'll make up for lost time when—

"Captain!"

Startled from his imaginary trip back home, Lane could tell by the urgency in Alexander's voice that something had gone terribly wrong. His first thought was of a frontal assault by the Chinese, but he quickly realized that there had been no preparatory firing from their mortar and artillery.

Grabbing his .45, Lane threw aside the poncho covering the door and bounded outside into the harsh afternoon glare. Glancing to his left, he saw Alexander running west along the ridgeline. Lane sprinted after him. Fifty yards farther on, bursts of fire from several of the quick-firing Chinese burp guns sent everyone diving into the trench.

At the sound of firing, marines carrying BAR's and M–1's began pouring out of every bunker all along the line, taking up their positions.

"What's going on?" Lane had piled in next to Alexander.

"Tenkiller."

Lane peered over the top of the trench while Alexander gave him the abbreviated version. At the edge of the woods, he could see where a struggle had taken place in the snow.

"I heard a yell! Looked down there and they was draggin' him into the woods!" Alexander checked his extra clips for the Thompson and his .45 while he talked. "He musta gone out to check his snares without telling nobody."

"How many men?"

"Four."

Lane saw the tops of the pine saplings stirring and knew the raiders were trying to make their escape. "Let's go!"

Alexander quickly pointed at six men to go with them.

As Lane stood up, he could see a clearing beyond the grove of pines. Tenkiller's hands were tied behind his back and he was being jerked and prodded along by his captors as they raced headlong down the slope toward the bottom of the valley.

Out in front of the others, Lane crossed the two aprons of barbed wire and had just entered the grove when he heard the muted thunking of mortars drifting across the valley from the enemy lines. "Incoming!" He dove flat out in the snow next to the stump of a tree blasted away the previous spring by artillery fire just before the first explosions jarred the earth.

Lane knew then that the Chinese had planned their mission well, that they had registered their mortars on the grove to cover the raiders. "Anybody hit?"

From behind came Alexander's booming voice. "Can't tell yet, sir!"

Up and running as fast as he could down the snow-covered, wooded slope, Lane hoped to be away from the area of fire before the next incoming hit them. Going through the deep, light powder was easy—almost too easy. It flowed out to the side with Lane slipping over the frozen pack underneath it.

Finding himself losing control in his accelerating slide downhill, Lane had to grab hold of branches every few yards to control his descent. Glancing behind him, he saw Alexander and five other men. *The mortars got one of 'em.* He knew that the corpsman would already be in the grove and that two more along with at least a squad of men would soon be following them down the hill.

A burp gun ripped the wooded silence. Lane latched onto a limb, flinging himself behind the trunk of a large pine. He had seen the bright flashes winking at him from a brush pile at the head of a ravine a hundred yards below.

Behind him, the other men had taken cover, not returning fire for fear of hitting Tenkiller.

Lane motioned to Alexander, pointing out the sniper's location. Alexander nodded and signaled to the other men. They fanned out, two on either side in flanking movements to hit the ravine from opposite sides.

Putting Lane's tree between himself and the sniper, Alexander rushed down the slope, diving next to the base of the big pine. "They're still there."

"One of 'em is for sure."

At that moment, bursts of fire erupted from the raiders, whining overhead like hornets, thunking into tree trunks and clipping branches off. Soft, powdery snow drifted down from the limbs of the trees like flour through a sifter.

Two of the Chinese bolted from behind the brush pile and ran down the ravine, prodding Tenkiller along ahead of them with their guns. Almost instantly, they disappeared into the gloom where the heavy forest began.

Seeing that their buddy was no longer in their line of fire, the four marines halted in their flanking movements and laid down a devastating wall of fire on the Chinese with their BAR's and Thompsons. The sound was deafening as heavy slugs ripped the brush pile apart.

In the middle of the barrage, Lane took advantage of the covering fire to plunge ahead directly at the ambush site. Fifty feet away, he dove behind the cover of another large pine, stood up quickly, and jerked his .45 from its holster.

Thinking all the marines were still far out in the woods, the remaining Chinese soldier sprang up to fire one last burst before he fled.

Standing at an oblique angle to the raider, Lane stepped from behind the tree, swinging his pistol up toward the Chinese soldier's chest. For a mere fraction of a second, the man stared directly at Lane, his eyes filled with the sudden and terrible fear of what was about to happen to him. In desperation he whirled the barrel of his burp gun around.

Lane squeezed the trigger of the .45 twice, feeling its heavy impact against his hand, up his arm, and into his shoulder. The first slug caught the man just below his collarbone in the right side of his chest, slamming him backward and to the left. A fraction of a second later the second shot tore away most of his jawbone on the left side of his face.

Before the Chinese soldier hit the ground, Lane was sprinting toward the right side of the ravine. He dove headlong, sliding up to the rim, his pistol gripped firmly. There was no longer any need for caution. The other soldier lay crumpled and lifeless at the base of the brush pile.

Two more and we've got Tenkiller home free. Lane slid down into the ravine, hit the rocky bottom, and was on the trail of the last two raiders before Alexander and the other four marines made it to the ambush site.

Following the trampled snow that marked their escape route, Lane was intensely concerned with catching up with Tenkiller's captors before they reached their own lines. Caution had been sidelined in favor of speed.

The slope of the hill was gentler now that it neared the bottom of the valley. Halfway up the trunk of a thick fir tree, Lane saw the burp gun winking brightly like an acetylene torch flashing on and off in the dark branches. Something struck the outside of his right hip just as the sound of the firing erupted in the stillness of the glade he had entered.

Diving into a snowbank, Lane got off three rounds toward the tree while he was in the air. He thudded into the snow and rolled over behind a stunted oak, its thin, twisted trunk and a few dry leaves still clinging to the limbs, providing little cover.

Lane heard the cracking of a limb and a heavy thudding sound as something hit in the snow ahead of him. Cautiously, he made his way along the edge of the trees. At the base of the fir tree the sniper lay on his back, his arms flung out behind his head. His left leg was twisted beneath his body, giving the man the appearance of someone trying to get back up. The round hole in the front of his padded jacket gave gruesome assurance that he would not.

Suddenly Lane heard a dry limb crack out in the forest to his right. Standing perfectly still, he tried to penetrate the shadowy gloom, knowing that he had now become the prey instead of the predator. In one swift motion, the Chinese soldier stepped from a heavy thicket of saplings and vines, his burp gun trained on Lanes' chest.

Time slowed to a standstill. In that fleeting moment, Lane could almost feel the shock of bullets ripping into his body and the first unbearable pain, could almost see himself thrown backward, torn and bleeding and gasping his last breaths.

Lane saw Catherine as clearly as if she had been standing in front of him. Then he saw the dark eyes of the Chinese shift suddenly, darting upward to stare at something above and behind him.

Beyond the enemy soldier, in the black-green haze of the woods, Lane saw Alexander, his Thompson trained on the soldier's back—but his eyes stared wildly at something in the clearing behind Lane. The Thompson remained rigid, unfired and impotent in Alexander's rough hands.

As though he had never been there at all, the Chinese soldier suddenly vanished like a vapor into the thick cover he had been hiding in.

Stunned, Lane saw Alexander walk deliberately out of the shadows, a look of wonder on his red, fleshy face. "He didn't fire! Why didn't he fire?"

Alexander stared over at the spot where the soldier had vanished, unable or unwilling to reply.

Lane glanced quickly behind him, seeing nothing but the trees and the snow and, above them, a hint of sky through the ice-covered limbs. "He was staring at something behind me. What did he see, Alexander?"

Alexander glanced at the same spot the Chinese had been staring at. He shook his head slowly, a look of disbelief in his eyes. "I don't know." Then he noticed Lane's webbed belt where the holster had been shot away. It seemed to bring him back to reality. "Looks like this is your lucky day, Captain."

Lane glanced down, having forgotten the sudden impact he had felt during the brief fire fight. He felt a slight burning sensation where the bullet had plowed some skin off his right hip, but knew immediately that

213

the wound was only superficial.

Snapping out of his near trance, Lane plunged into the thick woods after the Chinese, Alexander close behind. Two hundred yards down into the valley they found Tenkiller where the two raiders had left him before coming back to ambush Lane. The young marine lay propped against a tree as though he had sat down to rest, his hands still wired securely behind his back. A fluffy white rabbit's tail protruded out of one deep pocket. From the jagged bayonet wound in his neck, a dark rivulet of blood, frozen now in the intense cold, had spilled down the front of his field jacket. His eyes, drained of light, stared at something out beyond the dark wall of trees and the hard blue sky.

★ ★ ★

At the exact moment Lane began his trek down the snowy slope after Tenkiller's captors, Homer McCurley awakened on his single bed in the dormitory at the leprosarium in Carville, Louisiana, ten thousand miles away.

Lying still, Homer listened to the deep hum of a generator down the hall in the maintenance department. He slowly opened his eyes to dim light and shadow. Across the aisle, someone coughed and turned over in his sleep.

Homer had awakened from a sound sleep like this in the pre-dawn darkness many times before. He felt the same restless, urgent stirring in his spirit that he had come to think of over the years as "the quickening." Reaching for his flannel robe laid across the rail at the foot of his bed, he pulled it on and slipped into the fur-lined house shoes that Catherine had given him for Christmas. Taking his cane from the floor, he walked slowly down the aisle between the double row of beds.

Stopping at the door that led directly outside, Homer unlocked it and opened it slowly so as not to disturb the other patients. He shivered as the cold night air enveloped his thin body. Beneath the stars and the moon's pale shining he walked across the dew-wet grass toward his favorite bench beneath the ancient live oak where he had first met Catherine.

As Homer crossed the open lawn, he began praying for Lane Temple, making intercession for him, as the powers of darkness began marshalling themselves against this one frail missionary.

Coming to the bench, Homer fell to his knees in the knowledge that the spirit himself was also making intercession for him with groanings that could not be uttered. Alone under the vast glittering of the stars, he prayed fervently, throwing himself into the thick, fiery darkness of the battle.

Homer again lost all sense of time, knowing only that he would pray until released in his spirit. Sometimes it lasted until dawn and he would struggle back to his bed, utterly drained and exhausted, falling into a deep sleep that would last sometimes well into the following night. That was not to be the case this time.

Suddenly, Homer saw in his spirit a giant of a man clothed in light, wearing a long, pale robe. His hair was blond and fell to his shoulders, his eyes blazing with a pure, white fire. In his upraised hands he held a massive gleaming sword.

Homer felt peace sweep over him like a river, driving away the darkness and the fury of battle, and he knew that his months of intercession for Lane Temple had come to an end. He lifted his hands toward the heavens. "Precious Jesus! 'Who is this King of glory?

The Lord strong and mighty, the Lord mighty in battle
. . . The mighty One of Israel.' "

Exhausted now, Homer struggled to his feet, using
his cane for support. Walking slowly back toward the
dorm gleaming faintly beyond the open lawn, he felt
a gladness in his soul as he sang praises to his God.
He knew there would be other battles, that other en-
emies waited for him out in the endless dark, but he
had no fear of them. This was the life that he had chosen so long ago and he would remain faithful to it until he lay down that final time, never to awaken again
in this world.

THIRTEEN

THE CATS

★ ★ ★

Tony Vale, who has just been signed for his first starring role by MGM, announced at an impromptu party at Sardi's last night that he and his co-star, Ginny McCarthy, will wed in the summer. Good luck, Tony, and let's hope you can make that big leap from LP records to box office records.

Jessie sat on her balcony in the morning sunshine, staring at the Hedda Hopper column in the newspaper, unable to comprehend what she had just read. Not once in the six months that she had known Vale had there been even a hint that he was romantically involved with Ginny McCarthy.

The USO troop had gotten back from their tour the previous week and after a couple of days' rest, Jessie had returned to the studio for screen tests. She had seen Vale once for breakfast, and the day before, they had taken a drive up to Santa Barbara.

Jessie called back the beauty of the rocky shoreline

and the sun sparkling on the ocean. Vale had been especially attentive to her, catering to her every whim. She now realized that it had only been his way of saying goodbye.

Folding the newspaper and laying it on the table, Jessie stared at the ring Vale had bought her in a little shop next door to the restaurant where they had eaten lunch. The intricately scrolled gold band held an emerald set in a cluster of diamonds. She had protested that it was far too expensive, but Vale had had his way and she left the shop with the ring on her finger.

"It's just a trinket, Jess, but I hope when you look at it sometimes you'll remember how bright you've made these last few months for me." Jessie had memorized his words and now they taunted her like the sight of the ring. Taking the ring from her finger, she placed it carefully on the table next to a white vase holding a single rose.

Getting up and walking over to the railing of the veranda, Jessie stared out at the ocean. In the smoky morning light, with whitecaps all the way to the horizon and a heavy surf pounding the rocky shoreline, the Pacific proved to be nothing like its namesake. The early traffic on the Coast Highway hummed along from the mountains and beaches toward the city.

Jessie thought of all the wives who were preparing breakfast, dressing children, and sending their husbands off to work, starting another week with their families. She saw herself growing old alone, rising after a restless night to greet the day with her morning coffee and a calico cat.

This is stupid! I'm not even nineteen yet. I've got my whole life ahead of me. So what if Mr. Tony Vale, the Hollywood tomcat, is getting married? What do I care? I'm going to be a movie star myself. I'll have more men than I know what to do with. You can have your old Ginny McCarthy, you skinny, dried-up, two-timing Romeo!

Jessie felt the first teardrop hit warmly on her hand, gripping tightly to the railing. Then she felt tears flowing down her cheeks and heard a terrible sobbing. She glanced around, thinking that someone behind her had begun to cry, then realized that the sound was her own.

An hour later, still lost in her sorrow, Jessie heard the telephone ringing as if from a distance. Gradually she pulled herself up out of the grief and the tears, stepped into the house, and picked up the telephone.

"Jessie, this is Tony."

Jessie felt only numbness and a sense of being outside the ordinary matters of living.

"Jessie, are you there?"

"I'm here."

"Look, I've got to talk to you!"

Jessie stared out the sliding glass door at the emerald ring, gleaming in the morning light.

Vale's voice took on another level of urgency. "Jessie, this is important!"

"Okay."

"Will you meet me for lunch?"

Taking a deep breath, Jessie replied, thinking that her voice sounded like a recording. "I guess so."

"I'd pick you up, but I'm kind of tied up right now. Can you make it on your own?"

"Yes."

"I'll send a cab for you."

"Fine."

After Vale's call, Jessie summoned up all her strength, pulled herself together, and got ready for her luncheon engagement. She bathed, washed and dried her hair, and spent an hour putting her makeup on to perfection. Then she selected a black linen dress in the latest "siren sheath" design, taking a single strand of pearls out of her jewelry box to complement it. Sheer black stockings and black pointed shoes with spike heels completed her outfit.

★ ★ ★

Jessie sat at a corner table amid the hum of conversation and the bustle of patrons and waiters that defined the Brown Derby from noon until midnight. She fidgeted with her purse, fixing her lipstick and hair a half-dozen times. Glancing at the wall to her left, she noticed a caricature of Cary Grant.

Then as she stared across the restaurant at the front door for what seemed like the hundredth time, she saw Cary Grant in the flesh as he escorted Doris Day to a table. *My goodness, he's handsome!*

As Jessie gaped at Cary Grant, Vale entered the restaurant unseen and walked over to her table, stopping along the way to make the necessary greetings to anyone in the business who might be able to smooth his way to stardom.

"I see you're smitten with our Mr. Grant."

Startled, Jessie glanced up at Vale. He wore a brown silk jacket along with a slight frown betraying his concern that Jessie should be so interested in any other man while she waited for him.

For some reason it made Jessie feel better to see that Cary Grant was better looking than Tony Vale and to see that this obviously bothered Vale. She pushed it further: "He *is* the most attractive man in the movies. I think so anyway."

Vale didn't expect his meeting with Jessie to get underway this awkwardly for him. "Well, he doesn't have the box office draw that he did back in the forties, but he's not all that old yet. I expect he'll be around another four or five years."

Still in a daze from reading the news about Vale's marriage and also from her telephone conversation with him, Jessie felt even more confused at the way their luncheon had begun. "Why are we talking about Cary Grant?"

Vale smiled and slipped into the seat next to Jessie. "You're right."

A waiter wearing black tie and tails appeared as though by magic next to the table. "White wine for the lady and a double martini for me. Okay, Jessie?"

Jessie nodded.

Vale cleared his throat. "I think we've made enough small talk, don't you?"

"Is there a quota?"

"You're not going to make this easy, are you?"

"Easy?" Jessie found it almost amusing that Vale would act as though he was the one who was being wronged. "I think relationships are *all* easy for you, Tony. Especially the—*unique* way you have of ending them."

"One thing I want to say before we go any further. I didn't *announce* anything at Sardi's last night. I never planned for you to find this out in the newspaper."

The waiter returned and placed their drinks in front of them. "Will there be anything else?"

"We'll order later."

"Very good, Mr. Vale."

Vale took a swallow of his martini and continued. "Some Hollywood newshound must have overheard our conversation and got the word to Hedda."

Jessie sipped her wine, feeling very grown-up and

trying to sound as sophisticated as she could. "You could have let me know about you and—what's her name—months ago, Tony."

Vale smiled knowingly. "There was nothing to tell months ago, Jessie."

"Well, whenever you fell in love with her, then." Jessie felt foolish, wanting to get up and leave.

This time Vale laughed—not quite sarcastically. "What a child you are, Jessie!"

"I don't know what you're talking about," she pouted. "I only asked a simple question. The obvious one, I should imagine, under the circumstances."

"Love has absolutely nothing to do with any of this. I've known Ginny for ages—or it seems like it anyway." Vale was still smiling, but now because of the refreshing innocence of Jessie Temple.

"How can you marry someone and say that love has nothing to do with it?" Jessie felt a numbness and a sense of disbelief at Vale's words. "I'm sorry. You've lost me."

Vale shook his head almost sadly. "Do you really think it's just a coincidence that our marriage is taking place at the same time the picture is going to be released?"

"I never thought about it."

"It's good press, sweetheart." Vale talked to her like a teacher instructing a first grader on how to stay inside the lines with his crayons. "Do you have any idea what this marriage will mean in box office receipts?"

"No."

Vale saw the confusion and dismay in Jessie's face. His voice grew gentler. "It's just the way things work out here, kid. Nothing's real—on or *off* the screen."

Jessie had heard the stories of Hollywood romances with agents taking the place of marriage brokers, but had always thought them exaggerated. Most of her time since leaving home had been spent on the Korean USO tour or in preparation for it, so she'd had little actual experience with the Hollywood lifestyle. "I don't believe you. People can't *live* like that!"

"Hey, it's show business! Kind of like politics except the people are prettier." Noticing the hint of hysteria in Jessie's voice, Vale tried to make light of the situation. "We live by a script out here, Jessie, in front of the cameras *and* in our personal lives. It's not so bad, once you accept it."

"I could *never* accept something like that! Jessie took a long swallow of her wine. She found herself thinking of the many times she had listened to Vale sing love ballads, on records and in person, and of the special way it had always made her feel. *Grow up, Jessie. You're not living in a Walt Disney cartoon. This is the real world he's telling you about.*

"Don't knock it 'til you've tried it. The money's great and the fans adore you." Vale continued his commercial for the Hollywood lifestyle. "And some of us aren't even phonies. Take Jimmy Stewart, for instance. Then there's Hope and a few others."

Shaking her head slowly, Jessie stared across the restaurant where Cary Grant leaned over, whispering something in Doris Day's ear. She smiled and nodded her head in response.

"I've saved the best part for last," Vale continued with a conspiratorial smile. "We can still see each other."

"You mean *after* you're married?" Jessie felt that she must have misunderstood Vale. A sense of unreality fell over her like a cold vapor.

"Sure," Vale answered quickly. "Oh, not for a while. But in a few months we can get together—dis-

creetly, of course. Ginny's a good kid. She'll understand."

"Never!"

Vale's voice grew flat and unadorned. He laid aside
his bright smile. "I know, Jessie. I don't even know
why I brought it up. Yes, I *do* know why."

Jessie took another swallow of wine, hoping that
it would numb the aching that had begun in her
breast.

"I've never known anyone like you before, Jessie—
and I don't want to have to let you go, to never be with
you again." Vale reached for her hand.

Jessie snatched it away, clasped her hands together, and placed them in her lap.

Vale gave her a sad smile. "The people in this business—the people I've made my living with all these
years—my *friends* . . ." Vale spoke with a caustic note
in his voice now. "Well, let's just say they're a lot *different* than you are."

The waiter appeared next to the table, but Vale
waved him away impatiently.

Staring directly into Jessie's eyes for the first time
since he had arrived, Vale continued in a level voice.
"It's hard for me to put all this into words. That
sounds kinda funny coming from me, I know—but it's
the truth."

Jessie felt a slow anger burning its way through
the numbness that had seeped into her, to think that
she had been simply a matter of convenience for Vale.
She felt herself trembling slightly, hoping that he
wouldn't notice.

"You see, Jessie," Vale stared at the flash of day-
light across the room as someone entered the restaurant. "Whenever I was with you I felt, I don't know—

innocent, I guess you'd call it—almost like I was a child again."

Wary now of anything Vale said, Jessie couldn't help but feel that for this one time anyway he was being completely honest with her.

"I felt—clean inside." As though this minor confession had shaken his core values, Vale lifted his martini glass and drained it. "I haven't been around anyone like you in years—not since my mother died."

Jessie laid her hands on the table. "I wondered why you—why you never tried anything with me. Not that there were that many opportunities, but you had the chance a time or two."

"Guess you thought I was a real gentleman these past few months, didn't you," Vale laughed. "Like those southern boys you grew up with."

Suddenly, Jessie could almost see Austin sitting next to her in his relaxed, easy way, his infectious smile making her think he was planning some benign effrontery.

"You find this funny?"

Jessie hadn't realized that her mental image of Austin had caused her to smile. "No, not at all."

Somewhat miffed, Vale continued. "Well, it wasn't because I was being a gentleman at all. I just didn't want to do anything to lose that special way you made me feel."

Feeling that Vale had spoken his genuine feelings out loud, Jessie relented in her half-intentioned vow to never speak to him again. "I'm glad I made you feel that way, Tony. Maybe it'll be a good memory for both of us."

"I know it will."

Jessie gave Vale a weak smile, knowing that she was going to miss him: his attentiveness, his funny stories, being with him in all the exciting and exotic places they had seen together. Most of all, she would miss those few times when they were alone and he would sing to her. She would always remember the sound of his voice, intoxicatingly romantic. The emptiness *behind* the man, she would try to forget.

"Well, maybe you've learned something from this little dog-and-pony show, Jessie."

Jessie shrugged.

"If nothing else, that we're just a bunch of phonies out here—some of us pleasant phonies I hope," Vale smiled. "Don't take anything seriously if somebody in the business says it. Even if they're espousing some noble cause, remember, it was probably dreamed up by a press agent."

"I think you're being a little hard on yourself, aren't you?" Jessie laughed softly.

Vale gave her a thoughtful look. "The best I can hope for is to make people forget their troubles for a couple of hours once in a while. I'll settle for that."

Jessie gazed into Vale's eyes, and she could almost see him as a dark, serious ten-year-old, stocking the shelves in his father's little grocery store. She realized then that she had no true reason to be angry at him, that he had make no promises to her and that the marriage he was entering into held less meaning for him than a date to the senior prom. *How can I be mad at someone like that? What a sad, lonely life.*

Vale's tone of voice became more staid as he spoke again. "There's something important I need to talk to you about after we eat, Jessie."

"You mean something *else* important, don't you?"

"Yeah, maybe so," Vale shrugged.

"I'm not hungry."

"Me either. Let's go." Vale dropped a ten-dollar bill

on the table. "You don't mind if I bring you home, do you? I promise I won't go inside."

"No. I don't mind."

★ ★ ★

Jessie sat over against the passenger door as she rode down Hollywood Boulevard with Vale in his pale blue Cadillac convertible. The marquee above Grauman's Chinese Theater advertised *High Noon*, starring Gary Cooper and Grace Kelly. Turning, they stopped at the traffic light at Hollywood and Vine. She glanced over at the corner drugstore where, according to her bio, Lana Turner had been discovered.

Jessie thought back to the day when she had first moved to town and had taken a bus downtown to see the drugstore. She had ordered a chocolate malt at the soda fountain, thinking that she might be sitting on the exact stool that Lana Turner had sat on that fateful day. Since she had won the national USO contest, Jessie had felt no need to be "discovered," secure in the knowledge that her own career was already a certainty.

"That's where Lana Turner was discovered," Vale offered, pointing to the drugstore. "Or so they tell me."

Jessie nodded and glanced again at the store where three high-school girls in saddle oxfords, pleated skirts, and school sweaters entered the front door, giggling at some obviously hilarious story one of them had just finished telling.

Gazing at the people hurrying along the sidewalks, Jessie could see the bright hopes etched on the faces of the young women as though each of them also rested in the certainty, as she once had, that it was only a matter of time and a few breaks before they, too, had their names on the Grauman marquee.

Vale glanced over at Jessie, a shadow of concern falling across his face. "Bob Hope said he's never seen anyone with more natural talent than you have. And the way those boys over in Korea took to you, well, there's no way to teach that—you either have it or you don't."

"But . . ." Jessie could tell by the sound of Vale's voice that he had bad news for her.

"He believes in you, Jessie," Vale continued. "You don't get a personal interview with John Houston if you don't have that special 'star' quality."

"But . . ."

"Don't sound so fatalistic!" Vale turned onto Sunset Boulevard, heading west toward the Pacific Coast Highway. The afternoon sun gleamed on his dark sunglasses and his darker hair. "You've had three screen tests, Jessie. And not one of them even comes close to the performances you gave in Korea."

"What's wrong with them?"

Vale punched the cigarette lighter, took a pack of Old Golds from his inside jacket pocket, and stuck one in the corner of his mouth. As he lit it, the smoke streamed away in the wind. "You're—stiff, stilted, remote—you don't *perform* for the camera, you act like you're *afraid* of it."

"I just feel so stupid on those sound stages. Everything's fake." Jessie thought back to the thousands of uplifted faces of the men she had sung for in Korea—gaunt, hollow faces full of heartache, loneliness, and the fear of dying on some forgotten hill in a frozen land so far away from home.

Vale seemed to sense what her problem was. "You sang your heart out for those men overseas, Jessie. If you could just hold on to that same feeling, pretend the cameras and the microphones are a bunch of lonely G.I.'s, you'd be the hottest thing this town's seen since Judy Garland sang 'Over the Rainbow.' "

Jessie gazed toward the distant ocean, a faraway look in her eyes. "I did my best all three times, Tony. I guess I just don't have what it takes."

"You've got everything! You've just got to find a way to get it out of you when you get in front of the camera. That's where it counts."

"I'm hopeless."

"John Houston doesn't think so," Vale assured her. "Neither does Bob Hope."

"I don't know what to do."

"Work harder! That's what you do."

Jessie glanced over at Vale. She could see the intensity in his face and realized that he truly wanted her to be a success in this most elusive of careers. "I guess I could keep showing up every day—if they'll have me."

"That's the spirit." Vale seemed elated, flashing Jessie his Colgate smile. "We'll get you a drama coach at the studio and enroll you in acting classes on your off time. Your singing's already professional enough. I can still give you a pointer or two there though, just to make it perfect. That way I can still spend some time with you."

Vale reached over and patted Jessie on the hand. "Who knows? Our relationship might even change. It could easily become more—intense, if you know what I mean."

In the six months she had known him, Jessie had seen Vale's passing fancies in everything from clothes to the boys who ran errands for him on the set. *I guess he's gotten bored with the "innocent" phase of our re-*

*lationship. Or maybe he's only happy if he's got a wife
to run around on.*

Jessie gazed out at the blue Pacific as they turned
right on the Coast Highway. Her thoughts seemed to
be buffeted about by a strong wind—willful, unruly
things that she could no longer get a hold on.

In spite of Vale's encouragement, Jessie felt she
was going against insurmountable odds. And his final
innuendo disturbed her even further, making her see
that she had probably been shielded from most of the
sordid side of Hollywood so far, but that this fortunate
and probably unique phase of her apprenticeship was
rapidly coming to a close.

Vale turned onto the narrow road that wound up
the hillside to Jessie's house. At the foot of the long
flight of stairs leading up to the terrace, Vale parked
and turned off the ignition. "One drink for old times'
sake, Jessie?"

Jessie shook her head and got out of the car.

In spite of all the warning signs, the desire to see
her name in lights, to see her image on the "silver
screen," and to bask in the adulation of the fans
burned more intensely than ever in Jessie's breast.
The glamour and glitter of Hollywood still drew her
like a moth to flame even though she had had
glimpses of the darkness behind the bright lights.

Vale gave her his best smile and started the engine.
"See you at the studio in the morning. And don't
worry—you're going to make it, kid."

★   ★   ★

Jessie stood on the terrace, her robe pulled about
her against the chill wind blowing off the ocean. She
had been there most of the afternoon, agonizing over
whether to commit herself to making it in Hollywood.

Night had fallen and still she was no closer to a decision. Far below her the surface of the sea glinted like hammered silver in the pale moonlight. Gazing up at the ancient stars, she remembered that some of them had burned out long ago and still she was seeing their light.

Memory seemed to sift down on her like stardust from the heavens. She could almost see the lights twinkling on the surface of Capitol Lake as she and Austin sat in his car and talked of their future together; could almost feel his arms around her and the stirring inside her as they kissed. *Oh, Austin, do you still care about me; do you ever think of me? Is it too late for us? Maybe I really can't go home again.*

Noticing a movement just below her, Jessie saw her neighbor step out onto her small porch. She had seen the woman—gray-haired, frail, and in her sixties—almost daily since the studio had moved her into the house.

She had seen her up close only once, passing her as she was returning home from an early morning walk. The woman, wearing a frilly dress that would have suited a girl of sixteen, had applied powder and rouge and lipstick in such quantities that her face had a clownlike appearance. She had given Jessie a listless smile. The sad, faraway look in her eyes spoke of little time spent in the company of other people.

From her vantage point above the woman, Jessie watched her feeding her cats. She had adopted all the strays in the neighborhood and fed them nightly on her porch. They swarmed around her when she stepped through her door. It seemed to be her one consuming passion.

Jessie gazed once more out at the shining sea, listening to the muted roar of the surf throwing itself against the rocky shore. A hint of a smile came to the corners of her mouth. She walked over to the table and stared down at the emerald ring lying where she had left it earlier in the day next to the white vase holding its single rose. It gleamed like green fire in the faint light spilling out through the terrace door.

Scooping the ring up from the table, Jessie walked back to the railing. Below, her neighbor had knelt down among the cats. She cooed softly to them as they brushed against her and climbed across her legs, waving their long tails.

Casually, without looking at it again, Jessie tossed the ring out into the night. She watched it spinning downward, catching the light from the street lamps as it hit her neighbor's porch. Bouncing against the house, it came to rest next to a straight-backed chair.

Hearing the sound, the lady looked up from her cats, walked over, and picked up the ring. Jessie stepped back into the shadows as the lady stared at the ring, then looked all about her. Apparently satisfied that the ring's owner was nowhere to be found, she smiled placidly and slipped it onto her finger.

For a few moments, Jessie watched the woman admiring her new treasure, then walked back across the terrace and into the house. Picking up the telephone, she asked for the long distance operator.

"Hello."

The voice on the other end of the telephone line made Jessie feel safe and warm and loved. "Mama, this is Jess. I'm coming home."

PART FOUR
★ ★ ★

A SUDDEN
SWEET JOY

FOURTEEN

COMMUNION

★ ★ ★

Charlie Garrett, lean and athletic at six-foot-three, still maintained the 205-pound playing weight he had carried when he made all-American end at LSU. Wearing a dark brown tweed jacket that matched the color of his wavy hair, he walked through the door marked Assistant Principal and over to the high counter of the main office.

Light from the tall windows caught the wolfish gleam in Garrett's brown eyes as he gazed at the woman behind the desk, taking in the soft curves of her rose-colored sweater. "Catherine, can I see you for a minute?"

Looking up from her typewriter, Catherine smiled, thinking how fortunate she had been that Garrett had hired her. Even though Lane had his entire paycheck sent home each month, there never seemed to be enough money to pay all the bills until she went to work. "Be right with you."

Garrett turned to leave, calling back over his

shoulder, "Bring some coffee, will you?"

Catherine finished the letter, walked over to the coffeepot, and poured two cups. Adding sugar and cream to hers, she set the cups on a wooden tray along with her steno pad and carried it into Garrett's office.

He stood with his back to her, gazing out through the venetian blinds at the young saplings bending in the January wind. "Have a seat."

Placing the cup of black coffee on Garrett's desk, Catherine sat down in a heavy oak chair, her steno pad on her lap. She sipped her coffee and stared at Garrett's contrived pose. With his broad shoulders and lean waist outlined against the window, he stood next to his dozen or so football trophies gleaming in the pewter-colored light filtering through the blinds.

Catherine had learned to adjust to Garrett's theatrics. They had proven harmless; he was pleasant and easygoing, and his demands regarding her job were minimal. She enjoyed her work at the school, especially helping the children who came to her with excuses for being absent or tardy, checking out for one reason or the other, and the hundred other small happenings that brought them to the main office during the school day. Some had come to regard her as their "school mom."

"I'm ready for spring," Garrett smiled, turning toward Catherine. "How about you?"

"I think so."

Garrett sat down in his brass-studded leather chair. He handed Catherine a letter. "Have this mimeographed and see that every teacher gets a copy. Let's see—here are the new bus schedules and—there they are, the changes in the basketball schedule and the proposed seating arrangement for the PTA meeting on the tenth of next month."

Catherine took the sheets of paper individually, making notes on her pad.

"How's Jessie getting along these days?"

"Oh, she's just fine. She's back from the USO tour now."

Catherine knew that Garrett was genuinely interested in Jessie, as he had devoted a lot of time to her during difficult periods of her three years in his school. He was especially kind to Jessie after the Christmas Eve tragedy of a little more than a year ago.

"What a great thing to do for her country. I always knew she had a good heart, even if she did break a few rules now and again."

Garrett leaned back, the chair creaking in protest. "She certainly is a pretty girl, too, and she's probably got more singing talent than anyone who's ever gone to Istrouma—since I've been here anyway. Maybe I'll see her in the movies one day."

Catherine closed her notebook, placing it on her lap. "Not much chance of that now."

Garrett gave Catherine a puzzled look. "That was always her *one* big dream."

"I think it may have turned into a mild nightmare," Catherine smiled. "She called last night. Says she's coming home just as soon as she ties up a few loose ends."

"Oh yeah—the dreams of youth. I sure remember my young and reckless days." Garrett smiled almost sadly, glancing at his trophies, lined up in ragged formation on the windowsill. "Sometimes the things that look so good to us turn out to be nothing but pretty facades like those Hollywood movie sets. When you get around behind 'em, there's nothing there."

Garrett had alluded to his past glories and their sad demise several times before, but Catherine had no

237

inclination to spend time in the confessional with him, so she quickly changed the subject. "Well, she's finally coming home and that makes me happy. Now maybe she'll enroll in LSU's music school and do something worthwhile with her life."

Garrett caught the hint. "What do you hear from your husband?"

"Jessie saw him while she was over in Korea. Said he's all right except that he's kind of skinny," Catherine replied, glad for the opportunity to talk about Lane. Sometimes it seemed almost as though their marriage was something out of her dreams when she didn't talk about him with someone for a while. "I got one letter while his company was in reserve, but they're probably back on the line by now."

"That's a tough war," Garrett volunteered, his eyes narrowed in thought. "Since Truman fired MacArthur I'm not sure we even have any strategy left for winning it."

Catherine took her coffee in both hands, warming her fingers as she took small sips. "Lane was on the *Missouri* with MacArthur when he signed the armistice with Japan."

"No kidding." Garrett seemed genuinely impressed. "It was a real honor to be selected for that duty."

"Lane thought MacArthur was a military genius but not as good a general as he was an actor." Catherine lost herself in thoughts of her husband. "He always said MacArthur had a flair for the dramatic. Like that speech of his at West Point—'Old soldiers never die, they just fade away.'"

"That was a classic," Garrett agreed. "The newspapers played with that one for weeks."

Catherine finished her coffee and started to get up.

"If that's all, I'd better get back to work."

Garrett seemed unwilling for Catherine to leave his office. "I saw your boy play a couple of times this past football season. Can't wait for him to get out of junior high."

"Lane thinks Dalton's going to be good enough to play for LSU someday."

"I wouldn't doubt it." Garrett gazed directly into Catherine's eyes. "But before he gets there he's going to help Istrouma win a couple of state championships."

Catherine felt uncomfortable under Garrett's stare. "He certainly loves football, all right. I wish he thought about his studies as much as he docs about making touchdowns."

Seemingly in a daze staring at Catherine, Garrett started abruptly at the sound of the class bell ringing.

Catherine restrained her smile at his embarrassment. "Well, if that's all for now . . ."

Garrett took a pack of Lucky Strikes out of his desk drawer, tapped one out of the pack, and stuck it in the corner of his mouth. Fishing a silver lighter from his left front jacket pocket, he lit the cigarette, squinting through the blue-white smoke. Drawing the smoke deeply into his lungs, he let it flow out his nostrils, then between his slightly parted lips. "There's something I need to talk to you about, Catherine."

"Well if it's important, but I really have to get back to work." Catherine had the feeling that whatever was on Garrett's mind had nothing to do with her job.

Garrett gave her his all-American smile, the smile that had proven so irresistible to cheerleaders and sorority girls during his four years on the LSU campus. "I know how hard you've had it trying to make ends meet since Lane's been gone."

Here it comes. "It hasn't been so bad since I've been working here."

"Well, anyway," Garrett continued, clearing his throat. "I thought you might like to go out to dinner one night. You know, some place real nice."

"I'd love to."

"You would?"

"Why certainly," Catherine smiled sweetly. "I've been wanting to meet your wife."

Garrett's face went slack, his mouth slightly open. He quickly closed it. "Uh—I'm not sure she'll be able to come. She's—ah, been real busy lately."

"No hurry."

Garrett seemed at a loss for words. The long ash of his forgotten cigarette fell onto his trouser leg. Brushing it away quickly, he stubbed the cigarette out in a nearby ashtray.

Catherine's placid smile seemed to settle him down. "You're a nice man, Mr. Garrett . . ."

Flinching at the use of the word *Mister*, Garrett recalled that he had tried for weeks to get Catherine to use his first name in their conversations.

" . . . but we need to come to an understanding. It's been almost twenty-two years since I met Lane."

Garrett began the mental calculation in figuring out Catherine's age.

"Let me save you the trouble. I was fifteen." Catherine stood up, holding her notebook and papers across her breast with both hands. "There's never been another man in my life since then—and I don't expect there ever will be."

Garrett reddened slightly under his tanned skin. "I'm sorry if I offended you."

"Apology accepted. Now if it ends here, fine. If not—I'll start looking for another job."

"No, no," Garrett insisted. "I'm not a troll—couldn't take all that dampness under the bridge. I promise I'll be a perfect gentleman from now on."

Catherine smiled thinly, then gave him a direct and dubious stare.

Holding up three fingers, Garrett promised, his face staring at the wall behind Catherine, "Scouts' honor."

"That's good enough for me."

After a quick knock, the door opened and a pretty girl with carrot-colored hair and a sprinkling of freckles looked in, her pale eyes wide with excitement. "Mr. Garrett, there's a special delivery letter for Mrs. Temple."

Catherine gasped involuntarily, bringing her left hand up to her throat.

Seeing that Catherine's face had gone white, Garrett walked around his desk and took her by the arm. "Sit down, Catherine. I'll get it."

Catherine felt her heart pounding in her breast. Her mind raced back to the years during World War II when Lane had been overseas and she had seen the little green Ford that Mr. Appleby had driven all over Sweetwater, delivering telegrams from the War Department. She saw again the banners hanging in the windows of families who had men in the war and saw the blue stars changed to gold the day after Mr. Appleby's visit.

Later she would visit the funeral home with its powdery-sweet smell of gardenias and the sound of muffled weeping. Then came the hard benches in the church with the coffin closed and women holding palm-leaf fans, the men uneasy in their ties and everyone singing about precious memories and how they would understand it better by and by.

Then came the memories of the hillside studded with tilting old tombstones and the big tires of a black hearse crunching slowly along the gravel drive—listening to mockingbirds and, drifting out across the cemetery from the edge of the woods, the sound of a bugle playing taps.

And finally at the house, the dishes and platters of fried chicken and pork roast, the steaming pots of squash and okra and new potatoes—a mess of greens and a pone of bread—and blackberry cobbler. Always so much food, as though the very act of eating could keep death at bay or soothe away the grief.

And more than all these things, Catherine remembered the color of the star—the blue now turned to gold.

"Catherine, are you all right?"

So strong were her memories that for an instant Catherine wondered where she was and who this man with the concerned expression was as he leaned over her. The memories fled and Catherine stared at Garrett, her eyes dull with the beginnings of shock. "Yes. I'm all right."

Garrett held the letter in his hand. "Do you want me to read it for you?"

"No, I'll do it." Catherine held out her hand to Garrett. She took the letter, stared at the official return address, and opened it carefully as though she might harm Lane in some way if she damaged the letter.

Dear Mr. Mrs. Miss *Temple*.

We regret to inform you that your Husband Son Brother has been classified WIA and is presently undergoing convalescence in-country. As soon as he has recovered sufficiently, he will be transported back to the United States.

This letter will be followed up with a telephone call ASAP in order to provide you with additional information.

> Sincerely,
> Winston R. Batten, Lt. Colonel
> Dependent Liaison Section
> Office of the Commandant,
> USMC

Catherine folded the letter carefully, slipping it back into the envelope, her face a pale mask.

"Is he all right?" Garrett sat down next to her, leaning forward in his chair.

"He's alive." Catherine stared at the envelope as though it could answer all her questions, assuage her fears.

"Wounded?"

"Yes."

"Is that all it says?"

"Wounded In Action—WIA," Catherine said flatly, thinking how cold and sterile the words sounded. "They're going to call me later and give me more information."

Garrett stood up. "I'll drive you home, then."

Catherine gazed at the pale gray light streaming in through the blinds. "That won't be necessary. I do need to use your telephone though."

Garrett took Catherine's arm, escorting her behind his desk and pushing the heavy black phone over in front of her.

"Thank you." Catherine dialed the number, and waited a few seconds. "Austin?. . . . Could you possibly pick the children up at school for me today? . . . Thanks so much. . . . No. Everything's fine. I'll tell you about it later. . . . Okay. Bye."

★ ★ ★

Catherine pulled into her driveway, stopping for a

moment to stare at the front of her house. There were no banners with their blue or gold stars hanging in hers or anyone else's windows for Korea. No one in America seemed to care about this war very much— except those with husbands or sons or brothers who were fighting it.

Driving on back to the garage, Catherine parked the car and walked along the brick path toward the back porch. The fountain gurgled and splashed, gusts of wind blowing a cold spray in her ashen face. She went inside and brought the telephone out on its long cord, placing it on a wooden plant stand near the back door, then sat down in the porch swing to await the call.

Catherine remembered that stormy April night the past year when Lane had told her of his leaving for Korea. She could almost see him sitting next to her as the rain slackened, could almost hear again the bittersweet sound of "September Song" floating from a neighbor's open window.

The swing drifted slowly back and forth. Beyond the porch, the wind stirred the leaves of the live oak, rustling softly, lifting the Spanish moss that hung from its branches. Clouds hung low and gray and heavy over the city.

Catherine had come to think of this little enclave on the back porch as her own private place. She would come out on mild nights after the children were asleep to spend some quiet time and have "communion with her own heart," as she had grown to think of these moments.

Brrrring! Brrrring!

Catherine scrambled out of the porch swing. In her reveries and daydreams she had lost track of time. She hurried across the porch and snatched up the telephone. "Hello. . . . Yes, this is Catherine Temple. . . . Yes, I'm his wife."

★   ★   ★

Sitting in a cushioned chair with rounded chrome armrests, Catherine watched Austin pacing back and forth at the end of the concourse. She wore tan slacks and the brown leather jacket that Lane had given her years before. Her mind was torn between thoughts of her husband and the expectation of seeing her daughter after such a long absence. "Why don't you come sit down? You're acting like an expectant father."

"I guess I am at that." Austin, wearing his usual jeans and Istrouma letter jacket, gave her a sheepish smile, walked over, and sat down next to her. "Six months since I've seen her and it seems like six years."

Patting him on the arm, Catherine said reassuringly, "Well, I imagine she's just as eager to see you. She asked enough questions about you the last time she called."

Austin thought of Jessie's glowing, eager face and her dreams of stardom before she left for Hollywood. "I'm not so sure about that. After all those movie stars, I bet I'm gonna look like a real country bumpkin to her."

Catherine gazed into Austin's intelligent gray eyes. His high cheekbones and black hair spoke of the Indian blood that flowed in his veins. She had seen the unmistakable change in his life in the past few months and hoped that he and Jessie would remain close. "You don't look anything like a bumpkin, Austin—believe me. Being from Mississippi, I'm something of an expert on the subject."

Austin laughed, glancing again down the concourse.

"Although, as far as I'm concerned, we country bumpkins are some of the nicest people around."

"Mrs. Temple, I didn't mean to . . ."

Catherine smiled at her own joke. "I'm kidding you, Austin. Labels don't mean much to me. You always forget about them after you get to know the person behind them anyway."

"You set me up, didn't you?" Austin had come to know Catherine better since Jessie had been gone than when they had been going out together, but she usually seemed remote. "I'm going to have to keep my guard up around you."

Catherine gazed at the bustle of the airport lobby: men with business suits and briefcases rushing to make their flights; a young sailor waiting for someone, probably his girlfriend or wife-to-be, with the same eager expression as Austin; a couple in their sixties, the woman in a simple housedress and her husband in khakis, carrying his cardboard suitcase, who both looked as happy as newlyweds. "Austin, I really appreciate all the help you've given me over the past few months."

"I didn't really do anything." Austin stared at the floor, looking as though he felt an awkwardness accepting compliments. "It was fun picking up the kids once in a while."

"Well, it was certainly a big help to me. With Lane and Jess both gone, I felt—kind of *lost* sometimes. Those little odd jobs you did around the house saved me a lot of money that I really couldn't afford to spend."

Austin glanced once more at the concourse. "I was glad to do it. My folks already have things like that taken care of. They don't really need me for anything."

A shadow seemed to cross behind his eyes for a fleeting moment.

Bothered by Austin's choice of words and the brief glimpse she had of his downcast expression, Catherine felt she needed to reassure him. "I know you don't really mean that, Austin. I've spoken with your mother. She had nothing but good things to say about you."

Austin nodded.

"Well, I've certainly seen a change in you in the past few months." Catherine glanced at the big clock on the opposite side of the lobby. "I have to confess something."

Turning toward Catherine, Austin gazed at her with a perplexed expression. "A confession?"

"Yes." Catherine smiled warmly. "For a long time when Jessie was dating you, I truly didn't like you very much. I even tried to make her stop seeing you."

"I don't blame you a bit." Austin held Catherine's eyes with an unwavering gaze.

"But you've changed—or maybe I'm just seeing a different side of you." Catherine leaned toward Austin, shifting positions in her chair.

"I guess what I'm saying, Austin," Catherine continued, her voice soft and deliberate, "if you'll forgive a mother's interference, is that I hope you and Jess will keep seeing each other. I think you'll be good for her."

"Maybe you're right," Austin agreed. He grew thoughtful and quiet, as if suddenly sensing how valued he was by the Temples.

Catherine looked beyond Austin. In the distance, she saw a young woman with hair as bright as neon in the dimly lighted concourse. She wore the latest style dress in a jade green color, its narrow waist magnified by the bulky crinolines beneath it. With a carry-on bag and a tan coat draped over one arm, she walked with a graceful assurance that made men take a second look at her when she passed by.

Austin turned around, stood up, and walked toward the concourse with Catherine close behind. He forced himself to walk slowly, a smile spreading on his face that he thought would split his lips at the corners.

Jessie, preoccupied with her newfound elegance, didn't notice Austin until he was fifty feet away. She stopped, her eyes round with surprise, staring at him for a full three seconds. Then, completely forgetting the adult status she had recently adopted, she dropped her bag and ran toward him.

Austin closed the distance between them even faster, took her up in his arms, and whirled her around. "Jess! You look like a million dollars!"

"My goodness!" Jessie gasped, holding on tightly to Austin's arms as she caught her breath. "What a reception! I should leave home more often."

Catherine smiled brightly at her daughter, then walked toward her with open arms.

Jessie hugged her mother, feeling for the first time since that snowy day in Korea the comfort and security that comes only with the people you grew up with. "Oh, Mama! I've missed you—all of you so much!"

Catherine stared at her daughter, still finding it so difficult to believe that she had grown into a woman. "I'm glad you're back home, Jess."

Austin retrieved Jessie's bag, then watched her reunion with Catherine as he walked back.

"Well, let's go, you two," Jessie said, taking them both by their arms. "You've got to bring me up to date on everything that's happened in the last six months. And then I want some real South Louisiana cooking."

A shadow crossed Catherine's face. The reunion with her daughter demanded that she get the news over with as soon as possible. "Let's sit down for just a minute before we go to the car, Jess."

Jessie's face went pale. "Mama, it's not about Daddy, is it? He's not . . ."

"Settle down, Jess. It's not as bad as all that." Catherine led her over to a chair, sitting down next to her.

Holding on to her mother's hands, Jessie trembled in the face of the news that awaited her. A vivid picture of Korea's frozen mountains flashed in her mind. She remembered the wounded men she had visited in one of the rear area hospitals, saw again the pain and the relentless terror of combat in their eyes.

"Your daddy's been hurt."

"Oh, Mama!"

"Hush now. Let me finish." Catherine kept her voice calm, trying to give Jessie the news as if she were reading off a grocery list. "A piece of shrapnel went through one of his lungs. He got an infection and it was touch-and-go for a while, but he's out of danger now. He's convalescing in a hospital in Seoul. They said he should be able to call us in a few days."

Jessie began to cry softly, staring at her hands entwined with her mother's. "I was so selfish, Mama. I didn't even go down to San Diego to see him."

Catherine put her arm around Jessie. "Your daddy understands that, Jess. He told me he knew how busy you were, trying to get your big chance in show business."

"That's no excuse—it was a thoughtless thing to do." Jessie stared into her mother's blue eyes, thinking that for the first time she could understand some of the responsibilities and heartaches of being a woman. "I don't even think I realized how much I loved him until I saw him over in Korea. It just suddenly hit me then that he could actually get killed."

Patting Jessie on the shoulder, Catherine tilted her face over, placing it against her daughter's head. "It's all right, Jess. Your daddy's okay and we'll all be together again soon. Right now, why don't we just enjoy your homecoming?"

FIFTEEN

T-Beaux, Dippy, and Seritta

★ ★ ★

Austin drove Catherine's Chrysler north on Airline Highway. Humming along over the four-lane concrete bridge that spanned the Bonne Carre Spillway—designed to carry water from the Mississippi River across to Lake Pontchartrain in times when flood waters threatened the levee system—he gazed out over the cane fields, burned after the grinding season had ended. Lying blackened and fallow under the lead-colored sky, they stretched from the highway to the levee.

In the gray distance, the Goudchaux Sugar Refinery lifted its towering bulk from the surrounding fields. Austin remembered going to an end-of-grinding-season party at the refinery in late December five years before. Instrumental in getting the refinery some much-needed interim financing for an expansion, his father had been treated like royalty. Everyone from the field hands to the president of the company attended. The food supply was endless, and the drinking and dancing lasted until the red sun climbed above Lake Maurepas across the marsh.

"Let's stop in LaPlace," Jessie cried out. "I love their chicken andouille gumbo."

"Okay with you, Mrs. Temple?"

Catherine smiled at Jessie, seated between her and Austin. "Whatever Jess wants. It's her homecoming."

Austin turned into the oyster-shell parking lot of the restaurant. Originally built in 1937 as an automobile dealership, the sprawling, white art-deco-style structure, with its glass-block wall at the front entrance, boasted a theater-like marquee above the gas pumps. A large red, white, and blue sign in the approximate shape of a musical note attached to a derrick-like steel structure rose above the stainless steel marquee proclaiming, "Airline Motors Restaurant, Since 1939, Air Conditioned."

Entering the front door, Austin noticed the long counter running the length of the left wall. Almost every one of its chair-backed swivel stools held a mid-morning customer: bankers, car salesmen, construction workers, and a few off-shore workers who had just returned from a fourteen-day stint on the oil rigs. However, most of these roughnecks seemed to have gravitated to the bar in the far right corner of the large, open room.

Austin led the way to a table with a frost-white tablecloth, a silver napkin holder, and a bottle of Tabasco sauce. It stood next to one of the front windows. "Is this all right with y'all?"

Catherine nodded.

The dark-haired waitress, resembling a nurse in her white uniform, sported a "poodle cut" and eyeglasses sparkling with rhinestones. "What y'all havin' today, *cher*?" She pronounced the southern endearment like Coley did. Popping her chewing gum loudly, she smiled at Austin while she talked.

Austin noticed her name tag said "Dippy," then smiling, glanced down at his menu.

"How 'bout a little bit gumbo to start wit?" The waitress continued her impromptu commercial. "It some good! Make you tongue t'ink it died and went to heaven, yeah."

"That's exactly what I want," Jessie replied eagerly. "Only I want more than a 'little bit.' "

"You gonna be happy, you, when you finish de bowl gumbo I bring out."

Austin had bacon and eggs and Catherine contented herself with coffee.

"So, how's school?" Jessie took out a small gold compact, touching up her makeup while she talked.

"Pre-law," Austin remarked dully. "It's kind of like eating a dry cake with no icing."

Jessie snapped her compact closed and dropped it into her purse. "Why not go into something else, then?"

"I'm trying to keep peace at home." Austin thought of the scene with his parents when he told them he wanted to go to school in Baton Rouge. "My mother insisted that I go to Harvard Law School, so we compromised. Law school it is, but at LSU."

"You have any plans yet, Jess?" Catherine glanced in the direction of the bar where the men talked about their latest conquests and drank whiskey from shot glasses, chased with frozen schooners of beer.

"I'd like to get into the record business," Jessie said without hesitation. "I'd never make it as an actress, but then, all I'd have to do on records is sing."

Secretly hoping that Jessie would have been satisfied with getting a degree in music, Catherine felt a twinge of anxiety. "I think you probably need some contacts for that, even if you do have a good voice."

"I'll bet you made some out in Hollywood," Austin chimed in. "You're not holding out on us, are you, Jess?"

"No. I might have if I'd stayed a little longer—but I was ready to get out of *that* town."

The waitress returned with their food, setting the plates down with a clatter, glasses tinkling and tilting precariously on her heavy tray.

Jessie savored the smell of the gumbo—big white chunks of chicken floating in a thick, rich, spicy broth. She dumped the separate bowl of fluffy rice into it, stirring it in well, then, using the outsized spoon, took her first big bite. "Hmmm! You can't get food like this anywhere else in the country."

As Austin ate, enjoying Jessie's company after her long absence, he noticed a man with dark, oily hair held in place by a red bandanna worn Indian-fashion detach himself from the group at the bar and walk over to a slot machine that stood against the wall three tables from where they sat. In his mid-thirties, he wore greasy jeans and a fatigue jacket with the sleeves cut off. Beneath the word "T-Beaux," a tattoo of the traditional "Grim Reaper" figure complete with long robe and scythe decorated his right bicep.

Jessie looked up from her gumbo to speak to Catherine when she noticed the man leering at her over his shoulder. She quickly darted her eyes away.

Seeing her reaction, Catherine glanced around at the man. "Ignore him. He's probably drunk."

T-Beaux thumbed a quarter into the slot machine, jerked on the handle, and watched the three wheels spinning colorfully behind their tiny glass windows. "T-Beaux ain't drunk, no. But he gonna get dat way befo' de noon whistle she sound over to de refin'ry."

Catherine put her hand to her mouth, her eyes wide with alarm.

Austin shrugged it off, motioning with his hands for her to forget about it.

"Sure will be good to see the kids again," Jessie said in a shaky voice, glancing again at T-Beaux. "I didn't think I'd miss them as much as I did."

"I'm certainly glad to hear you say that," Catherine joined in. "You can spend all the time you want hauling them around while I work."

Jessie smiled, thinking of Sharon and her brothers. "I think it'll be fun again, for—"

"Hey, little girl! You got chirren, you?" T-Beaux's gravelly voice boomed across at them.

Jessie gasped, her hand to her breast, as she stared at him turning around to face her.

"Don't be afraid, little girl. T-Beaux got nuttin' but good t'ings in mind for you." The man started across the three-table space that separated them.

Austin felt a spark behind his eyes, but determined that he would not let the anger flame up in him. Almost unconsciously Austin sized up the man who called himself T-Beaux as he walked toward them. The first thing he noticed was the way he flexed his hand, carrying the right arm a little higher than the left. That big looping right was probably his main and perhaps *only* real weapon. It was with a sense of relief that he saw how heavily the man moved, his big boots scraping along the floor in a shuffle, the feet slewed outward at a forty-five degree angle.

"You fine as wine, little girl." T-Beaux pulled at his chin whiskers, then stared down at Catherine. "Yo' sister ain't half bad either. Purtiest blue eyes in St. John Parish, I gar-roan-tee."

"She's not my sister. She's my—"

"It's all right, Jess."

T-Beaux glared down at Austin. "You mighty rude, you. Interrupting like dat."

Austin smiled up pleasantly.

Taken a little off balance by Austin's reaction, T-Beaux retaliated. "What'd you win that letter jacket for, sweetheart? Playing jacks?"

Austin's eyes danced with light. *Do good to them that spitefully use you.* The scripture that Austin had read only the day before flashed across his mind. He took a deep breath, replying calmly, "No, actually it's for chess. I usually don't go in for anything as strenuous as jacks."

"Dat's good," T-Beaux smirked. "You ain't got no use for deese girls den. Hey, Savoy! Come over here, you."

A dumpy little man with a hooked nose and one eyetooth missing climbed down from a stool at the bar, walking a little unsteadily over to the table.

Austin didn't give him a second look.

"Deese ladies t'ink you and me de best lookin' men in Sout' Louisiana."

"Dey smart, yeah."

Austin felt himself coming to the end of his capacity for doing good to a guy like T-Beaux. He stood up, his eyes glinting with a cold gray light. "I enjoy having a good time as much as anybody, but—"

"You ain't never pass a good time in yo' life, little boy," T-Beaux interrupted.

Austin fought to keep his temper under control, "—you're upsetting the ladies, so I'll have to ask you to leave."

Savoy thought Austin's request uproariously funny.

"Axe all you want," T-Beaux grinned at Savoy. "Don't bother me none."

"Me neither," Savoy agreed, his words hissing through the space where his eyetooth used to be.

The men at the bar were enjoying the show, making odds on how much longer Austin would remain conscious. On the other side of the room, behind the counter, Dippy, nervously adjusting her rhinestone glasses, held the telephone to her ear, nodding her head and staring at T-Beaux as she spoke.

"Let's just leave, Austin."

"Okay." So far the men had used no profanity and hadn't touched Catherine or Jessie. Unknown to them, these were Austin's unspoken rules for allowing them to continue with their fun. He suddenly realized that being the butt of their jokes didn't seem to bother him very much.

"Leave?" T-Beaux shook his head slowly, an expression of mock bewilderment on his face. "You tell anybody they could leave, Savoy?"

"I ain't said nuttin', me."

"Fun's over, boys—you win. We're going home now." Austin thought it ironic that he had fought so many times over so many insignificant matters and now that he had a reason that any rational man would consider valid, he was walking away. But it was not to be.

A split second after T-Beaux placed his grimy, calloused hand on Catherine's shoulder, his breath left him in a great *whooshing* outrush.

Austin took Catherine by the hand, leading her away from the table and ushering her and Jessie over toward the counter at the front of the restaurant.

T-Beaux hunkered down on his knees, spluttering for breath, his right hand on the floor for balance and the left across the pit of his stomach where Austin had buried his left fist.

The men at the bar began fishing out their wallets, paying off the only man who had bet on Austin.

"How come you know he could do dat to T-Beaux," one of the roughnecks wearing a grease-stained Levi's jacket asked as he counted out the bills, slapping them down on the bar.

The big winner, a wiry little man with a black handlebar mustache and a leathery face, smiled impishly. "I seen his pitcher in de paper, me."

"So?" his friend shrugged.

"When he won de state boxing championship over in Lafayette. You oughta read more, you."

T-Beaux gasped a few more times, then took a deep breath. His face ashen, he knelt on the floor, squinting over at Austin, sizing him up for the first time.

Austin sat down in a chair ten feet away, crossing his legs and leaning forward on both elbows as he gazed directly into T-Beaux's dark eyes.

"I ain't never been hit dat fast, no," T-Beaux muttered. "I been hit harder—but not dat fast."

Austin continued to stare at the man, beginning to like him for some strange reason.

"I could take you, me."

"I know you could," Austin grinned, glancing at the man's bulging biceps and the ridged muscle across his shoulders and broad back.

T-Beaux grinned. "But it would take me a long time, yeah."

"I know that too."

T-Beaux stood up, pulled a chair over, and sat down. He rubbed the hard stubble on his chin. "And I t'ink maybe my girlfriend don't know who dis face belong to when we get finish."

"Maybe."

T-Beaux threw his head back and laughed. "You okay. I t'ink you make a good Cajun, you."

Austin knew it was over then.

"C'mon over here. I buy you a drink, me."

Austin shook his head, glancing over at Catherine and Jessie. He saw a deputy with a huge belly hanging over his gun belt and a nightstick gripped in both pudgy hands talking with Dippy. She nodded her head, both hands out in supplication. The deputy glanced at T-Beaux, slipped the nightstick into his belt, and left.

"Thanks, but we really have to go."

T-Beaux shrugged and walked heavily back to the bar and into a storm of good-natured insults from his friends.

★ ★ ★

With its red-tiled roof and graceful arches, Foster Hall reflected the original Mediterranean look of the early LSU Campus of the 1920s. Austin sat on a concrete bench under the colonnade that ran the entire length of the building. He watched the January rain and the leaves of the live oaks turning black-green, glistening in the tin-colored light. Students laden with books, their umbrellas shuddering in the occasional gusts of wind, plodded along toward their eleven o'clock classes.

On the far end of the colonnade Jessie stepped out of the downpour, closed her umbrella and shook the water off. Wearing her tan raincoat over a brown sweater with matching scarf and a full skirt, she stared down at her mud-spattered saddle oxfords. "What a day to meet Austin. Welcome back to South

Louisiana, Jessie," she said out loud to the geyser of water pouring off the gutter of the building.

Jessie walked along under the lofty arches and the high, heavy drumming noise of the rain toward Austin, wearing his usual jeans and letter jacket as he glanced through the newspaper. She knew the clothes, especially the jacket, identified him as blue collar North Baton Rouge and had come to believe that he wore them as a sort of penance or perhaps rebellion—she couldn't quite decide which—for being born into money.

"I wouldn't get out in this kind of weather for just anybody, you know."

Austin glanced up from his newspaper. "Just testing you. I knew this was going to happen."

Jessie smiled. She had seen a softer light in Austin's gray eyes since she had gotten back from California and his ways had gentled to the point where she no longer noticed the mild anxiety that she used to feel whenever she was around him. When she was with him now she felt safe almost the way she felt when, as a child, her father would take her up in his arms when she hurt herself playing.

Thinking about the incident at the Airline Restaurant, Jessie realized that Austin would be willing to stand against anyone or anything that threatened to harm her. Even on this chilly, rainy January day she felt safe and warm and secure being with him. She determined in that ordinary moment that this was something to cherish. "Anything interesting in the news?"

"That scarf just matches your eyes," Austin said, staring at Jessie as though seeing her for the first time.

Jessie laughed softly, tossing her head, the fine blond hair flashing with light. "That's the idea, college boy. I'm glad you noticed. I don't think most men would."

Austin forced his gaze away from Jessie's eyes with their long curving lashes. "Now for the latest breaking news," Austin continued in a flat radio announcer's voice, popping the newspaper open at arms' length.

Jessie sat beside him, noticing that his hair hadn't reached its full growth after the head-shaving tradition all freshmen had to submit to.

"Somebody gave Richard Nixon a cocker spaniel puppy and Trisha, his six-year-old, named it Checkers," Austin peered at Jessie over the top of the newspaper. "Now, that's a shocker! I'm surprised they'd put something like that in a family publication."

Jessie spoke dryly, "Austin, maybe you should leave the humor to Bob Hope. Anything else?"

Austin turned the pages. "I see that movie you've been waiting for is playing at the Paramount this weekend."

"You mean *A Place in the Sun*? Oh, Austin, let's go. It's supposed to be a wonderful film."

"Film? Maybe we should wait until they develop it. It'll be a whole lot easier to recognize the actors." Austin hid his face behind the newspaper.

"That's what it's called in the business, silly." Jessie pushed the newspaper down. "Oh, you know very well what I meant. Picture show, then—is that better?"

"Much better. Now you sound like a real Mississippi redneck," Austin laughed. "And you're not fooling me with that 'wonderful film' business either. You want to see it because you think Montgomery Clift's eyes are 'so dreamy.'"

"Well, that too," Jessie admitted, standing to her feet. "Now, are you going to feed me or not?"

Without answering, Austin stood, pulled Jessie to

him, his arm around her shoulder, and opening the umbrella led her down to the end of the colonnade and out into the rain. Turning left, they walked down a set of steps with rounded iron railings, across a concrete area peppered with raindrops, and into the basement beneath Foster Hall.

Inside, the warmth hit them like a soft wave. Water and steam pipes running along the ceiling and walls gave the coffee shop the appearance of a converted boiler room, which it may have been. Jessie found a booth for them while Austin went through the serving line, returning in a few minutes with po-boys and bottles of Coke on a battered tray.

"What am I having?"

"Don't worry—you'll like it." Austin opened a bottle of Tabasco, shaking some onto the fried oysters inside the crusty, chewy French bread of his po-boy.

Jessie opened her sandwich, heavy with fried shrimp, mayonnaise, sliced tomatoes, and lettuce. "I think that Tabasco's a little too hot for me."

His mouth full of food, Austin handed her the Louisiana Hot Sauce.

Jessie added a few drops and took a big bite of the po-boy. The shrimp were lightly battered, crispy on the outside and tender and succulent inside. She chewed happily, gazing across the table at Austin.

"Hi, Austin, I haven't heard from you in months." A slim girl of about nineteen with long, dark hair and obsidian eyes stood next to the booth, smiling down at Austin. Her black sweater made her skin appear even paler than it was. She supported a mound of books with both arms.

"Mbfff," Austin mumbled through a huge mouthful of food. He glanced at Jessie, saw her eyebrows raise a quarter of an inch, and held his hand up to the girl asking her patience while he finished chewing.

The girl smiled sweetly at Jessie, then turned her gaze back on Austin, watching him desperately try to swallow his food.

Austin cleared his throat. "Hi, Seritta. Uh, this is Jessie Temple. Jessie, this is Seritta—I'm sorry, I've forgotten your last name."

"Caldoni."

Austin grinned sheepishly at Jessie. "Caldoni."

"Nice to meet you," Seritta cooed, resting her books on the table as she held her hand out limply to Jessie.

Jessie took the proffered hand. "You too, Seritta."

"Austin's told me all about you, Jessie," Seritta went on in her throaty voice. "How you went out to Hollywood and on that USO tour to Korea and everything, and what a good voice you've got. I feel almost like I know you."

"I'm afraid you have me at a disadvantage then, Seritta," Jessie said evenly, nodding to the girl with a forced smile, then turning on Austin. The smile didn't make it up to her blue eyes. "Austin never mentioned *you* at all."

Seritta frowned at Austin. "You bad ol' thing. After all those nights on the lake."

"*One* night, Seritta!" Austin shot back quickly. "It was only *one* night!"

"Well, I've got to run now." Seritta winked at Austin. "Nice meeting you, Jessie."

Jessie glared at Seritta's back as she sashayed across the coffee shop to a table full of football players.

Austin picked up his po-boy, holding it in front of him as though it would shield him from Jessie's flashing blue eyes. "One night, Jess. It was only *one* night."

"What makes you think I *care* if it was *one* night or a *hundred* and one nights?"

"Besides, she's strange. Reads Jack Kerouac." Austin shrugged and took a big bite of his sandwich.

"Seritta?" Jessie stared coldly at him. "Is that really her name?"

"Mbfff." Austin held his hand out again until he finished chewing and swallowing. "I think so. I only saw her that one time. It was during rush week and we met at this party and decided to go for a drive and—well, we just ended up parking out by the University Lake and—"

"I'm not interested in the sordid details of your life while I was away, Austin."

"Sordid? Nothing happened at all. We just—"

"Austin!" Jessie cut him off. "I'd rather not discuss it, if you don't mind. I didn't expect you to be a cloistered monk while I was away, but Seritta? My goodness, couldn't you have at least picked a Jane or a Mary?"

"Yeah, well I bet you went out with some of those Hollywood hotshots while you were out there, didn't you?" Austin tore a big bite of his sandwich off with his teeth, chewing furiously.

"That's different."

"Mbfff." Austin glared at Jessie until he had swallowed enough to talk. "Different? What's different about it?"

"You wouldn't understand."

Austin's voice raised an octave. "Try me, Miss Silver Screen 1952."

"It's just part of the business," Jessie explained in her most practiced sophisticated manner. "You know, being seen with the right people in all the right places."

264

"People like Tony Vale."

"How'd you know that?"

"Somebody showed me a *Photoplay* magazine. I could barely make you out, but it was you, all right. I didn't recognize the dress you *almost* had on though."

Jessie went on the defensive. "There's nothing wrong with that dress—or with Tony."

Austin replied smugly. "Not if you're a divorce lawyer, there isn't. I'll bet they all just *love* him."

Jessie stared at Austin's face, a faint grin coming to her lips, then laughed softly.

"What's wrong?"

Putting her hand to her mouth, Jessie stopped laughing. "That red sauce. It's smeared up your cheeks from the corners of your mouth. Makes you look like Emmett Kelley."

"Who?"

"Emmett Kelley. You know, that clown with the Barnum and Bailey Circus."

Austin touched his mouth with his fingers, then smiled at Jessie. "I bet I do at that."

"Nothing happened with Tony either, Austin."

"I knew that." Austin bit into the po-boy again, determined this time to finish before he tried to talk.

SIXTEEN

LANCELOT

★ ★ ★

Standing in the sun-dappled glade, the whitetail, a ten-point buck, gazed at Austin with his big liquid brown eyes. A fox squirrel, its legs splayed out against the trunk of a towering red oak, stared down fearfully at a bobcat lurking below him in the shadows of a canebrake.

"I love this place." Austin gazed through the plate glass protecting the *Louisiana Upland Forest* diorama in Foster Hall above the coffee shop where they had just eaten. "Makes me feel like I'm really out in the woods."

Jessie surveyed the peaceful scene. "Daddy took me squirrel hunting one time when I was eight years old—just a few months before he went in the Marines. Dalton wanted to go with us, but he was only three at the time. I remember he pitched a fit because Mama made him stay home."

Austin could tell that Jessie's concern for her father never left her for very long at a time.

"I wasn't really crazy about the idea. You know, killing and all that rugged outdoor stuff," Jessie continued, her eyes staring back through the years. "But once we got out in the woods, it was just beautiful."

Jessie's voice, even in speech, was like a soothing balm to Austin. He felt that he would never tire of the sound of it and her singing always made him feel weak in the knees, although he had never told her so.

"I remember we walked along the river and there was a mist on the water, and for some reason, I can still remember a rooster crowing way off in the distance. Strange, the things that stick in our minds, isn't it?" Jessie walked down the hall where it turned, then turned again in the U-shaped diorama area of the building. The entire bottom of the U was dedicated to an exhibit of the Louisiana coastal marshes.

Austin caught up with her. "Well?"

"Well what?"

"What about the rest of the hunting trip?" he asked in an agitated tone of voice.

"That's it," Jessie responded absently. "I told you how pretty everything was and about the rooster."

"Well, what about the *hunting*?" A vein at Austin's temple bulged slightly. "That's why you went, wasn't it? You said you went on a *hunting* trip."

"Oh, I don't want to talk about that part," Jessie declared bluntly. "I didn't like it."

Austin rolled his eyes back in his head. "A hunting story with no hunting in it!"

"Makes perfect sense to me." The hunting forgotten, Jessie continued on to the end of the hall, gazing at the blue-green expanse of the Gulf Coast and the variety of waterfowl and shore birds in various stages of flying and feeding. One mallard swam head down with his feathery tail pointed to the sky as he sought his breakfast in a marshland pool. "Now, this is where I'd like to go. I bet you can just see forever."

Strolling over to the exhibit where Jessie stood, Austin tried to put the huntless hunting story out of his mind. "I think that's over in Cameron Parish. Maybe I'll take you there sometime. Then we can tell everybody back home about the birds we saw in the marsh, but we'll leave all the birds out of the story."

Jessie turned slowly around, facing Austin, her eyes narrowed, right arm akimbo.

"Okay, I take it back," Austin relented. "We won't leave *all* the birds out of the story—we'll put in one rooster."

Jessie's frown softened into a smile. She stepped close to Austin, her face uptilted, offering him a kiss.

Austin took her up on the offer.

A few seconds later, the sound of footsteps echoed through the corridors. Jessie pulled away, brushing her hair back from her slightly flushed face.

"Well, so you're going to register for the School of Music in the summer," Austin breathed thickly, trying to sound casual and controlled.

Jessie glanced at the little bald-headed man in his rumpled gray suit as he walked briskly past them on his way back to the Zoology Department. "I've told you once, *whoever* you are," she replied, in a voice louder than conversation level. "I *don't* want to talk to you!"

The little man stopped, turning his birdlike face toward Jessie. "Is this young man bothering you?"

Jessie glanced at Austin, then smiled at the professor. "I'm sure it'll be all right now, thank you."

"Are you *quite* sure?"

"Oh yes. He's harmless."

The man stared suspiciously at Austin.

Austin, his face glowing, turned and walked down to the opposite end of the diorama, staring intently at a blue heron in graceful flight.

"Well, I'm right down the hall if you need anything."

"Thank you so much."

The man turned and continued on his brisk way, glancing back once more at Austin.

As soon as Jessie heard the man's office door close, she burst into laughter.

Austin plodded deliberately over to her. "You think that's funny?"

"I think—I think it's—hilarious," Jessie replied between spasms of laughter.

Austin smiled weakly, then chuckled softly. "I guess you're right. You had that little fellow all fired up. He would have taken me on in a second."

"I wish you could have seen your face!" Jessie tried to suppress another fit of laughter.

"I'm glad you're having such a good time today, Jess," Austin muttered. "Anything else I can do for you? Would you like to throw a pie in my face or something?"

Jessie wiped tears of laughter from her eyes. "Sorry. I just couldn't stop. I'm okay now."

"Good. I thought I was going to have to take you over to the infirmary for a minute there." Austin's tone became more solemn. "You *are* going to enroll in school out here in the summer, aren't you?"

Looking away at the flight of the coastal birds, Jessie spoke halfheartedly. "Maybe."

Austin stepped around in front of her. "What do you mean *maybe*? I thought it was all set—we were going to go to college together."

Jessie gazed directly into Austin's eyes. "I want to

be a singer. Hollywood's not the place for me—I know that now. But there are *other* places I can sing."

"Like where?"

"Places I can get a start in the business, work my way up to a record contract maybe."

"You didn't answer my question."

"Nightclubs!" Jessie blurted out. "Now—I've told you! Are you happy?"

"Nightclubs! Are you nuts?" Austin's voice grew louder. "Your mother would *never* let you do that!"

"I'm almost nineteen. It's my decision." Jessie spoke calmly, her arms crossed stubbornly over her breast.

At the sound of Austin's voice, rising almost to a shout, the little man in the rumpled suit appeared at the end of his dimly lighted hallway. "Would you like me to call campus security for you, miss?"

Austin raised his arms to the ceiling. "Aw, great! Lancelot's back to save the queen!"

"Hush, Austin!" Jessie turned to the little man. "No, everything's all right." She held her hands out toward him in supplication.

"Maybe I'd better stay here and keep an eye on your friend over there, just the same." Glaring at Austin, the little man crossed his arms over his narrow chest.

"I've had about enough of this! A man can't even look at a duck in peace around here!" Austin spun around and stormed down the hall.

Jessie shrugged at her diminutive bodyguard and hurried after Austin.

Leaving the Natural History Museum, Austin walked along the colonnade and sat back down on the bench where he had waited for Jessie. The wind had died and the slow, chill rain covered the campus like a gray curtain. Austin glanced at his watch, thinking of the wet run he would have to make over to Himes Hall for his one o'clock American History class.

Jessie walked over and sat down next to him. "What's so bad about singing in nightclubs?"

Austin took her by the hand. "You've only been home a week. Why don't you think about this for a while?"

Jessie glanced at her little defender from the museum as he left the building under a black umbrella, trudging down a sidewalk toward the quadrangle. "I have, and I'm singing Friday night at the Pastime."

Austin shook his head sadly. "I don't think you really want to do this, Jess."

"A *lot* of singers got started this same way," Jessie insisted. "Tony for one. Besides, there's a good chance I might get to sing at the Blue Room in New Orleans. Some of the biggest names in the country perform down there."

"It's your life, Jess," Austin admitted reluctantly. "I just think you're heading down the wrong path."

Jessie took Austin's face in her hands, her eyes wide and her soft voice on the verge of a plea. "I don't want this or anything else to come between us."

"It won't—nothing will." Austin took her hands in his, giving her a quick kiss on the mouth. "Except for my class that I have about two minutes to get to."

Handing Austin her umbrella, Jessie pulled him up from the bench. "C'mon, I'll walk with you."

★ ★ ★

Pabst and Dixie Beer signs glowed dimly through the blue-white haze of smoke hanging in the stale air. Crew-cut college boys in jeans bought mugs of draught beer for their dates, who wore fashionable full skirts and saddle oxfords; college professors, businessmen, and lawyers—ties loosened, briefcases left in their cars—sat at the rough wooden tables next to construction workers whose ball caps and hard hats hung on the backs of their chairs. More people jammed the doors leading from the outside and the bar, trying to get a seat for the ten o'clock performance.

Kay Starr's plaintive version of "Wheel of Fortune," blaring from the jukebox beneath the blue neon *Restrooms* sign, made little headway against the heavy drone of five dozen conversations interspersed with random and raucous laughter.

On the small stage built into a corner of the large room, a heavyset balding man with a face like well-formed biscuit dough adjusted the chrome microphone. Behind him a slim man with greasy dark hair sat behind his full complement of drums. A piano, guitar, and saxophone rounded out the unwholesome-looking ensemble.

Austin, wearing tan slacks and a navy sport jacket, sat alone at a two-chair table in the corner on the opposite side of the room from the band. A bottle of Coke and a small glass of ice sat before him next to glass salt and pepper shakers, an ashtray, and a half-full bottle of Heinz ketchup.

"Mind if I join you?" The boy was about Austin's age, tall, slim, with flaming red hair and a face full of freckles. He tucked in the tail of his white dress shirt, stained down the front with spilled beer, and stuck out his hand. "My name's Greg Crosby."

Austin shook his hand, noticing that the place was packed. "Help yourself."

Crosby plopped down in the chair, poured his Jax beer, cold and frothy, into a glass identical to Austin's, and took a long swallow. "Boy, that's good."

Austin frowned at the heady smell of the beer, feeling almost stifled by the heavy pall of cigarette smoke, growing even thicker as the evening wore on. *How can people stand these places?* Then he remembered the times past when places like these had seemed so enticing to him.

"You don't like beer?" Crosby turned his head to the side and belched loudly.

Austin took a sip of his Coke. "Not particularly, but don't let that bother you."

"Oh, don't worry. I won't," Crosby mumbled, taking another long swallow.

Somehow I didn't think you would. Austin felt that he may have been too hasty with his hospitality. *Well, at least he's not smoking.*

"I'll tell you one thing you'll like for sure though." Crosby belched again.

"What's that?"

"Jessie Temple's singing."

"She's good, huh?"

"Man, she's the greatest." Crosby took a pack of Lucky Strikes and a book of matches out of the inside pocket of his seersucker jacket. After three tries he managed to get a crumpled cigarette lit, then promptly broke into a coughing fit.

"Are you okay?"

Crosby held his hand palm outward toward Austin, coughed twice more and wheezed, "Fine. I'm just fine."

"Maybe you should quit smoking."

Crosby gave the people around him a conspiratorial glance. "I probably should, but there's a plan behind the madness. Women love it."

Austin thought he surely must be joking at first,

then realized he was dead serious. "They do?"

"Sure." Crosby seemed appalled at Austin's na-
iveté. "Haven't you seen those Humphrey Bogart movies—the way he handles a cigarette? That's why the
women are nuts about him."

"Oh."

"Anyway, like I was saying, you're in for a real treat
with this Temple dish tonight," Crosby continued.
"Did you catch her show last Friday?"

"No. I missed it."

"Well I didn't," Crosby said, pursing his lips, his
head nodding for no apparent reason. "There wudn't
too many people here then, but the word's out now.
That's why this place is packed to the rafters."

"You know a lot about the music business."

"Well I don't like to brag, but . . ." Crosby tried to
blink away the tears caused by the trail of smoke rising from his cigarette. No matter where he held it, the
smoke seemed to drift directly into his eyes. Finally
he gave up and stubbed it out in the ashtray. "I do
know a thing or two about it. I even gave this little
Temple nightingale some help."

"You did?"

"Oh, yeah," Crosby assured Austin. "Breath control, diction, you know. 'Course, I've known her a long
time."

Austin found himself intrigued as well as sad-
dened by Crosby's apparent alienation from the truth
and perhaps from reality itself. "You have?"

"Sure," Crosby continued his story as though from
actual memories. "We go way back. Our families used
to go on vacation together when we were kids. Jessie's
had a crush on me since the first grade."

Austin gazed out over the crowd, wondering how
many of them were as desperately lonely as Greg

Crosby. He suddenly felt a surge of pity for Crosby and was about to tell him there was a better way to live when the jukebox suddenly shut down.

"And now ladies and gentlemen, here's the reason only half of you could find a seat tonight and the rest of you don't mind standing up—Miss Jessie Temple."

A pale blue spotlight found Jessie and followed her as she threaded her way through the crowd to enthusiastic applause. Wearing a white, form-fitting satin gown, she stepped over to the microphone, smiled and, with no cute remarks for her audience, began to sing.

"Because of you there's a song in my heart . . ."

A hush bordering on reverence swept over the crowd. Austin stared at the people nearest him under the spell of Jessie's voice. Then he noticed the rapt expression on Crosby's face. It seemed somehow quiet and relaxed, the tension drained out of it, his eyes now serene. *She's got something, all right. Something that doesn't come along very often.*

Jessie sang eight more numbers and finally had to beg off after two encores of "Hello, Young Lovers."

As she left the stage, the emcee walked over to the microphone, holding his hands up for quiet. "Now I want all of you to promise me one thing. Don't let RCA or Capitol Records find out about Jessie or they'll come down here and take her away from us. That's our show for tonight, folks."

In the mild clamor and controlled thronging of her fans, Jessie made it over to the table where Austin waited for her with Greg Crosby.

Austin watched Crosby's face go slack with defeat as Jessie came closer to them and he finally realized that he was going to have to confront her.

Jessie kissed Austin on the cheek as he stood up to

greet her. "Well, how'd you like it?"

Austin rubbed his chin with thumb and forefinger, a pensive look on his face. "Well, you're no Tennessee Ernie Ford, but it wasn't too bad."

"I should have known better than to expect a sensible answer out of you," Jessie scolded, making a small fist with her slim fingers and hitting Austin on the shoulder.

Crosby eased out of his chair, stood up quietly, and turned around to leave.

"Jess, I want you to meet your number one fan." Austin took Crosby by the arm before he could take his first step. "Greg Crosby. Greg, this is Jessie Temple."

Crosby turned to face Jessie, a stunned expression on his face when he realized that Austin had no intention of humiliating him. "Hi," he said weakly.

"Hello, Greg," Jessie smiled, taking his hand. "It's nice to know *some* people"—she glanced toward Austin in mock reproof— "appreciate my singing."

"Oh, I really do think you're the *best* singer I've ever heard," Crosby beamed, "and that includes Rosemary Clooney and Jo Stafford."

"You've got me in pretty good company, Greg," Jessie replied, noticing Crosby's disheveled appearance. "Maybe someday I'll sell as many records as they have."

Crosby merely nodded, captivated by the sound of Jessie's voice.

Jessie turned to Austin. "We'd better go. I don't want to be out too late."

"Okay. Greg, it was nice meeting you tonight." Austin shook hands, unable to shake off the unassailable pathos he felt when he looked into Crosby's sad, rheumy eyes.

"My pleasure for sure." Crosby stood up a little straighter, holding on to the back of the chair to balance himself. "I'll be waiting to buy your first single and I just know there'll be an album after that, Miss Temple."

"Jessie, please."

"Jessie." Crosby beamed again.

★ ★ ★

The street lamps winked through the limbs of the live oak trees as Austin drove down Park Boulevard toward City Park and the university. They passed in front of a massive Tudor home. Flanked by ancient magnolias, it rose cold and stony and remote beyond its low brick wall. Farther along, a Victorian mansion, with Corinthian columns arcing gracefully along its curved front porch, stood among flower beds, newly weeded, the earth turned in preparation for spring planting.

Spinning along Dalrymple, Austin gazed out across City Park Lake, its surface gleaming in the pale moonlight. As he turned left on Lakeshore where it formed a landbridge between City Park and University Lakes, a cloud, its edges nimbused with light, drifted across the moon.

A few blocks farther on, Austin pulled off near the walking path across the street from his house.

"Why're we stopping here?"

Reaching into the backseat for his leather jacket, Austin got out of the car, walked around to Jessie's side, and opened her door. "It's a nice night. We can just sit and talk awhile, and look at the lake."

Jessie stepped out of the car and let Austin drape his jacket around her shoulders. Then she glanced down at her fragile dress. "Sit, in this?"

Austin held a forefinger up beside his face. "Not to worry." He stepped behind the car, opened the trunk, and took out a director's chair.

"You think of everything," Jessie smiled.

Austin unfolded the chair, placing it next to the lake beneath a willow tree. Bowing, he offered the chair to Jessie as though it were her throne. "Madam."

"Thank you, noble sir." A little awkward in her heels, Jessie walked across the grassy bank, sat down in the chair, and gazed out across the lake.

Austin sat down at the base of the tree, leaning back against its rough bark. He took a deep breath. "You certain this is what you want out of life, Jess?"

"I don't know for sure," Jessie answered somberly. "The view's nice, but I think just sitting here would get awfully boring after a few years."

"That's pretty funny." Austin quickly squatted behind Jessie, grabbed the back of the chair, and began a steady pull, tilting it backward on two legs.

"Wait! You'll make me fall!" Jessie tried to scramble out, but the angle of the chair was too great.

Austin now supported Jessie's weight in the chair, her legs flailing as she tried to get out. "I always react to bad jokes like this, Jess. Can't seem to help myself."

"Stop! I'll get my dress dirty."

Austin leaned forward, his face only inches from Jessie's as she lay back almost parallel to the ground. "Give us a kiss and I might let you up."

Feeling herself in no danger of falling now, Jessie relaxed. "Oh, all right."

Feeling the touch of Jessie's lips against his, Austin lost himself in the softness and warmth of her kiss. It had always escaped him how so simple a thing as a kiss could hold such mystery, such promise, and give him such pleasure. Having known others, before and after Jessie, he realized that it went far beyond the mere physical act of touching and had come to believe that it was something that he may never find again.

"That was nice." Jessie's voice was as soft as the night breeze stirring the reeds at the edge of the lake.

Austin tilted her chair forward, then sat back down again under the willow, stretching his legs out on the cool damp grass. "I think *nice* is something of an understatement."

After a few moments of silence, Jessie remarked casually, "I got an offer to appear at the Blue Room."

Austin stared out at the dappling of headlights shining on the lake's surface as the traffic moved along Dalrymple. "When did you find out about it?"

"Just tonight. They sent someone up to hear me sing."

"Kind of quick, wasn't it?" Austin glanced over at Jessie's face, almost luminescent in the pale light.

"Well, I told you I'd talked to them before. They'd already heard about me winning the national USO contest and going on that tour with Bob Hope's troupe. They know he won't take just *anybody*."

"You gonna take the offer?"

"I'd be silly not to," Jessie replied quickly. "They're putting me on the same bill with Joni James."

Austin leaned back, watching the winking light of a lone airplane move slowly across the purple dome of the sky.

"Anything wrong with that?"

"I don't like all those guys gawking at you," Austin answered flatly.

"They gawked at me when I sang in church."

"I don't think you had a bunch of drunks sitting out there in church watching you sing."

"Oh, sober gawkers are all right, then."

"You know what I'm talking about, Jessie." Even though Jessie's pale hair, big brown eyes, and trim figure gave her a striking appearance on stage, Austin knew it was her voice that drew the customers back. "I think it's just the places you sing in with all the booze, and cigarette smoke so thick you need fog lights to find your table."

Jessie spoke the next words without thinking. "You used to not mind those places." The response she got from Austin was not what she had expected.

Austin gave her a thoughtful stare. "You're absolutely right about that."

"Well . . ."

"Well, I'm a different person now."

Jessie had seen a change in Austin before she had left for Hollywood and it was more pronounced since she had come home. It was as though a kind of nameless serenity had replaced much of the restlessness that had previously marked him. She had never questioned him about it, somehow almost afraid of what he would tell her, as though he had gone someplace where she would not be allowed to follow. "Different—how?"

"Almost a year ago now something happened right here where we're sitting. Maybe that's why I wanted to bring you out here tonight."

Feeling a slight chill at the back of her neck, Jessie reached over and took Austin's hand.

Austin's eyes softened and the corners of his mouth lifted slightly as he began to speak. "Well, there's this older couple, Tom and Sarah Edmonson. I've been watching them walk along the lake here for years. It was almost dark. . . ."

Jessie's eyes grew bright with tears as she listened to Austin's story. She pressed his hand tightly with her own, as though by holding on to him she could also grasp the marvelous gift that he had been given.

When Austin had finished he realized that Jessie was the first person he had ever told his story to. A feeling like warm oil flowing through his veins swept gently over him. He felt almost giddy, as though his smile was too big for his face.

Jessie took the handkerchief Austin offered her, wiping the tears from her eyes. While Austin spoke, the memory of that terrible Christmas Eve of more than a year before had lurked in the dim recesses of her mind. Unable to block it out, she now felt that she needed to talk to Austin about it. "Do you still think about Ellis and Janie much?"

Austin's eyes grew dark with sadness. "Yes."

"I've had so many nightmares, I've lost count."

"I did too, Jess—for a long time," Austin confessed. "But now I've got a peace that I really don't understand. Oh, I still miss them both—I guess I always will. I just wish I'd realized what a good friend Ellis was before he got killed."

Jessie felt a sudden frightening chill as though something hard and scaly had brushed against her soul. Standing up, unmindful of her white gown, she sat down in Austin's lap. Laying her head against his shoulder, she took his hand in both of hers. She felt comfortable and warm, and safe from the memories and dreams that waited for her when she was alone in the dark. Then she began to sob.

SEVENTEEN

BILLY

★ ★ ★

Torn between the dread of seeing what the war had done to Lane and her almost overwhelming longing to be with him again, Catherine stood on the station platform peering both ways, trying to find him in the throng of passengers leaving the train. Suddenly she caught a glimpse of him in his green uniform beyond a dolly piled high with luggage. Carrying a musette bag over his shoulder, he stepped carefully down from the Pullman, stumbled, and grabbed the rail to keep his balance. She felt a quick pang of sorrow mixed with her joy when she saw how thin he looked.

Catherine had worn her blue dress with the white lace trim at throat and bodice. It had been Lane's favorite since the day she bought it. Her eyes bright with tears, she walked hurriedly, then ran to welcome her husband home from another war. "Lane. . . . Oh, Lane! Thank God you're safe!"

Catherine saw Lane glance around as she rushed toward him. The empty, hollow feeling of the past months lifted as she entered his arms, feeling safe and warm and complete for the first time since he went away.

Feeling no need to speak, they clung to each other there on the platform, content in their embrace as the noisy crowd surged around them.

After a while, Lane stepped back, giving Catherine a weak smile. He started to speak, then shook his head slowly as he took a deep breath.

Wiping her eyes, Catherine smiled warmly at him as she noticed the hollow, dark sadness of his eyes, the new sprinkling of gray around the temples of his closely cropped hair, and the skin of his face pallid and drawn taut across his cheekbones. Putting her arm around his waist, she felt him lean on her for support as they walked toward the station. "It's so good to have you home, darling."

In a few moments, Lane stopped and turned toward her, his hands on her waist as he stared directly into her eyes. "They almost got me this time, Cath."

Catherine rose on tiptoe, took his almost gaunt face in her hands, kissing him warmly on the lips, then pressed her soft cheek against his, whispering to him as she had done to their children when they had awakened afraid in the night. "It's all right, darling. We're together now."

"Yeah." Something flickered in the depths of Lane's eyes. "We are, aren't we?"

Catherine took him by the arm as they walked toward the depot. "Let's go pick up your luggage."

"I don't have anything but my duffel bag and they're shipping it on to Baton Rouge." Lane's eyes still held a dull, dazed look. "Cath, do you think—I don't know, maybe we could go somewhere, just the two of us before we head on home. I think I need to ease back into things."

"I know what!" Catherine suggested brightly. "Let's go take a walk along Lake Pontchartrain. It's a beautiful day to be near the water."

"Whatever you say," Lane agreed as they walked past the depot. His '39 Ford coupe was parked at the curb. "Where's the Chrysler?"

"Jessie needed it to drop the children off at school. She hates to use your old car. Wanna drive?" Catherine asked, holding the keys out toward Lane.

"No, you go ahead. I think I've probably forgotten how." He walked around to the other side of the car, got in, and tossed his bag into the backseat.

★ ★ ★

"I thought I'd never get out of the French Quarter," Catherine said, heading down Canal Street away from the river. "One wrong turn in this town and your family might never hear from you again. All those narrow little one-way streets and old buildings all look alike to me."

"I thought you did just fine."

As they continued on toward the lake, Catherine brought Lane up to date on their family, deliberately leaving out Jessie's performing in nightclubs. "Coley can't wait for you to start handling your own cases again. Says being in politics has made him lazy."

Lane smiled, but made no response.

"Are you all right now, Lane?" Catherine felt awkward asking the question, as though she were prying into the personal affairs of a stranger. It occurred to her then that they had to reacquaint themselves with each other because of the changes each of them had undergone—especially Lane—during their separation. She felt a distance between them, although he sat right next to her on the seat of the car.

Turning his head toward her, Lane had a puzzled expression on his face.

"I—I mean," Catherine stammered, trying to find the right words. "You aren't in any pain, are you?"

"Not much." Lane seemed to reconsider his answer. "I may act a little funny to you, Cath. I know we've been through this before when I got back from the Pacific, but—I don't know, maybe it was because I was younger then, maybe—it's just a lot of things I can't explain."

"We don't have to hurry into anything, Lane." Catherine spoke in a soothing voice. "We've got lots of time now, remember."

Lane continued in a dry monotone, as though all emotion was being kept in check. "When a man sees so many boys dying, just high-school kids a lot of them, he kind of—backs into himself where it won't bother him so much, so he can just keep living one day after the other." He gazed blankly through the windshield. "I guess that doesn't make much sense, but it's the best I know how to explain what happens."

Catherine remained quiet, feeling that the mere act of speaking about the war seemed to have brought Lane a step closer to his old self. Driving along Pontchartrain Boulevard in the midmorning traffic, she watched the fronds of the tall, slender palm trees swaying gently in the breeze from the lake. Many of the houses took on a Mediterranean appearance with their white stucco fronts and walled gardens.

Catherine pulled into the white shell parking lot of Fitzgerald's Restaurant, stopping beneath an ancient magnolia tree whose deep green leaves gleamed in the sunlight as though they had just been varnished.

Lane still seemed in a kind of daze, staring out across the water at a sloop as it cut through the waves, its canvas popping loudly in the stiff breeze.

Catherine took his hand, squeezing it gently. "You sure you feel all right, darling?"

"Maybe a little disoriented," Lane replied, his voice a hoarse whisper. He cleared his throat. "It seems like it was just yesterday . . ." he continued, his eyes now staring at something far out beyond the lake, ". . . or maybe a hundred years—time's kind of mixed up for me now—that I was out there in those mountains in Korea with Alexander and Tenkiller— now, he was the one who didn't last very long, he got . . ."

"Let's not talk about it now, darling." Catherine could see Lane's lips grow thin and white, the muscles along his jawbone working under the skin as his memories came flooding back. "We've got all the time in the world."

They left the car, walking across the shells— crushed and packed as hard as cement by years of traffic—to the wooden bridge that led to the restaurant built over the water. Waves slapped against the huge creosote pilings beneath the building as they walked along beside the railing and out to the wide deck at the far end facing the lake.

Catherine stood close to Lane, her arm around his waist, gazing at the sunlight winking off the water. A lone gull, white against the dazzling blue sky, sailed by, its cries muted and swept away in the wind.

"It's been a long ol' road since that day in Sweetwater when we met, Cath." Lane's voice took on a note of nostalgia underlaid with the joy of being home again.

"Twenty-two years," Catherine replied, leaning

closer to Lane. "I can't remember that boy's name. The one who tried to make a pass at me that day."

"Rayford Mott."

"You sure put him in his place," Catherine smiled, remembering how brave she thought Lane was to defend her against the hulking brute who had spilled her groceries along the sidewalk. "I can still see the look on his face."

"And the day Jessie was born," Lane continued, his face growing more relaxed. He seemed to be clothing himself with memories, using them as a man would use a heavy coat against the cold. "That was one of the happiest days of my life."

Catherine thought back to the little hospital in Oxford, Mississippi.

"I don't think I ever talked to you about this before, but the first time I ever saw her was when you were nursing her right after she was born." Lane's eyes filled with light as he spoke. "I never had a feeling like that in my whole life. It almost took my breath away, Cath, seeing the two of you together. It's like a camera inside my head took a picture of you and Jess. It'll always be there."

Catherine moved against Lane, tilting her head slightly upward, feeling the touch of his lips on hers and his arms around her as she had imagined a thousand times since he had gone off to war. When he pulled back she saw that the smile on his face was the same as when they had been kids together. The troubled sadness fled from his eyes.

Then Lane embraced her as tenderly as he had on their wedding night, and she felt her own loneliness disappear as a vapor in the wind. As they had done at the train station, they held each other, oblivious to their surroundings. The wind off the lake blew

Catherine's hair into a swirling brightness about her head, the waves lapped against the pilings, and the traffic out on the boulevard caused little more than a rumor of noise.

Catherine placed her hands on Lane's chest, gently easing back from his arms as she gazed up into his face. "You've really come back to me, Lane—I mean just now. I can feel it."

"I think you're right." Lane stared out across the wide expanse of water, a look of wonder in his eyes. "It's almost like a door opened inside me to let the world back in again."

Catherine could almost feel the dark spaces between them vanish.

Lane smiled again, the old smile, nodding his head slowly. "I guess I had to be around you for a little while so I could separate *you* from my dreams of you. I've thought about you so much and dreamed about you so much in these past few months that it's hard to tell where the *dream* stops and the *real* you starts."

"But you know now, don't you?"

Lane took Catherine's face tenderly in his hands, gazing directly into her eyes, blue as a rain-washed sky. "Yes. I know now—and I'm ready to go home."

★ ★ ★

"Daddy! You're really back!" Jessie bounded down the back steps, running along the brick walk toward the car as Catherine parked it just outside the garage. "I'm such a mess too. I didn't expect y'all so soon."

Lane opened the door and stepped out just as Jessie rushed up and threw her arms around him. "Uhh . . ." Lane grunted as he fell back against the car, catching onto the door handle to keep from losing his balance.

Jessie took him by the arm. "Oh, I'm so sorry! Are you all right? It's just that I'm so glad to see you. I've thought about you so much over there in that terrible cold and snow and about how all the men—"

"Jessie, will you settle down a little?" Catherine walked around the car, taking Lane by his free hand. "I know you're glad to see your daddy but you don't have to talk his ears off the first ten seconds."

"I'm glad to see you too, Jess." Lane stepped back, admiring his oldest child, noticing her freshly scrubbed, straight-from-the-shower look. Her hair was pulled back and pinned behind, and her face shone with health. Wearing jeans and a white blouse with a Peter Pan collar, she looked almost like a little girl. He glanced down at Catherine. "You know, Jessie's the only one who cared enough to come see me over in Korea!"

"That's right," Jessie agreed, pushing Catherine aside playfully as she put her arms around her father and hugged him tight.

Lane pulled his daughter close, pressing his cheek against hers as he gazed at Catherine. "Yep, Jess's the only one who really loves me, all right."

"I don't know which one of you is the silliest." Catherine shook her head, turned, and walked away toward the back door. "C'mon, let's go see how the only one who really loves you did with her cooking."

"I fixed a special treat for you, Daddy," Jessie cried happily. "I hope you like it."

"If you cooked it, I know it'll be great!" Lane grinned, walking with his daughter toward the back porch.

"You go ahead and wash up and when you get back, I'll have everything ready."

Five minutes later the three of them sat down together at the dining room table.

Lane drove his fork into one of the plump fried oysters on his plate, dipped it lightly into Catherine's own homemade tartar sauce, and bit into it. "Hmmm. You certainly have learned something about fixing seafood since we moved down here. This is better than any restaurant."

Jessie gazed down at her own plate of shrimp roumalade. Lane had already wolfed his down as an appetizer. "I remembered how much you always liked them."

"South Louisiana's not perfect, but it's sure got the best food in the country."

Marveling at the remarkable change in Lane's behavior in the past three hours, Catherine watched him enjoy his food.

Lane glanced up. "Aren't you eating?"

"You know how I like to watch you stuff yourself," Catherine nodded, taking a bite, enjoying the cool, spicy taste of the sauce mixed with the firm texture of the fresh Gulf shrimp. "I have to admit it, Jess. You beat me at this kind of cooking."

"I gotta take the boys fishing, Cath. Make up for some lost time." Lane still had his head turned downward as he ate. "That's all they talked about when I finally got to call home—going down to Coley's camp and catching a bunch of fish. I always feel better myself when I get to spend a little time out there in the swamps."

"Well, they'll sure be tickled to death," Catherine smiled, reveling in the fact that Lane's appetite was so good. She could almost see the hollows of his body filling out.

"We'll go Friday as soon as they get home from school. I'll call Coley, soon as we finish eating."

A shadow crossed Catherine's face. "Lane, couldn't you make it next weekend?"

"Why?"

"I wanted us to go somewhere together—the whole family!" Catherine answered ardently.

Lane placed his fork on his plate. "We can do that anytime—next weekend, whenever you want. I promised the boys I'd take them fishing as soon as I got back."

"Friday's the only night we have," Catherine explained. "Billy Graham's preaching at Memorial Stadium."

"Who?"

"Billy Graham. He's a young evangelist and he's really a good preacher, Lane. I think you'd like him."

"You and the girls go ahead," Lane said, returning his attention to his food. "We'll see him next time he comes to town."

"I can't go either, Mama."

Catherine felt disappointment settle over her like a cloud. "Not you too, Jess."

"I have to sing Friday night." Jessie immediately regretted her words. She had promised Catherine that she would break the news to her father in her own way, and now it was out in the open.

Lane chewed his food contentedly and swallowed. "Sing where?"

Jessie glanced nervously over at her mother.

"Sing where?" Lane repeated, his eyes now fixed on his daughter.

"At the Pastime!" Jessie spat the words out, immediately going on the offensive.

Lane's eyes grew wide in disbelief. Then he pushed his chair back, throwing his napkin on the table. "Are you *crazy*? That's a nightclub!"

"Friday's the last time, Daddy. Then I sing down in New Orleans at the Blue Room."

"You've already *had* your last time!" Lane stood up abruptly, knocking his chair over. "No daughter of mine is *ever* going to sing in a place like that!"

Jessie stood up to face her father across the table. "Next week I'll be on the same bill as Joni James!"

"I don't care if you're on the same bill as Laurel and Hardy, you're not singing in a nightclub!"

"I'm almost nineteen!"

"And I'm still your father and you'll do what I tell you to!" Lane shouted.

"That's enough, you two!" Catherine stood up, taking Jessie by the arm. "Now calm down. Both of you."

Lane's eyes sparked with anger. "Is this what's been going on in my family while I was on the other side of the world?"

"Lane, please sit down," Catherine spoke in a calm, controlled voice, "and be quiet."

Opening his mouth to speak, Lane saw the look of reproval on his wife's face and realized that he had lost control of his temper. He sat down.

Catherine led Jessie down the hall into the living room at the front of the house. She pointed to one of the two tapestry-patterned Queen Anne chairs that sat at oblique angles to the bank of windows looking out on the front yard.

Jessie plopped down in the chair. "Why does he have to act like that?"

"First of all, you know I feel exactly the same way your father does about your singing in nightclubs," Catherine reminded her as she sat down.

"Mama, you know I'm not going to do anything wrong. Don't you trust me?" Jessie gazed through the diaphanous curtains at the lawn, cast into shadow by the ancient live oak that grew near the sidewalk. A smoke gray cat crouched in the grass, stalking a sparrow that was pecking around under the tree.

"Of course I do, Jess. But you have no business in places like that. It may seem harmless at first, but the end of it is always trouble."

Jessie leaned forward slightly in the chair and continued to stare out into the yard. With a sudden rush, the cat leaped into the air, its forelegs stretched out parallel to the ground. At the last moment, the sparrow shot upward in a flurry of wings, barely escaping the cat's extended claws.

"Now, let's get back to your father," Catherine continued. "He's been through a rough time. Worse than either of us can imagine, although you should know more about it than I, since you were actually over there."

"I know all that, Mama."

"He never knew from one day 'til the next whether he'd ever see any of us again, Jess." Catherine said gently, but with resolve, "You can't know *all* about that until you've lived through it."

Jessie remembered the happiness she had felt seeing her father in Korea; remembered that, maybe for the first time in her life, she finally realized how very much she loved him. A single tear coursed down her cheek. She felt it drop warmly on her hand like a gentle reminder of that memory of her father in the cold, hard mountains of Korea—and of how very fragile life is.

Without saying a word, Jessie got up and walked back to the dining room. "Daddy, forgive me. I don't want us to be mad at each other ever again."

"I'm sorry for yelling at you, Jess." Lane pulled her close, brushing the tear from her cheek. He spoke softly now. "That doesn't change the way I feel about what you're doing though—singing in those kinds of places."

Catherine watched her husband and daughter from the doorway.

Lane stepped back and took Jessie's hands, the warmth in his eyes saying more than his words. "But I want you to know that I love you, no matter what you do."

★ ★ ★

"This fellow must be *some* preacher." Austin, wearing gray slacks and a pale blue button-down collar shirt, pushed Coley along through the press of the crowd and up the concrete ramp that led out into Memorial Stadium.

"Why do you say that?" Coley, clad in his usual jeans and gray sport jacket, glanced back over his shoulder at Austin.

"'Cause you turned down a fishing trip with Lane to come out here tonight and hear him."

"I just wanted you to realize what a spiritual giant I am, Austin," Coley grinned. "Besides, I'm going down to meet Lane and the boys first thing in the morning."

Wearing a pastel green dress of soft cotton, Catherine walked along behind them next to Jessie, with Sharon holding tightly to her hand. "I'm so glad you decided to come with us, Jess."

"Well, I can't stay for the whole thing," Jessie reminded her mother. "I have to be at the Pastime early enough to make the ten o'clock show, so I'll have to leave by 9:30 at the latest."

As they reached the top of the ramp, Austin pushed Coley to the side, out of the way of the people filing into the stadium. A uniformed city policeman noticed them and walked over just as Jessie stepped through the entrance.

"Hey, aren't you Jessie Temple, the singer?" The young officer, taking in the soft curves of Jessie's lavender dress, obviously admired more than her singing. He had dark eyes, sharp features, and a thin mustache. A name tag above the left chest pocket of his uniform identified him as *D. Fortenberry*.

"Yes, I am."

"I love your singing. You're better than Teresa Brewer."

"Thank you."

"Are these people with you?"

"Why, yes, they are."

"Well, come on, then. Let's get you seated." The officer turned to several teenage boys seated on the front row. "All right, boys. Let's get moving. We got a man in a wheelchair here."

Amid grumbling and muted threats, the boys got up and started up the steps.

"Here we are, folks."

Austin backed Coley's wheelchair next to the end of the long stadium bench and took a seat next to him. Being careful of her new spring outfit, Jessie sat next to Austin with Catherine and Sharon on the other side. All around them people milled about, gazing up the tiers of the stadium looking for seats, engaging in animated conversations, waving at friends, and generally enjoying the mild April night.

A wooden platform stood out in the very center of the football field. Musicians sat in folding chairs next to an upright piano while a choir, dressed in their best Sunday morning outfits, arranged themselves on a small set of bleachers. The song leader, with dark,

curly hair and a warm smile, stepped to the microphone and raised his arms.

"This is my story, this is my song . . ."

The song carried Catherine back through the years
to a hotel room where she gazed through a rain-
streaked window at cars hissing by on the mirrored
streets and at the tops of umbrellas in the hands of
people hurrying along the sidewalks. Standing there
on the brink of eternity, she had felt as cold and empty
and alone as the tiny park below, abandoned in the
winter rain. That was the day Catherine Temple truly
began to live.

After a few brief comments and more songs, a tall,
angular young preacher with a thick shock of unruly
brown hair stepped to the microphone. He carried a
heavy brown Bible in his left hand. "God has called
me to bring you His glorious gospel through 'the *foolishness* of preaching.' "

Catherine glanced at Jessie, fidgeting on the seat
next to her, glancing down nervously at her watch.

The preacher opened his Bible, placing it on the
pulpit. "Tonight I want to take my text from the eight-
eenth verse of the first chapter of Corinthians. 'For the
preaching of the cross is to them that perish *foolishness.*' "

As Catherine listened to the sermon, she recalled
the times she had awakened in the night, burdened
for her family, and had knelt by her bed or gone downstairs to pray, feeling so often that her prayers were
merely dry, dead words, accomplishing nothing,
heard by no one. She felt that way now, but she prayed
anyway because her Bible instructed her to do so.

The preacher told again the old, old story of a child
born in a stable in Bethlehem, raised in the little town
of Nazareth in Galilee, and crucified on a rocky hill

outside Jerusalem, and of how He came back from death on the third day.

Toward the end of the message, Catherine closed her eyes yet again in prayer.

"All those Jesus called, He called publicly. There's something about coming down and standing before the world that makes your commitment to Him final. He said that if you're ashamed of Him before men He'd be ashamed of you before the heavenly Father. Come to the cross of Jesus.

"The things of this world—money, power, fame— won't satisfy you. Paul, one of the most learned and intellectual men of his day, said, 'God forbid that I should glory, save in the cross.'

"Come and have your names written in the Lamb's Book of Life. Only Jesus can satisfy the deep longing of the heart."

The preacher crossed his arms over his chest, bowing his head to rest his chin on one hand as the choir began to sing.

> Just as I am, without one plea
> But that Thy blood was shed for me,

"I'll go with you, Jess."

Catherine heard the words, but her mind didn't grasp their meaning until a few moments later.

> And that Thou bidd'st me come to Thee,
> O Lamb of God, I come! I come!

When Catherine lifted her head she saw Jessie, holding on to Austin's hand, walking across the field with him toward the foot of the platform that had become an altar. The high, glaring arc lamps gleamed down on her pale hair, bathing her in light.

Catherine remembered that long-ago time in the little hospital in Oxford when she had first seen Jessie, remembered cradling her at her breast and felt again the sudden, sweet ineffable joy of birth.